# Dear Ken,

They say that life begins at forty. Well, now I've turned forty and it's time for my life to begin.

I love you and the boys very much, but I need to know what it's like to be taken care of and looked after.

I have withdrawn one thousand dollars from the savings account. Let's call it my birthday present. I know it's a lot of money, but if you had remembered my birthday, you probably would have bought something extravagant, right? Forty is a landmark. I don't want jewelry or a fur. I would rather spend the money on something I really need—time, peace, solitude.

I assure you, I'm fine. I'll call you once I'm settled in somewhere. And I'll see you in about a month.

I do love you, Ken. Take care of the boys and wish me a happy birthday.

Love,

Lila

# ABOUT THE AUTHOR

Just as heroine Lila Chapin reaches a personal landmark in *Change of Life*, so does author Judith Arnold. It is her twentieth book for Harlequin. From her first book for American Romance, *Come Home to Love* #104, to this, her latest, Judith writes stories filled with humor, poignancy and heart-wrenching emotion. Her talent and versatility have been showcased by Harlequin since May 1985. Judith, her husband and two young sons live in Massachusetts.

## Books by Judith Arnold

### HARLEQUIN AMERICAN ROMANCE

201-PROMISES*
205-COMMITMENTS*
209-DREAMS*
225-COMFORT AND JOY
240-TWILIGHT
255-GOING BACK
259-HARVEST THE SUN
281-ONE WHIFF OF SCANDAL
304-INDEPENDENCE DAY
330-SURVIVORS
342-LUCKY PENNY

*KEEPING THE FAITH SUBSERIES

### HARLEQUIN TEMPTATION

122-ON LOVE'S TRAIL

# JUDITH ARNOLD

# CHANGE OF LIFE

Harlequin Books

TORONTO • NEW YORK • LONDON
AMSTERDAM • PARIS • SYDNEY • HAMBURG
STOCKHOLM • ATHENS • TOKYO • MILAN

Published October 1990

ISBN 0-373-16362-2



Printed in U.S.A.

# *Chapter One*

The day began like so many others: with a fight.

"You stole my pencil!" Michael shrieked.

"Did not!"

"Did too! You're a little thief. That was my best pencil—and look, you got gunk all over it. How'd it get in your drawer?"

"Well, you got all the good pencils," Danny whined. "I don't have any pencils with erasers on them."

"That's on account of you're an idiot. You don't think before you write. So you write stupid stuff and then you have to erase it. That's how come you use up all your erasers."

"I'm not an idiot! *You're* an idiot!"

"*You're* an idiot," Michael declared, and then proceeded to list several orifices into which Danny might consider inserting his eraserless pencils.

"Do something with them, would you?" Ken muttered from inside the walk-in closet, where he was searching for a tie to wear with his charcoal pinstripe suit. "I can't stand listening to this."

Lila's head pounded. She couldn't stand listening to it, either. She finished smoothing the blanket across the bed and then lifted her robe from the hook on the back of the closet door. Flinging her arms through the sleeves, she stumbled out of the bedroom and down the hall to Danny's room.

Danny had on his underwear; his pajamas lay in a heap on top of his unmade bed. Michael stood near the dresser, brandishing a pencil. He was clothed except for his shoes. "Look at what he did, Mom!" he roared indignantly, waving the pencil inches from Lila's face. "There's, like, chewing gum or something on this!"

"Well, I don't have any pencils with erasers," Danny complained in a querulous voice. "Michael has all the good pencils. He stole them."

"*You* stole them, Danny!"

Lila shut her eyes and held up her hand. "Hush, both of you," she commanded. After a brief exchange of snarls, they finally fell silent. "Now," she said, opening her eyes and staring at her two sons. "I'm going shopping today. I'll buy a new package of pencils and divvy them up, half for each of you, and that'll be the end of it."

"Hey, that's not fair!" Danny protested. "He's already got a hundred—"

"Half for each of you," she interrupted sternly. "But if I hear one more word about it, neither of you will get any. Is that clear?"

They gazed up at her, their features nearly identical despite the two-year age difference between them. Both had scruffy reddish-brown hair, dark eyes, triangular chins and childish button noses. Michael appeared a touch smug, Danny resentful, but neither of them dared contradict his mother.

"Okay. Finish getting dressed. I'm going to make breakfast."

Exhaling wearily, she turned and plodded down the stairs to the kitchen. Her headache seemed to have sprouted wings which fluttered relentlessly against her temples. She reckoned she ought to get some aspirin, but she didn't have the energy to climb back upstairs. Instead, she turned on the radio for the weather report, but got a more immediate weather report by looking out the window above the sink. She saw a morning sky dark with swollen rain clouds, and shut the radio off.

Within a few minutes Ken, Michael and Danny had joined her in the kitchen. The boys engaged in a minor scuffle over who would get to read the back of the Cheerios box while they ate. Ken glanced at his English muffins, mumbled, "Sorry, hon—I really don't have time," and gulped down half his mug of coffee without bothering to sit. Time, she knew, wasn't at issue as much as nerves. Sometime this week he would be finding out whether he'd gotten the promotion. Not knowing was driving him crazy—and he, in turn, was driving her crazy.

He thumped his mug down onto the table, splattering brown drops of coffee across the front page of the newspaper, and left the kitchen. When he returned, he was carrying his raincoat. He brushed Lila's cheek with a hasty kiss. "Wish me luck," he said before stalking through the mudroom to the garage.

As soon as he was gone, Danny and Michael resumed their quarrel over the Cheerios box. Lila removed it from the table. "Five minutes till the bus gets here," she alerted them. They scampered off to brush their teeth, their bowls still full of cereal.

Lila gazed at the table, the array of breakfast foods uneaten, the stained newspaper and the mess of Cheerios under Danny's chair. On some mornings she would simply shrug at such a dismal sight. On some mornings she would curse.

Today she had to fight back tears.

She hustled the boys out to the bus stop, cleaned up the mess in the kitchen, went upstairs and took a couple of aspirin. Then she got dressed and drove to the supermarket. She spent a hundred and ten dollars, including ninety-nine cents plus tax for a box of pencils. She drove home wondering how much of the food she'd purchased would actually be consumed and how much would wind up on the floor under Danny's chair.

By eleven o'clock the groceries were all put away and she left the house again, this time driving to the soup kitchen in the basement of Mt. Zion Methodist Church in Roxbury. She arrived too late to help with the food preparation, but Claudette told her not to worry about it. "I got most of it done," she said. "Just carry in the apples. We haven't got much today."

Lila surveyed the day's offerings: macaroni and cheese, two large bowls full of limp green salad, milk, coffee, graham crackers and a bushel basket of Macintosh apples. "No meat?"

Claudette shrugged. "What are you going to do? We take what we can get."

Lila nodded. She thought of the food wasted at home and of the people lining up in the rain outside the church basement door, eager to partake of a free hot meal. She should have bought something extra at the supermarket that morning, some sandwich meat or canned fish, or something. That she was here didn't seem enough.

At noon the door opened and the people—clients, Claudette called them—filed in. Most of them were men, but a few women were scattered among them, some with children in tow. Lila scanned the line in search of Mitzie. She spotted her and waved.

Mitzie waved back. A few years younger than Lila, she was dressed, as usual, in a grubby sweat suit and tattered denim jacket. Her hair was the color and consistency of straw, lying in an uneven shag around her drawn, pallid face.

"Is it still raining?" Lila asked Mitzie as she slid her tray along the counter.

"Yeah, a little," Mitzie answered. Thanks to the precipitation, perhaps, her face was less grimy than usual.

"Have you got a dry place to stay tonight?"

"Don't worry about me," Mitzie said.

"Fat chance of that," Lila said gently. "I *will* worry about you."

"Thanks," Mitzie said, smiling bashfully. "Thanks for the food, Mrs. Chapin." She waved again and carried her tray to one of the long tables set up throughout the room.

Lila sighed and tucked a stray strand of pale brown hair behind her ear. Her head hadn't stopped throbbing, but hearing Mitzie say "thanks" had done more for the pain than the aspirin she'd taken that morning. She smoothed out her apron and shaped a smile for the unshaven man across the counter from her.

"How are you doing?" Claudette asked her once the flow of clients had ebbed to a trickle. "You look beat."

"Just tired," Lila replied. "I'm feeling tired and old."

"Old!" Claudette let out a hoot. She stacked the empty macaroni pans and carried them into the kitchen, calling over her shoulder, "I'd like to be as old as you are." Claudette was in her fifties, but she was so youthful and energetic Lila often forgot that the woman was a grandmother.

By two-thirty, all the pots and pans were scoured, the remaining apples had been distributed among the clients and the basement was clean. "See you Wednesday," Claudette said as she and Lila parted company in the parking lot behind the church.

"I'll try to get here earlier next time," Lila promised.

Claudette swatted the air with her hand. "Whenever you get here, I appreciate it."

Lila smiled and climbed into her car.

Michael and Danny were already home from school by the time Lila pulled into the garage. Danny had found the new box of pencils on the kitchen table and was sharpening them. Michael was storming around the basement, complaining about the lack of good materials for a science project. "Mark Nugent's dad got dry cells and switches and everything," Michael moaned. "He's gonna get a better grade than me."

"I'm sure you can put together a decent science project with what we've got," Lila said, attempting to encourage him. "Maybe you can make a weather chart out of oaktag and paint."

"I don't want to make a chart. You don't get an A-plus for something like a weather chart. I want to make something neat, like, something with electricity."

"Why don't you do dinosaurs?" Danny hollered down the stairs.

"That's kid stuff."

"I'm doing dinosaurs in my class," Danny noted.

"Yeah, on account of you're in third grade. In fifth grade we do better things—electricity and stuff. How come we never have any neat things to do science projects with, Mom?"

Lila suppressed the urge to snap at Michael. "I'm sure we've got something down here you can use for your project," she said, surveying the shelves lining the walls. They were crammed with toys, art supplies, tools and seasonal items. "Maybe you could do something with ice," she suggested, inspired by the cooler chest.

"Yeah, what?"

"I don't know. It's your project."

"Ice melts. Big deal." Michael shoved his hands into the pockets of his dungarees and sulked.

"How about mold? You can grow bread mold."

His face brightened. "Hey, yeah, that's an idea. It's not as neat as dry cells and switches, but yeah, maybe I could do that." Michael bounded up the stairs, leaving Lila to turn off the lights.

She helped Michael to set up an experiment with slices of bread, then prepared dinner. Ken got home late, and his piqued expression conveyed that he hadn't heard anything about the promotion. Lila gave him a reassuring hug, which he returned. "What do they say about the waiting being the hardest part?" he lamented before heading upstairs to change his clothes.

Dinner featured the usual scenario—Danny rambling on about the intrigues of his class and Michael griping about how his meat was too dry. Lila picked at her own food, her appetite gone. Tired and old, she thought, trying to tune out Michael's long-winded criticism of her cooking. Tired and old.

After dinner the boys went to their bedrooms and Ken buried himself in the newspaper. Lila cleaned the kitchen, oversaw the boys' preparations for bedtime, tucked them in and returned to the den, where she settled in the recliner to watch television. She waited, glancing occasionally at Ken, wondering whether he'd remembered but knowing, deep in her heart, that he hadn't, that the day was lost, that this was her life and nothing was ever going to change.

He was a handsome man, his body trim and fit in a pair of jeans and a cotton sweater, his thick auburn hair swept across his forehead and dropping to his collar in the back, his eyes framed by faint laugh lines and the skin beneath his jaw as smooth and taut as that of a man half his age.

He looked younger than she did, she thought. Despite his preoccupation with his status at work, he looked young and rested and at peace with himself.

She waited, resolutely dry-eyed but aching in her soul.

At ten o'clock he tossed aside his reading, stretched and grinned at her. "How're you doing over there?" he asked, patting the sofa beside him.

"All right," she said, refusing to move from her chair.

"I'm about ready to head upstairs. How about it, Lila?"

Sex, she thought. Her reward for having endured another long, hard day. Making love with Ken would be pleasant, but tonight it would be too little, too late. "I'd like to stay downstairs a while longer," she said.

He measured her with his gaze, then shrugged apologetically. "I know, Lila—I've been awful lately. It's just so aggravating, watching them parade all those outside prospects through the office—"

"I know," she murmured.

"And I'm sitting there, thinking, 'Come on, guys, how can you bring someone in from outside the company, when I'm right here under your nose?' "

"I know."

"It's just . . . it's frustrating, that's all. And I've been a real bastard. But I promise I'll make it up to you."

"That's all right. You haven't been a bastard."

"Then come upstairs," he cajoled, moving across the room and circling her chair. He dug his fingers into the knotted muscles at the nape of her neck and massaged.

She smiled sadly, her eyes growing damp. Even now, after so many years, his hands could work wonders on her. It would be so easy to say yes, to go upstairs and tumble into bed with him. He would make love to her and she would forget everything for a while. She would forget her exhaustion and anger and disappointment.

She didn't want to forget, not tonight, not on this day of all days. "I'm sorry, Ken," she said, swallowing the tremor in her voice. "Okay?"

He stopped rubbing her neck. "Okay. I'll see you when you come up." He leaned over and kissed her cheek, then forced a smile and wandered out of the den.

She remained where she was for a long time, listening to his footsteps on the stairs, to the hiss of the shower and the creaking of the radiators and the mechanical laughter from the television set. Eventually—hours later, it seemed—she rose, turned off the TV and crossed to the desk. In the side drawer she found a pad, in the center drawer a pen.

*Dear Ken,* she wrote, *They say that life begins at forty. Well, now I've turned forty, and it's time for my life to begin.*

# Chapter Two

"Ken? Have you got a minute?"

Ken glanced up from the printouts he'd been skimming. It was after one o'clock, but the half-empty cup of tepid coffee occupying the corner of his blotter was as close as he'd come to eating lunch. The computer records Pam had dumped on his desk earlier that day didn't have to be reviewed until next week. But Ken had found that the only way to survive the stress of not knowing about the promotion was to immerse himself in his work. So he'd spent most of the morning doggedly plowing through the customer records, figuring out where Allied-Tech's new system was doing well and where it was performing below expectations.

When Larry Talbot beckoned, however, Ken couldn't hide behind the printouts. The vice president in charge of finance was standing in Ken's office doorway—slouching, actually, his red suspenders curving on either side of his potbelly like bright parentheses. A mysterious grin quirked his lips as he stared at Ken through the thick lenses of his eyeglasses.

"For you, Larry, I've always got a minute," Ken said expansively. "What's up?"

"Let's take a walk," Larry suggested. "There's something I want to discuss with you."

Ken struggled to decipher Larry's cryptic smile. Good news or bad? Promotion or no promotion? Ordering himself to stay calm, he tossed down his pen, stood and lifted his jacket from the back of his chair.

"You won't need that," Larry said, gesturing toward the jacket.

*Bad news,* Ken deduced, masking his intense disappointment behind an impassive expression. Damn. Years of dedication, months of maneuvering, weeks of hoping, and the senior management went and imported an outsider to fill Ed Healey's job as head of East Coast marketing. Ken knew it. If he'd been tapped for the opening, Larry would want him to look spiffy, wouldn't he? He'd advise him to straighten his tie and don his jacket and look like a proper executive. Damn it to hell.

He joined Larry in the hall outside the office. They walked side by side down the carpeted corridor, neither one talking. Ken kept his hands in his pockets and his head bowed, not wanting Larry to detect his pain. No matter how stoical he strived to be, he knew that his discontent would show in his eyes—Lila was always telling him that when he was upset his eyes gave him away.

Lila. Oh, God, how was he going to explain this to her? He'd been so short-tempered lately, so impatient, so detached from the family. He'd snapped at the boys and neglected Lila. The poor woman had had her hands full trying to keep things in balance while he'd been obsessed for months about the promotion. And after all that, to come away empty-handed...

What if she pitied him? He wouldn't be able to stand it.

"Hey, Chapin!" Diane Suralik shouted through the open doorway of the personnel department's offices. "Way to go!"

Way to go? He turned sharply to Larry, whose grin widened slightly. "What is it, Larry?" he asked. "Did I get the job?"

"Patience, my son," Larry intoned.

A slow grin crept across Ken's lips. "Come on, man—tell me!"

"It's not what you're thinking," Larry insisted, motioning toward the stairs. "Or perhaps I should say, it is and it isn't."

"Quit the Zen routine, Larry. Did I get the promotion?"

"Yes and no."

"What do you mean, yes and no?"

"Patience, my son," Larry repeated, his eyes sparkling with mischief.

He started up the stairs, Ken at his heels. Why were they going upstairs? Moving into Healey's job shouldn't require a trip upstairs. If he'd gotten Ed Healey's job, they could have taken care of the paperwork in personnel.

If he fished for information Larry would admonish him to be patient, and he'd be tempted to throttle Larry. Exercising restraint, he followed in silence, refusing to get too excited or expect too much.

The third floor of Allied-Tech's corporate headquarters was smaller than the other two floors, a single hall lined with doors to the spacious private office suites of the senior vice presidents, the president and the C.E.O. Ken was acquainted with everyone in the uppermost stratum of management. They played softball together at the company picnic and they swapped lawn care tips in the lunchroom downstairs. Still, there was an aura about the third floor, a rarefied atmosphere, something that demanded a certain degree of reverence. The carpeting was thicker, the doors oak rather than painted metal, the secretaries assigned one to an executive, rather than shared among several managers. Without his suit jacket, Ken felt underdressed up here.

He expected to be led to Larry's office, but they walked past that door. Ken clamped his mouth shut to keep from badgering Larry with questions. Eventually, they reached a door near the end of the hallway. Larry opened it and gestured Ken inside, past a tastefully decorated secretarial office and through another door to a spacious inner office.

It was obviously vacant. The large teak desk was bare, the matching built-in teak bookshelves empty. A nail protruded from the wall above the credenza; no doubt a painting had once hung there. "Wasn't this Cecile Patterson's office?" he asked.

"That's right. You knew she took the job as Head of West Coast Operations, didn't you?"

"Yes, but . . ." A glimmer of understanding flickered in Ken's brain. "I get it—you're moving into this office. It's bigger than your old one, isn't it?"

Larry shrugged. "I considered asking for it, but I couldn't stand the thought of moving. You've got to pack everything and then unpack it—you can't count on the maintenance staff to do it for you. I didn't think it was worth the effort. I guess nobody else wanted the hassle, either. So we decided to give this office to you."

"Me?" Ken was dumbfounded.

"Well..." Larry leaned against the credenza and folded his arms across his chest. Ken didn't miss the amused gleam in his associate's myopic eyes. "We figured, why give you Ed Healey's job? You've been with Allied-Tech for ten years. You opened the Southwest for us. You've got the technical background, the business acumen, the guts, the loyalty, and an unhittable curveball. So what the hell—we decided to name you Vice President of Marketing."

"What?" Ken realized that with this breathless single-syllable stammering he was coming across as an imbecile. But a vice president... All he'd aspired to was Ed Healey's job. He hadn't dreamed of any position beyond that. "Me? Are you sure?"

"As a matter of fact, no," Larry teased. "I for one think you're too young. You haven't even gone bald. I resent that. I happen to think anyone who reaches this level in the company ought to be at least thinning on top."

"Cecile wasn't bald," Ken joked.

"Which was why she got shipped out to San Francisco. What do you say, Ken? Do you think you could tear out some of your hair to make us happy?"

Ken laughed. "If being a vice president is anything like what I imagine, I'm sure I'll have plenty of occasion to tear out my hair."

"Then the job's yours," Larry declared.

Ken meandered through the room, dazed. He felt the way he had on the morning of his eighth birthday, when he'd gone downstairs and found a three-speed Royce Union bicycle with a genuine leather saddlebag, standing in the middle of the living room, waiting for him. He'd wanted that bike ever since he'd seen it in the window of Fuller's Cycle Shop, but it had cost thirty dollars and he hadn't dared ask for it.

He hadn't dared ask for a vice presidency, either. He'd assumed that when Cecile took the West Coast position, Allied-Tech would hire a head-hunting firm to lure a marketing executive from some other company. It had never occurred to Ken that they'd consider him for the position.

Not that he couldn't handle it, of course. Not that he didn't deserve it. But still... "What about all those people you've been interviewing? I thought—"

"We've still got to fill Ed Healey's position, right? We've narrowed it down to three candidates, and we'd like you to meet with them before we make the final decision. What does your calendar look like over the next few days?"

"I don't know." He floundered, unable to digest his sudden rise through the ranks. "I—uh—I'll have to check."

"Have Theresa check for you. You'll probably want to keep her on as your secretary up here. Cecile swore by her. She's terrific."

"Fine. I'll..." He shook his head and laughed again, astounded by the realization that he would no longer have to keep track of his own appointments. "I guess I'll talk to her." He turned to gaze out the window, which overlooked a steady stream of traffic on Route 128. He couldn't complain about the view—his previous office hadn't had a window at all.

Vice President of Marketing. Unbelievable.

He rotated back to Larry. "I've got to call Lila," he said.

"Fine. Call your wife, and then Diane Suralik has some paperwork for you to go through. There's the matter of your increased salary—"

"Oh. Right." Ken shook his head and laughed. "I'm not usually this dense, Larry."

"If you were, you wouldn't be standing in this office right now," Larry pointed out. "It's a nice raise, but there isn't much room for negotiation. You know the tier system we've got here."

"Right."

"And then you'll have to start packing to move up here. Maintenance will get you some cartons." He gave Ken an intense perusal. "You okay?"

"Never been better."

"You look a little pale."

"I'm in shock, that's all," Ken said with a grin.

"You think this is shocking? Wait till you see how much work we pile on you. Go call your wife," Larry suggested, giving him a congenial slap on the shoulder. "Ask her if she can line up a baby-sitter for Saturday evening. Joyce and I are having a little party—to welcome you on board, if that's all right with you."

"Oh, no. A party in my honor?"

"Yeah. Prepare a presentation," Larry joked. Then he extended his hand. "Seriously, Ken—congratulations."

Ken shook it. "Thanks. Thank you, Larry," he said, no longer caring whether he sounded imbecilic. He was entitled to be in shock. This brisk Tuesday afternoon in October belonged in the pantheon of Great Days in the Life of Kenneth Chapin, right up there with the day he'd met Lila, the day they'd gotten married and the days his sons were born. He'd been giddy and mildly incoherent on those days, too, and he hadn't apologized for it. Larry actually seemed tickled by Ken's bedazzled state.

Together they went back downstairs. "Go call Lila," Larry said, "and then meet me in personnel. Diane has those papers for you, and we can all talk numbers."

"Right." Ken knew that the numbers—his salary increase, his investiture status, his bonus package—were important, and Lila would want to hear what the promotion entailed, but he couldn't wait to call her. He jogged down the hall to his office—his *former* office, he reminded himself with a grin—and closed the door behind him. Without bothering to sit, he reached across the desk for the phone and punched his home number.

It rang unanswered.

He cursed, then laughed at his own impatience. It wasn't Lila's fault that she wasn't sitting by the phone at home when he had such exciting news to share with her. She was probably doing her volunteer work at the soup kitchen... No, today was Tuesday, and she did that on Mondays, Wednesdays and Fridays. Maybe she was at the boys' school, involved in some project with the P.T.O., or out shopping. Hell, she wasn't obligated to check in with him whenever she left the house.

Sighing, he lifted the framed photograph of her from his desk. Also on display he kept a photograph of her with the boys taken on the Cape last summer, but the picture of her alone was one of his favorites. The photograph showed her gazing off into the sunset, the tawny curls of her hair blown back from her face. Her skin was smooth, her nose dappled with girlish freckles, her pale blue eyes fringed with surprisingly dark lashes, and her lips curved in a Mona Lisa smile. Her delicately sculpted chin was sharply delineated by the slanting light of dusk, and her throat appeared sleek and graceful above the open collar of her blouse.

"Oh, Lila," he whispered to the picture. "Sweetheart, we've made it."

All right—so she wasn't home. He would surprise her with the news when he saw her. That was it: he'd stop off on the way home tonight and buy some champagne, and they'd party. He'd hand her the champagne, gather her into his arms, bury his lips against that warm, lovely throat of hers and kiss her silly—and he'd ignore the boys, who would stand around snickering and making smooching noises. He would kiss her and hug her and then tell her.

This moment belonged to both of them. The promotion was hers as much as it was his. After all, he and Lila were a team.

He placed the photograph back on the desk and gazed around the office. "Unbelievable," he murmured one last time before bounding out of the room.

"LILA?" He had to kick the mudroom door open; what with the champagne, the roses and his briefcase, his hands were too full to cope with the doorknob. "Lila! I'm home!"

He entered the kitchen and dropped the flowers onto the table. Then he set down the bottle and turned on the light. "Lila?"

From the den he heard juvenile giggling. He crossed to the doorway and peeked in. Danny and one of his neighborhood buddies were seated inches from the television screen, playing a video game. "Hey, Danny," Ken called to his son.

Danny jumped and spun around. "Oh. Hi, Dad," he said, directing his attention back to the screen and toying with the control stick.

"Where's Mom?"

"I dunno."

Ken nodded politely toward Danny's friend, then left the den. Loosening his tie, he scanned the kitchen once more, poked inside the laundry room and then headed upstairs, figuring he would find her there.

Michael's room was closest to the top of the stairway. His door was open and Ken glanced inside. Michael was at his desk, reading his math textbook, twirling a new pencil between his fingers and listening to his Walkman. Ken entered the room and plucked the headphones from Michael's ears. The tinny sound of rock music emerged through the padded yellow circles.

"Yo, Dad," Michael said.

"Where's Mom?"

"Beats me."

Ken frowned. "Is she home?"

"I haven't seen her."

"Didn't she tell you where she was going?"

"I haven't seen her since I got home," Michael answered, taking his headset back and putting it on. "I've gotta finish this homework, Dad, okay?"

Ken was disturbed by his sons' evident disinterest in their mother's whereabouts, but he didn't bother interrogating Michael any further. They should have asked where she was going. If Lila wasn't in the house, she was probably somewhere nearby. She should have told the boys where she was going, though.

He peered into Danny's room, a scene of absolute chaos, and then strolled down the hall to the master bedroom. The bed was neatly made, the closet door closed, the shades all meticulously adjusted to the same height. The air in the room was still, the early-evening light lending an eerie pinkish wash to the cream-colored walls. Shrugging off the strange sense of foreboding that overtook him, Ken decided to change out of his suit first, and then continue hunting for Lila.

He pulled his wallet from the hip pocket of his trousers, crossed the room to his chest of drawers and saw the envelope.

She'd propped it up against the small walnut and brass tray on top of his bureau. The tray was where he stored his loose change and his keys when he emptied his pockets at the end of the day. It was the first place he went each evening when he came upstairs to change his clothes.

And now an envelope was there, waiting for him.

His heart began to pound crazily, and his throat contracted into a knot. He grabbed the envelope, tore it open, yanked out the folded sheet of paper and read:

Dear Ken,

They say that life begins at forty. Well, now I've turned forty and it's time for my life to begin.

I love you and the boys very much, but I need something more. For too long, I have put everyone else's needs first and my own needs last. I wouldn't mind so much if I felt that someone else put my needs first sometimes. But no one ever does.

I am the one who makes sure everything gets done and everything runs smoothly and everyone else is happy. Other than that, I may as well be invisible. I'm tired of it, Ken. I need to know what it's like to be taken care of and looked after.

So, since no one else seems willing to do it, I am going to take care of myself and put myself first for a while. I am going to spend some time by myself. I am doing it because if I don't, I know I will explode.

If this comes as a surprise to you, it shouldn't. I've been asking for help for a long time—maybe asking too nicely, or too quietly. You get four weeks of vacation from Allied-Tech every year, and the boys get vacations from school. I've been working this job for nearly half my life. I need some time off, too.

I have withdrawn one thousand dollars from the savings account. Let's call it my birthday present. I know it's a lot of money, but if you had remembered my birthday, you probably would have done something extravagant, right? Forty is a landmark. I don't want jewelry or a fur or some sterling silver dust-collector. I would rather spend the money on something I really need—time, peace, solitude.

I assure you, I'm fine. I'll call you once I'm settled in somewhere. And I'll see you in about a month.

I do love you, Ken. I will miss you. Take care of the boys and wish me a happy birthday.

Love, Lila

He took a deep breath. The letter demanded rereading, but he didn't think he could stomach it. Instead, he crumpled it into a ball and hurled it violently across the room.

He took another breath, this one to calm himself down. He wrestled with the urge to smash something. How could she do this to him? How could she steal a thousand dollars of his money and vanish for a month? Did she honestly think he'd take her back after this?

Another breath, and another. Slowly, each step an agonizing effort, he moved across the room to where the letter had landed on the floor. He lifted the wad of paper and smoothed it out. Then he sat on the edge of the bed, turned on the bedside lamp and forced himself to read it again, poring over Lila's delicate script, pausing at the end of each sentence. By the time he reached *Love, Lila*, his rage had dissolved into grief and remorse.

Her birthday. For God's sake, her fortieth birthday. He'd forgotten it. Somewhere in the back of his mind was a vestigial memory that her birthday fell in early October, but family birthdays weren't the sort of information he considered crucial. He'd never forgotten his sons' birthdays, but he'd been in the delivery room on those two miraculous days, holding each newborn son and beaming with joy. When it came to other birthdays—his parents', his sisters's and brother's—Lila kept track of the dates, purchased the cards, reminded him to sign them, addressed the envelopes for him and made sure they got mailed on time. As for Lila's birthday... Well, he tried to not let it slip his mind from one year to the next, but really, once you were an adult, birthdays weren't supposed to matter that much.

They mattered to her, though. Despite his indifference to the occasion, she had insisted on hosting a small dinner party for his fortieth birthday a couple of years ago, and she'd bought him a hand-knit Icelandic wool sweater, which must have cost close to a hundred dollars and which he rarely wore because it was too fancy for casual wear and too casual for work. It was a beautiful sweater, though. As they said, it was the thought that counted.

And when it came to Lila's birthday? Ken had been so wrapped up in his professional situation that he'd literally forgotten what day it was. His entire focus yesterday had been on himself, his job, his career.

It was the thought that counted, all right.

The money she'd taken didn't bother him. They could afford a thousand dollars—especially now that Ken was Allied-Tech's Vice President of Marketing. He castigated himself for having impulsively accused her of taking *his* money. He and Lila were a partnership, all their assets under joint ownership for philosophical as well as pragmatic reasons. What Lila had taken was only hers—not just the money, but also the time.

Had he really been thinking, less than five minutes ago, that if she returned home he wouldn't take her back? Now all he could think of was, what if she didn't return home? What if a month went by and she didn't come back? How would he survive without her?

"Daddy?" Danny's voice broke into his ruminations. "What's for supper?"

He twisted around to face the door. Danny and Michael hovered in the doorway, watching him. He was stricken by the sad irony that his son had asked not about Lila, but about dinner. From Danny's perspective, his mother's whereabouts weren't worth questioning as long as there was food on the table.

This, Ken realized with a painful stab of recognition, was what Lila had walked away from: the understanding that she wasn't as important to her family as the meals she served.

He opened his mouth and then closed it. He couldn't remain immobilized on the bed, reeling under the weight of his insight, while the boys gaped at him from the threshold. "Give me a minute to change my clothes," he improvised, "and we'll go to Papa Gino's. How does that sound?"

"Yeah!" Danny yelled. "Papa Gino's!"

"I like Pizza Hut better," Michael objected.

"Fine. Pizza Hut it is." Shaking off his stupor, Ken rose from the bed and pulled his tie free of his collar.

"Where's Mom?" Michael finally asked.

Ken ducked into the walk-in closet to buy some time. As he struggled to drape his trousers smoothly over the rod of the suit hanger, he tried to sort out his thoughts. How much truth could the boys handle? How much did they need to know? How much could they bear?

He himself could scarcely bear the truth. Nor could he bear the understanding that at this moment, when he wanted nothing more than to scream and kick things and rage against the heavens, he had to put up the strongest, most dignified front he could muster for the sake of the boys.

He stepped into his jeans and emerged wearing what he hoped was a reassuring smile. "Mom's gone away for a little while," he said.

"Where?" Michael pressed him.

"We'll talk about it over dinner." He silently chastised himself for putting off the dreaded conversation. Michael eyed him suspiciously, but Danny was oblivious, much too jubilant about the prospect of going out for pizza to sense his father's tension.

Not so oblivious, however, that when they trooped downstairs to the kitchen he didn't notice the roses. "What are the flowers for, Daddy?" he asked as he zippered his jacket.

*Damn her*, Ken fumed. Her little tantrum had managed to destroy every bit of happiness he'd been feeling about his ascension into the stratosphere of management at Allied-Tech. This was supposed to be his moment of glory, his crowning achievement, his shimmering triumph...

*Me, me, me. Keep thinking that way, Kenny-boy, and you're going to wind up forgetting her birthday next year, too.* If she came back by then, he thought morosely. If he hadn't already lost her for good.

"I'll—uh—I'll just put them in some water so they'll stay fresh," he mumbled. He would store the champagne in the basement. To leave it in the refrigerator, chilled for an imminent uncorking, might be overly optimistic.

The boys followed Ken through the mudroom and into the garage. Of course, her car was gone. Ken had been so wrapped up in his self-satisfied glee, he hadn't even noticed when he'd arrived home. *Me, me, me,* he thought with self-loathing. Couldn't he have even paid that much attention to his surroundings? Couldn't he have noticed that Lila had driven off somewhere? Or was she truly as invisible as she feared?

The drive to Pizza Hut took fifteen minutes. Michael and Danny sat in the back seat, Danny smirking and Michael brooding. Ken mulled over how he was going to explain Lila's absence to them. If she'd wanted to take a powder for a month, why couldn't she have enlightened everyone about her intentions before she decided to disappear? Why did she have to leave Ken to do her dirty work for her?

Cripes. If he kept on swinging back and forth between guilt and fury, he'd be schizoid before long.

The restaurant was fairly empty. They took a booth, the boys facing him. He gazed at them, his two finest contributions to the world, both of them infinitely more significant than an exalted title and a third-floor office at Allied-Tech. They looked so much alike, yet their personalities were markedly different. Danny was cheerful, disorganized, sloppy and adorable. Michael was intense, somber, aggressively goal-oriented. Michael was a prize-winning show dog, Danny a lovable mutt.

Ken realized that both of them forgave him for having neglected them the past few weeks. With Michael and Danny, forgiveness could be purchased with a pizza. Then again, if Ken had forgotten their birthdays...

If he had, Lila would have covered for him. She would have bought presents and said they were from Ken. She would have ordered a cake and planned a party, blown up balloons and hung streamers. What had Ken's contribution been to Danny's eighth birthday party last May? He'd taken a few photographs of the relay races and he'd helped to pour the apple juice. Lila had done everything else.

No—he mustn't keep thinking this way. He'd be better off hating her than hating himself. It hurt less.

An energetic young waitress came over, and he ordered a large cheese-lovers' pizza and three colas. As soon as she brought over the sodas, Danny tore the end of his straw wrapper and blew it across the table. Michael ignored his soda. "So, where did Mom go?" he asked.

"I'm not sure." Ken couldn't lie to his sons. He'd blunt the edges if he could, but he wouldn't lie. They were in this together.

"What do you mean, you're not sure? Didn't she tell you?"

"No, she didn't."

"She just went away, just like that?" Michael glared accusingly at Ken, obviously aware that his father was keeping something from him. "Mom would never do something like that."

"Well, she did," Ken retorted. He instantly regretted his sharp tone. Taking a deep breath, he added, "I think she wanted to surprise us."

"She sure did," Danny piped up. "It's kinda like a mystery, huh?"

Michael methodically unwrapped his straw and poked it into his glass. He stirred the crushed ice for a minute, meditating. "When is she coming back?" he asked, his scowl informing Ken that he was not the least bit reassured by his father's vague answers.

"In about a month."

"Yeah? Who's gonna make lunch?" Danny asked.

"I guess I will," Ken conjectured, frantically trying to recall what Lila put in the boys' lunch bags. "You guys are going to have to help me."

"Are you gonna stay home from work?" Michael asked.

Ken clamped his mouth shut to keep from cursing. He couldn't take time off from work, especially not when he had just accepted a new position with new responsibilities. If anything, getting a feel for the job would likely entail putting in longer hours for a while, not shorter ones. What was he supposed to do, hire a baby-sitter to take care of the boys from the time they got off the bus until he finally arrived home from work?

"I can't do that, Mike," he said slowly. "You're ten-and-a-half, now. You're a big boy. I guess I'm going to have to put you in charge."

"Yeah?" Michael sat straighter in his seat.

Danny, in contrast, looked miffed. "Does that mean I've gotta listen to him?"

"He has to listen to you, too," Ken explained. "You're going to be a team. Michael will be the senior member and you'll be the junior member."

"Did you and Mom have a fight or something?" Michael asked.

Ken wished to high heaven they *had*. He wished Lila had given him that much of a chance to state his case, to apologize, to do whatever it would have taken to stave off this disaster. But it wasn't in her to fight. She was soft-spoken and reasonable. She shied away from confrontations. Her gentle nature was one of the things he loved most about her.

What had she written in that letter? *I've been asking for help for a long time—maybe asking too nicely, or too quietly.* If only she'd asked noisily and nastily, he might have heard her before it was too late.

On the other hand, if she'd asked noisily and nastily, she wouldn't have been the Lila Moore Chapin he knew and loved.

Something told him that when she came back from her month-long retreat—*if* she came back at all—she might not be the same Lila Moore Chapin he'd been married to for the past sixteen years. She might be someone else, someone not so quiet and nice. The possibility panicked him. He didn't want her to change. He'd been content with the way she was, the way things were.

Apparently, however, she hadn't been content at all.

"No," he answered his son, "we didn't have a fight. She just... She needed a vacation."

"Yeah?" In Danny's mind, vacations were the next best thing to nirvana. "Where'd she go? Did she go to Disney World?"

"We all went to Disney World last February during your winter recess, remember? I don't think Mom would want to go back again so soon."

"I would," Danny declared.

The waitress delivered their pizza, and the boys bent to the happy task of devouring it. Ken managed to consume a single slice, but it wasn't easy. Chewing exhausted him; his throat balked at swallowing. Loud music spilled from a jukebox across the room, and a few tables away a toddler in a high chair pounded a spoon against her tray with heroic force. This wasn't the romantic evening he had envisioned when he'd all but floated out of Allied-Tech's headquarters less than an hour ago, mapping out a route to the nearest florist and then to the wine store on Route 20. This wasn't his idea of a swell way to toast his arrival into the ranks of the mighty.

*Me, me, me...* Was he truly that selfish, or had Lila's note skewed his self-image? Hell—it hadn't been for himself that he'd wanted to celebrate. It had been for her. The flowers and the champagne had been intended not to congratulate himself, but to thank her for having stood by him and supported him, for having loved him and believed in him and given him the only incentive he'd ever needed to aim high. The first thought he'd had when Larry had delivered the good news was to call Lila, to share his delight with her, to make her as much a part of it as possible.

And now her ugly little letter had robbed him of faith in his own decency. God, but he hated her.

"You know what I think?" Michael said somberly. "I think maybe Mom's sick of us or something."

Ken flinched. "Mom loves you very much."

"She's got to because she's our mother. But you know..." He twirled an elastic string of mozzarella around his finger. "Like, she always says she's sick of us playing war games and stuff."

"I explained to her," Ken assured Michael, "that boys play those kinds of games."

"Yeah, but maybe she got sick of it. Like, maybe she wanted to spend some time with girls or something."

Ken was impressed by Michael's sensitivity. "Maybe."

"Or maybe she left 'cuz we forgot her birthday," Danny said as he reached for another slice of pizza.

"You knew about that?" Ken exclaimed, gaping at his young son. "You remembered her birthday? Why didn't you do something? Why didn't you warn us?"

"I didn't remember till today," Danny answered, his mouth full of pizza. He chewed and swallowed, then elaborated, "Ms. Fairview, she was talking about Columbus Day and all that stuff, and I was sitting there trying to figure out how come I always think of birthday cake around Columbus Day. Cuz my birthday's in May and Michael's is in March and yours is in between ours, in April. And then it came to me..." He smacked his hand melodramatically against his forehead. "Mom!"

"We didn't have a birthday cake for her last year," Michael argued.

"She bought us cupcakes."

"Oh, yeah, that's right."

Ken nodded, reminiscing. In honor of Lila's birthday last year, she'd bought the boys a treat. But they'd given her something, he recalled—homemade cards and a couple of carnations constructed out of Kleenex and white thread. Ken had given her pearl earrings.

Ah, but this year she didn't want jewelry or furs or any of the rest of it. Just a pricey solo vacation. What would she have done if the boys had knocked themselves out making her new cards and Kleenex carnations? Would she have said, "Thanks, but I'm on my way"?

Or would she have stayed? Like last year, would she have said with tears in her eyes, "For me? You did all this just for me?"

He hadn't wanted the boys to feel guilty about missing her birthday, but it was too late. They both looked woeful. And maybe they *should* feel guilty. After all, they had taken her for granted as much as Ken had. Why shouldn't they carry a little of the responsibility for having driven her away? The Chapin men were in this thing together. They might as well share the blame, as well as the sorrow.

Ken asked the waitress to wrap up the leftover slices of pizza, and he and the boys headed for home. As soon as they entered the house, Danny begged for dessert. Ken refrigerated the pizza, tossed the boys a package of chocolate chip cookies and poured himself a bourbon. He rarely drank, and never alone. Then again, ever since Lila had entered his life, he'd never really felt as if he were alone.

Until now.

He sat at the table across from the boys, sipping his drink and watching as they munched on their cookies. On the counter the roses stood in a jar of water, mocking him with their empty sentiment. A month? A month of this torment, just because he missed her birthday? Wasn't there something in the Bill of Rights about the punishment fitting the crime?

The phone rang. He took a long drink, then rose to answer it. Two pairs of big brown eyes followed him as he crossed the room and lifted the receiver. "Hello?"

"Ken, it's Lila."

The familiar huskiness of her voice was enough to make him want to scream, curse, beg, weep. His fingers tightened around his glass and he nodded to the boys, answering their unspoken question. "Hello," he said in a strained tone.

"Are you all right?"

His gaze wandered from the roses to the table, strewn with cookie crumbs, and from there to the highball glass in his hand. Was he all right? Was the earth flat? Was the moon blue?

"Sure," he lied. "I'm all right. How are you?"

She didn't respond immediately. "Ken…look, I…" She sighed. "This isn't easy for me, either," she said, her voice cracking slightly.

*So come home, you idiot! Stop making us all miserable!* "Who says it's not easy for us?" he shot back, his tone caustic. "We're having a grand time here. Stay away as long as you like. One month, two—live it up. We're doing just swell without you."

"Ken, please." She sounded stronger now, more determined. "I've probably handled this badly—"

"Oh, no," he refuted, his words dripping with sarcasm. "You handled it wonderfully, Lila. I mean, a letter! How personal!" *Don't,* he cautioned himself. Perhaps this minute he was furious with her. But the way he'd been going, it wouldn't take long for the pendulum to swing back the other way, leaving him desolate and guilt-ridden. He choked back his bitterness and said, "Okay, Lila. I'm sorry. I'm sorry about your birthday. We're all sorry. Okay?"

"Don't worry about it," she responded. "I've given myself something I really wanted."

"Right. A ticket out of here."

"It isn't one-way," she said gently, as if explaining to a child. "I'll be back."

"You'll be back. Wonderful. What am I supposed to do in the meantime, wait with bated breath?"

Another woman would have responded with an equal measure of rancor. But Lila was different, which was one of the reasons Ken adored her. "What you're supposed to do," she suggested quietly, "is try to keep the house functioning while I'm away, and spend a little more time with the boys. You might find it's a special treat to have a little time alone with them."

"I'm supposed to thank you for this, is that it?"

"No," Lila said, a hint of anger creeping into her voice. "I gave up expecting to be thanked a long time ago." She paused, then said, "I'd like to talk to the boys, please."

"Wait, wait a minute," he said, suddenly contrite. He'd wasted this entire conversation spewing invective instead of attempting to straighten things out with her. "Where are you?" he asked.

"Don't worry about me—"

"I'm not worried," he fibbed. "I just want to know where you are."

She hesitated, evidently weighing how much she would reveal. "I'm at a very nice rooming house near the water," she said.

"Where? What water?"

"Not too far away."

*Great,* he grumbled inwardly. *Let's play Twenty Questions.* "Listen, if you're afraid I'm going to come after you, I won't. I just want to know where you are. In case there's an emergency or something."

"I'll call every night," she promised. "If there's an emergency, I can wait until dinner time to find out about it."

"Yes, but—" He bit his lip. If he continued pressuring her, she'd hang up on him and not call back. Only if he exercised restraint could he hope to hear from her tomorrow, at which time he might learn what he hadn't been able to learn today. "Okay. I'll put on the boys," he relented, suffering a growing sense of futility. She was where she was. She'd call when she'd call. If her purpose was to hurt him, she would succeed magnificently. It was out of his hands.

He beckoned the boys over and then drifted across the room, half listening to their end of the conversation. Danny went first. He babbled energetically about how his team had won a basketball game in gym that day, and how in history they were learning about Columbus, and how he'd had Garrett Kline over after school and they'd played Nintendo, and how he thought this was a really awesome mystery she'd given the family. Then, Michael took the phone. He soberly informed her that his bread hadn't sprouted any mold yet, but he imagined that sort of thing took time.

"Yeah, I'm okay," he told his mother. "Yeah, I'll be good. I'm sorry about your birthday, Mom. I really am. We all are. We talked about it at dinner tonight." He listened for a minute, then said, "Okay, Mom, we'll talk to you tomorrow." He hung up and turned to Ken. "I think she's sad," he announced.

"I think we all are." Ken set down his glass. "It's getting late, boys. Why don't you go on up and get ready for bed, and I'll pack some lunches for you."

"Trim my crust," Danny requested before racing out of the room. Michael reluctantly trailed his brother up the stairs.

It took Ken several attempts before he found the drawer where Lila kept the lunch bags, and another few tries before he located the aluminum foil. He made two peanut butter sandwiches, wrapped them, stuffed them into the bags and realized he hadn't trimmed Danny's crust. To hell with it, he thought churlishly. Let Danny learn to deal with the crust himself.

He threw some cookies into each bag and put the package away. He didn't notice the crumbs sprinkled all over the floor beneath Danny's chair until he was already at the door. To hell with that, he decided. He'd clean it up later, when he came back downstairs to finish his bourbon.

He trudged up the stairs, listening to the boys bickering over whether Michael was hogging the toothpaste. Wisely, Ken remained outside the bathroom until they emerged. He went with Danny into his room, admiring his son's agility at picking a path through the obstacle course of toys and clothing on the floor. Danny jumped onto the bed and threw the blanket over his head.

"Good night, Danny," Ken said, wondering whether he was supposed to kiss Danny through the blanket. Was that how Lila did it?

"Goood niiiight," Danny chanted in a spooky voice from under the covers.

Ken opted for giving what he guessed was Danny's head a loving pat through the blanket, then turned out the light and closed the door.

"Open!" Danny shouted from under the blanket. "Leave my door open, Dad!"

"Oh—sorry," Ken mumbled, opening the door. What else didn't he know? What else was he going to do wrong?

Shrugging off his feeling of inadequacy, he walked into Michael's room. Michael was rewinding the tape on his Walkman. "Bedtime," Ken announced.

Michael nodded and shut off the machine. Then he moved to the bed, smoothed the elastic waistband of his pajama bottoms and slid under the blanket. Ken switched off the lamp and leaned over the bed to kiss Michael.

"Dad?" Michael asked, his high, clear voice reminding Ken of how young both his sons were.

Ken gazed down at Michael, absorbing the earnest concern in Michael's dark eyes, the apprehension tugging the corners of his mouth downward. "Yes, Mike?"

"Are you and Mom getting a divorce?"

"No," Ken said, praying that it was the truth.

Michael thought for a minute. "I didn't want to ask in front of Danny, 'cause it might have upset him."

"That was very sensitive of you, Mike."

"But—like, if you're going to, you'll tell me, won't you?"

"We're not going to," Ken vowed.

"You love Mom, don't you?"

"Yes." Ken's voice wavered; his eyes began to grow misty.

"Does she love you?"

*Dear God, I don't know.* "I hope so," he whispered. "I hope so." He ruffled his fingers through Michael's hair, then straightened up and left the room so Michael wouldn't see him cry.

# Chapter Three

Lila hung up the telephone and burst into tears.

Danny had sounded reasonably normal, crowing about his skill at hoops and video games. Michael had come across as more reflective, but that was his nature. They could accept what she'd done—at least for the moment. Children, whether rightly or not, tended to assume their parents knew what they were doing. Lila only wished she could share that naive assumption.

She missed them. She missed them so much her soul ached. How could she have abandoned them like this? How could she have walked out on them? She shouldn't have done it. She should have stayed at home to greet them as they romped off the school bus. She should have hugged them and then suffered in silence as they recoiled, grimacing. She should have prepared a snack, which they would have made a mess with, and counseled Michael through some new academic crisis and listened to Danny's long-winded speeches about his classmates, all the while keeping her own crises and speeches to herself.

She should have smothered her frustration, ignored her despair and put her family's needs and interests ahead of her own. Wasn't that what she'd always done?

She wasn't blind enough to think that anything would be different when she returned home a month from now. Once her family got used to having her back, she would wind up spending most of her time and energy smoothing out life's rough patches for her loved ones, just as she'd done up to now, and no one would pay any attention to her unless, heaven forbid, she missed a rough patch and they stumbled over it. She would continue to receive complaints whenever something went wrong, but no kudos when everything went right. She would once again become invisible.

Yet she missed the boys so much. And Ken...

Pulling the blanket tighter around her, she buried her face in its soft wool folds and wept. The boys might forgive her for leaving, but Ken never would. She, of course, was supposed to forgive him for forgetting her birthday, but he would never forgive her for celebrating her own birthday by taking this vacation. She had heard his rage across the telephone wire, his bitterness tainting every word. He would never let her live this down.

Not that she blamed him. So he'd skipped her birthday—it wasn't as if he'd committed first-degree murder. He'd been so distracted lately, so worried about things at work. If she viewed things from his perspective, she would understand his lapse.

But why should she view things from his perspective? When had he ever bothered to view things from hers? When had he ever tried to understand her? A few more sobs escaped her, self-pity mingling with self-disgust, fear blending with a heavy sense of inevitability.

With a shudder, she sniffled away her tears and lifted her head to survey her surroundings. The cozy room she'd rented, in a charmingly dilapidated Victorian bed-and-breakfast overlooking the water in Hull, was almost offensively cheerful. Daffodil-yellow paper covered the walls and the voile curtains were held back with lacy yellow swags. The furniture—the night tables, the six-drawer dresser, the headboard and the cushioned easy chair on which she sat—was white wicker. In spite of the evening fog rolling inland off the water, the room was bright.

Ken would hate it. His idea of a good hotel room was one with air conditioning, cable TV and a stall shower. Lila was enchanted by the claw-foot tub and the pedestal sink in the bathroom adjoining this room. She adored the rattly windows, the uneven hardwood floors, the braided rugs and the faded chintz upholstery of the easy chair. If only the room were about fifteen degrees warmer, she would be content.

She had been lucky to find Bayside Manor. She had wanted a waterfront location, but her funds were limited. Fortunately, Bayside manor had low off-season rates, and the grumpy woman behind the desk downstairs had given Lila an extra discount for paying for a month's stay in advance. The woman had informed Lila that a continental breakfast would be served in the parlor every morning. Given the uncanny silence of the second-floor hallway, however, Lila suspected that one pot of coffee and a half-dozen pastries would more than meet the needs of the hotel's few guests.

She heard a knock. Gathering her blanket around her, she rose from the easy chair and edged toward the door. "Who's there?" she shouted, uncomfortably aware of her vulnerability as a woman alone.

"It's Jimmy, from maintenance," a male voice penetrated the locked door. "I'm here to fix the radiators."

Lila cautiously inched the door open. A young man in a gray UMass sweatshirt and jeans stood in the hallway, carrying a small toolbox and an aluminum pot. "Can I come in?"

She stepped aside and he entered. He gave her a long, curious appraisal, registering bemusement at the way she'd wrapped the blanket around her. "You must really be freezing, huh," he deduced, moving directly to one of the old-fashioned freestanding radiators abutting the outer wall. "This always happens in October, when they turn on the heating system for the first time. The radiators need to be bled."

"Bled?"

Kneeling down at one end of the radiator, he pulled a wrench from his tool kit and used it to loosen a valve. A loud hiss escaped, and he slid the pot under the valve to catch the drips of water. "Air pockets in the pipes," he explained. "They accumulate over the summer, when the heating system isn't being used. You've got to bleed them out."

"I see." Lila lowered herself onto the bed and watched him work. He appeared to be in his mid-twenties, his skin still glowing with a lingering summer tan, his blond hair shot through with streaks of platinum and his feet shod in expensive-looking leather sneakers.

"Newer heating systems don't have this problem," he went on, taking advantage of his captive audience. "I told Mrs. Tarlock when she hired me, she's got to start updating the facilities here. I mean, sure, she's done some work on the electrical system, renovating the wiring and replacing the fuse box with circuit breakers and all. But the heating and plumbing..." He shook his head. "She says she doesn't want the place to lose its flavor. If you ask me, a little flavor is fine, but not when she's got customers shivering in their rooms."

"I'm not shivering," Lila argued. As far as she was concerned, the quaintness of the rambling Victorian rooming house was a big part of its appeal.

Jimmy peered over his shoulder and gave her a dimpled grin. "Sure, you're not shivering—because you're all bundled up in that blanket."

She glanced down and loosened her grip on the blanket. Then, she politely returned his smile.

Jimmy turned back to his work, inspecting the thin, steady flow of water to make sure there were no more air pockets before he closed the valve and tightened it with his wrench. He rose, moved to the room's other radiator and repeated the procedure. "So," he said as he worked, "are you here on vacation?"

"Yes."

"You know, most people think the only time to vacation at the beach is in the summer. Not me. I like the beach better in the fall. It's less crowded, less muggy... I don't know why more people don't come here in October."

"I'm glad they don't," Lila commented. "If they did, I might not have been able to get a room."

"Good point. It's nicer having Hull all to ourselves." He shoved up the sleeves of his sweatshirt and jiggled the wrench in an attempt to loosen the sticky valve. "I grew up around here," he continued, "and my favorite time of year was always right after Labor Day, when all the summer people cleared out."

"That's not a good attitude to have when you work at a hotel," Lila chided him gently. "Without all those summer people, you'd be out of a job."

He laughed. "I'm only doing this on a temporary basis," he said. "I was living up in Portsmouth till last spring, and then my dad took ill and I decided to stay closer to home for a while. Anyway, my girlfriend ditched me, and my job up there wasn't so hot."

"How is your father now?" Lila asked. She wasn't sure why she was enjoying talking to this garrulous stranger. She didn't think it was because she was starved for company; she hadn't been away from home long enough to be lonely. Rather, it was that he was polite and amiable, and he had a friendly smile.

"He's improved some," he answered. "He has a heart arrhythmia. They wired him with a pacemaker in June." He held the pot under the valve, collected the dribbles of water and then tightened the valve with his wrench. "I don't mind hanging out in Hull," he insisted. "Especially now. The way I figure, I'll give this town a few more months and then head up to Boston and try to find something better up there. That way I'll be close to home if my dad takes a turn for the worse."

"He's a lucky man to have such a devoted son," Lila observed.

Jimmy appeared embarrassed by her compliment. "Nah. Like I said, my girlfriend up in Portsmouth was giving me a hard time. I needed an excuse to split." He placed his wrench in the toolbox and stood. "Is everything else okay?" he asked.

The question startled Lila. No, she almost replied, things weren't okay. She had just shattered the serene complacency of her family's world, and her husband detested her for what she'd done. She'd just turned forty and she was frustrated and anxious and more than a little bit frightened.

It dawned on her that Jimmy was referring to the room. "Everything's fine," she answered.

He stared at her for a few seconds, his bright hazel eyes taking in her stockinged feet, her disheveled curls, her freckled cheeks and defiantly raised chin. After weighing her words for a moment, he accepted them with a grin. "Listen, if you've got any problems, you just tell Mrs. Tarlock to send me up," he advised. "Mrs. Tarlock is kind of grouchy, but that's just her personality. Don't let her turn you off. I'll make sure everything gets taken care of."

"Thank you," Lila said.

With a wave and a wink, he was gone.

She closed the door and fastened the chain, then unwound the blanket and spread it out on the bed. Other than the metallic clanking of the radiators as they steamed to life, the room was quiet: no cacophony of boys engaged in a dispute, no babble of television noises, no *ka-chunk, ka-chunk* of a dishwasher motor or synthetic tunes from the Nintendo game in the family room. She embraced the tranquilizing silence as she had earlier embraced her blanket.

Sighing, she crossed back to the wicker easy chair by the window and sank into it. The night sky offered a shifting purple-gray panorama as great rolls of fog continued to rise off the water. New England fog was different from West Coast fog. It wasn't as dense as the fog she remembered from her Bay Area days, but it was chillier, more isolating, more shroudlike. She hadn't been to California in years, yet she remembered the San Francisco fog as somehow less threatening.

Well, those were happier times, she conceded. She was young and madly in love. She had few obligations and many illusions. The world was a kind, welcoming place.

Not that she'd ever been particularly carefree. The only child of two teachers, Lila had been the sort of girl people always described as "mature beyond her years." She did well in school, she was obedient at home and her parents were quite pleased when she decided to follow in their footsteps and prepare for a career in education.

By the time she began her graduate studies at U.C.-Berkeley, the days of militant street politics were history and the city exploited its colorful past primarily for tourist purposes. Vendors hawked leather goods on street corners; sidewalk cafés sprouted like weeds after a rain; boutiques sold candles and tie-dye shirts and People's Park decals; and the graceful lawns of the university campus were trampled by countless Frisbee players. And Lila met a brilliant, mercurial doctoral candidate named Ken Chapin.

She didn't realize at first that he was a computer whiz. She met him at a party one of the graduate school's deans had thrown at his house up in Bolinas, on the Pacific shore. Leaning against a porch railing near a keg of beer, she watched a group of young men playing a rambunctious game of volleyball in the dean's spacious backyard. Specifically, she watched one tall, lanky fellow with profoundly dark eyes, a sturdy chin, a contagious laugh and a wild mane of auburn hair that rebelled against the constraints of the red bandanna he'd rolled into a narrow strip and tied around his head. She observed the resilient strength of his legs as he jumped, the limber grace of his body, the freewheeling power of his hands as he spiked the the ball over the net and the gentle precision of those same hands as he set the ball for a teammate. She marveled at his exuberant laughter, when he scored a point, when he lost a point, when he collided with another player and wound up sprawled across the grass.

She probably fell in love with him during that game. She spied on him, sipping her beer and admiring his agility, his unflagging humor and his rugged good looks. After the game, sweaty and out of breath, he loped up the porch steps to the keg and filled a paper cup with beer. "Great game," he declared, flashing her a dazzling smile. "Did we win?"

"I don't know," she admitted.

He took a long drink, then lowered his cup. "My goal in life," he said, his grin growing mischievous, "is to own a piece of land big enough to set up a volleyball net. What's your goal in life?"

"Nothing that ambitious," she joked, instantly feeling comfortable with him. "I'd like to become a teacher, whatever that's worth."

"In dollars and cents, not much," he remarked. "In spiritual rewards and intellectual challenge, it's worth a lot. Now me..." He took another long drink, then refilled his cup. "If I were going to work in a school, I'd want to be a volleyball coach. If you ask me, the trouble with most public schools is that they haven't got volleyball teams. Football, yes. Basketball, baseball, track, field hockey for the girls... But volleyball?" He shook his head. "When I run the world, that's going to change."

"Is running the world another of your goals in life?"

He laughed. "It's probably the only goal I've got that's even remotely attainable. I, dear lady, hold in this outrageous brain of mine the secrets of—" he paused for effect "—digital microprocessing."

"Really?" she asked, suitably awed.

"Computers. The artificial intelligence of the future. By the time I get my Ph.D., no man will be safe from my genius. Women are already gravely at risk around me. I suppose I ought to warn you of that up front."

The warning came too late to save her. She was bewitched by the seductive glow in his beautiful brown eyes, the radiance of his smile, the lean male power of his body. In retrospect, it shouldn't have surprised her when, later that evening, as the party wound down and the fog swept in from the ocean to engulf the house, she agreed to return to Berkeley in his car. She went out for an espresso with him at one of the sidewalk cafés and strolled around the campus with him, telling him about her schoolteacher parents and the modest house where she'd grown up in a suburb of Philadelphia. In turn she listened as he told her about his father—a professor of philosophy—and his mother—an independent filmmaker—and his sister—a lawyer—and his brother—a studio musician in Los Angeles. He told her about his undergraduate days at Cal-Tech, his exemption from service in Vietnam due to a heart murmur, and his passion for sports.

It shouldn't have surprised her that, less than nine hours after she'd met him, she was making love with him.

That sort of thing happened in those days—never before to Lila, but many women wouldn't have thought it odd to make love with a man they'd only just met. With Ken, though, Lila felt that she knew him, knew him intimately, understood him. She understood the haunting darkness in his eyes and the innate solemnity underlying his humor.

He was gentle. This man, who had played volleyball with the untamed energy of a frisky puppy and talked about his research like the proverbial mad scientist, made love with a tenderness and reverence she'd never experienced before. When he brought her to a peak, he groaned in triumph, as if he considered her satisfaction more important than his own. Afterward, he held her tight, whispering to her that she was wonderful.

When she awakened the next morning and found herself lying beside him in his bed, she suffered no doubt or regret, nor even confusion. She felt that she was exactly where she belonged. And when he blinked himself awake a few minutes after her, a beguiling smile illuminated his face at the mere sight of her. "I didn't dream you, after all," he murmured before kissing her.

One week after Lila received her master's degree, she and Ken were married. During the final year of his doctoral studies, they lived off his fellowship and whatever she picked up from substitute teaching jobs. Then he accepted a research position with a small computer firm in San Jose. It took Lila many long months to secure a teaching job in San Jose, and after a year Ken accepted a better position in Dallas. After another year, Lila began to piece together a career for herself with regular substituting assignments. Then Ken moved to Allied Technologies in Phoenix and she was unemployed again.

"It's all right," he would assure her. "We're a team. We work together. From each according to his abilities, and all that."

Which Lila understood to mean: from Ken, the ever-increasing earnings, and from Lila the maintenance of the house. Somebody had to make sure the refrigerator was well stocked and the laundry done, she supposed, and Ken couldn't very well do those things, especially after he'd enrolled in night classes in the business school at the university. Somebody had to make sure the floors were clean, the car serviced and the lawn mowed. And then Michael was born, and two years later Danny.

Ken moved out of research and into marketing at Allied-Tech. He traveled frequently; he worked long hours. "I'm doing this for us, Lila," he asserted, whenever she grumbled about his absences. "I don't like it any more than you do, but we're building something here. It's not going to be like this forever. I need your support, Lila. We're a team, aren't we?"

She needed his support, too. She had two young sons, a house to manage and no outside employment. The more money Ken earned the shorter his hair became, and the grander his promises about how his job would eventually entail less traveling. "I'm paying my dues, Lila," he'd explain. "Allied-Tech is grooming me for something better, and once I have it things are going to be great for both of us."

By the time Ken was transferred to the corporate headquarters outside Boston, Lila had given up on a career in teaching. She'd been away from it for too long; the accepted educational methods had changed and people fresh out of graduate school were vying for the best positions. Michael and Danny attended nursery school and then elementary school, and Lila continued to take care of them and maintain the house.

Two years ago, she volunteered to help out at the soup kitchen in Roxbury. It had been an impulsive idea at first; Ken had gone into a frenzy at the mere thought of it. "That's a slum, Lila!" he railed. "You're going to get mugged!"

"I could get mugged here in Wayland, too," she countered. "There are hungry people in Boston. I love you and the boys, Ken, but I'm bored. I've got to do something with my life."

"Fine. Volunteer for the town beautification committee. Give tours at Drumlin Farm. Help out at the DeCordova Museum. You don't have to go into Roxbury."

"I think I do," Lila argued.

In the end, she won. She worked three days a week at Mt. Zion Methodist. She helped Claudette Wiley, a social worker who ran the project, to prepare the meals, serve them and afterward straighten up the room they used in the church basement. During those precious few hours every Monday, Wednesday and Friday Lila didn't feel invisible. She didn't feel taken for granted. No matter how bland and boring the food she dished out might have been, the clients thanked her for it.

Pulling herself out of her reverie, she resolved to drive to Roxbury tomorrow. She rose from the wicker easy chair and closed the drapes. Just because she was taking a vacation from her family didn't mean she had to take a vacation from the soup kitchen. Her family would survive without her, but Mitzie and the other clients filling the church basement every weekday at noon might not.

She would put in her hours there, then she would come back to Hull, and the rest of the day would belong to her and her alone. She would be free to eat when she wished—or not eat at all. She wouldn't have to cook or clean up afterward. She wouldn't have to deal with anyone but herself, or answer to anyone but herself. If she chose to, she could stay up half the night reading—she would definitely have to visit the bookstore in town tomorrow—and sleep until ten the following morning. If she chose to, she could take a thirty-minute bubble bath, and nobody would pound on the bathroom door and demand to know what was taking her so long in there.

Perhaps, after a while, the solitude would drive her crazy, but for the moment she relished the sheer novelty of it. Indeed, the way she felt right now, a month seemed like much too short a time.

SHE ARRIVED at Mt. Zion Methodist at a quarter to eleven the following day. It was easy to get there on time when she didn't first have to send the boys off to school, hose down the kitchen and run a zillion errands. Lila had started this day in a much more relaxed manner, with a leisurely cup of coffee and a doughnut in the first-floor parlor of the

Bayside Manor. A couple of honeymooners also partook of the continental breakfast, but they were utterly engrossed in each other and didn't even ask Lila to share the single copy of the *Boston Globe* Mrs. Tarlock had left on the glass-topped coffee table along with the percolator and the plate of doughnuts. The starry-eyed couple whispered to each other, and a vacuum cleaner purred somewhere in the distance. It was the most quiet, peaceful breakfast Lila had had in a long, long time.

Once she'd finished her coffee, she refolded the newspaper and left it on the table. She went upstairs to her room—"*my* room," she murmured with unforgivable possessiveness—where she washed her face, attempted unsuccessfully to brush the humidity-induced frizz out of her hair and added a cardigan to her skirt and blouse. Then she drove into town to stock up on reading material—three current bestsellers—and from there to the church in Roxbury.

Claudette seemed pleased and somewhat surprised by her early arrival. "You're looking bright-eyed and bushy-tailed today," the older woman said as she lifted a hefty carton from the back of her station wagon. "Feeling a little less old and tired, are you?"

Lila grinned and lifted another box, smaller than Claudette's but backbreakingly heavy, filled with cans of tuna and cream of mushroom soup. Tuna casserole, she guessed. Fish was better than no meat at all.

It probably should have troubled her that she was looking bright-eyed and bushy-tailed. After talking to the boys last night, she'd been besieged by doubt and worry. This morning, however, those emotions had faded, leaving an almost transcendent serenity in their wake. She could miss the boys and not feel guilty. She could love Ken and not feel she'd done the wrong thing by leaving him for a few weeks. And she could indulge in the hope, however unrealistic, that they loved and missed her just as much as she loved and missed them—and that they understood why she had left. When she wasn't talking to Ken, she could almost pretend he didn't hate her for what she'd done.

"I'm still feeling old," she informed Claudette, "but not so tired."

"I'll tell you what makes me feel old and tired: this constant drizzle," Claudette muttered, as she heaved open the basement door. She and Lila lugged their cartons directly into the kitchen and dropped them onto the spacious worktable at the center of the room. "Woody's bursitis is really acting up. He keeps saying he thinks we should move down south somewhere once he retires, somewhere warm, like Florida. I can't bear the thought of being that far from my granddaughter, though."

"Maybe you could spend your winters in Florida and then come up here once it warms up again."

Claudette let out a wry laugh. "Sure. And who's going to pay for these two houses we'll be living in? Besides the fact that it doesn't get warm in Massachusetts till about June, and then by the end of September, it starts freezing up again."

She set two huge pots of water to boil on the stove while Lila tackled the cans of soup and tuna with a can opener. "I guess you couldn't really leave town in the winter," Lila noted. "Who'd run the soup kitchen if you did?"

"Is that your way of telling me you want to take over?" Claudette teased.

Lila shook her head emphatically. "Three days a week is all I can handle."

"Other obligations, I suppose," Claudette agreed. "When my children were younger, I wanted to be within shouting distance when they got home from school, too.

Too many hazards out there in the world. You've got to keep an eye on the young ones all the time."

Lila suffered a twinge of guilt. She attempted to ward it off with the rationalization that Ken was as much the boys' parent as she was, and that if he didn't feel guilty about traipsing to his office at Allied-Tech five days a week, year in and year out, she shouldn't feel guilty about taking off for a few weeks of desperately needed R and R.

Rationalization was right. She wouldn't have to come up with one if she didn't feel so guilty in the first place. By her own choice she was no longer within shouting distance of Michael and Danny. What if they had to shout? What if no one heard them? What if something happened to them, and it was all her fault for having abandoned them?

Stricken, she almost lashed out at Claudette when the older woman innocently asked, "How are those boys of yours, anyway? Doing well in school this year?"

"Yes, so far," Lila said, disguising the quaver in her voice. The boys would be all right. Lila had plenty of neighbors within shouting distance—and Ken would keep his ear attuned every now and then, too. What law said that only the mother was supposed to keep an eye on the young ones? "Michael's turning into a real whiz kid like his dad," she said with an optimism she had to fake. "Danny's doing well, too. He's such a bubbly boy, very active and popular..." She realized that in the two years she'd known Claudette, she had never really bragged about her sons. She might have occasionally alluded to them—Claudette had fussed sympathetically during Danny's bout with chicken pox a year ago, and she'd enjoyed hearing about their summer camp outings last July. Every spring Lila showed off her new batch of school photos of the boys, and Claudette always responded with the appropriate comments about what handsome children they were.

Similarly, Lila clucked and cooed over Claudette's pictures of her granddaughter.

But Lila had never been the sort to gush over her own children. In part, she knew how boring such gushing could be, having been on the receiving end of it too many times. In part, too, she felt that when a woman spent too much time talking about her children, she was inadvertently conveying the message that she had nothing more going on in her life, that because her entire universe revolved around her offspring she had nothing else to talk about.

Yet she couldn't stop herself from boasting about the boys today, just a little bit. Separated from them, she appreciated them more. After a day without them, she found it almost impossible to remember how messy Danny could be, or how bossy and supercilious Michael sometimes behaved. All she could think of now were her sons' virtues.

She experienced another brief twinge of emotion, less guilt this time than wistfulness, nostalgia, a compulsion to give each of her boys a crushing hug. Too late for that, though. God only knew whether they'd ever let her get that close to them again.

Once she and Claudette had the casserole ingredients spread into broad commercial baking trays and heating in the oven, they prepared the salad. A delivery truck from a local grocery store arrived with two crates of oranges and a few gallons of milk. A parishioner showed up on schedule, at twenty minutes to twelve, with her regular contribution: a jumbo package of paper plates and a box of plastic flatware. The coffee urn was set up, the serving counter sponged down and the preparations kicked into high gear.

At noon, the door opened and the clients poured in.

Lila scoured the first wave in search of Mitzie. Spotting the slight young woman, she waved. Mitzie waved back.

"That girl," Claudette mumbled under her breath, with a shake of her head.

"What about her?" Lila asked.

"If only she dried out for a few days... She isn't stupid, you know. Uneducated, but not stupid. She's got potential, more than a lot of the folks here. If she could just wean herself from booze and learn how to read..."

Lila scooped a portion of salad for the grizzled older man standing in front of her, but her mind lingered on Claudette's statement. "Mitzie is illiterate?"

Claudette nodded.

"Maybe I could teach her to read," Lila proposed.

Claudette guffawed. "And weren't you just telling me three days a week serving food here is all you can handle?"

"Well..." Lila scooped another mound of salad onto a plate held by a tattooed, snaggle-toothed young man, who offered his thanks in a gravelly voice. She told him he was welcome. Then, turning back to Claudette, she said, "I could tutor her for an hour or so after we close down the kitchen. Or before we set up. It wouldn't really cut into my time." She warmed to the idea. "I could work with other clients, as well. If there are others here who are illiterate..."

"Slow down," Claudette cautioned. "What makes you think you could teach reading and writing to these folks?"

"I have a master's degree in education," Lila informed her.

This revelation gave Claudette pause. She considered, then shook her head. "Yeah, it sounds nice enough," she said with a sigh. "And when you're done teaching them how to read, you can clean up the environment and establish world peace."

"Don't be cynical," Lila scolded with a smile. "If I were trained in environmental science, I would clean up the environment. I'm a teacher—and I became a teacher so I could help people. You can give people food, provide housing and free medical care, but if they lack an education they'll never be able to do anything for themselves."

"I know the quote, Lila," Claudette broke in. "The one about teaching a man to fish."

"It's the truth," Lila asserted. "We're feeding these people, not teaching them how to feed themselves. We've got a real opportunity to do some good—"

"Honey, you want to talk about real?" Claudette plopped a gooey mound of the casserole into an outstretched plate, then rotated to face Lila. "The reality is this: we haven't got the money to start a literacy project here."

"I wouldn't expect to be paid," Lila clarified. "We don't get paid for feeding the clients, either."

"Salary is the least of it. You can't teach reading without books, right? And paper and pencils. These people don't even have a roof over their heads, some of them. Do you think they can just march into the local five-and-dime and buy themselves a spiral notebook?"

"Well..."

"You know how we run things here: I beg. We live on donations, on whatever the local supermarkets are kind enough to give us, on Mrs. Galt bringing us paper goods, on leftover produce from the restaurants and caterers—and most of all, on this space from the church. They give us this basement for three hours every day, three hours when they could be renting it to someone with money, or holding Bingo games to raise funds for the Sunday school, or at the very least closing it up so they don't have to pay for the extra utilities. For you to sit around giving reading lessons after hours would mean trying to wrangle more time from the church, and they can't afford that."

Refusing to admit defeat, Lila issued a perfunctory "you're welcome" to a client while her mind tossed around possibilities. "Maybe I could find a room at a school, somewhere..."

"Where, in Wayland? Here in Greater Roxbury they like to keep the children in school as late as they can, because once they leave they'll be on the streets with the crack dealers."

"I couldn't do it in Wayland," Lila complained. "I would have to do it where the clients are."

"Fine. Then do it on the street corners, in the alleys, in the bus station—and hope nobody jumps you for the change in your pocket. Ten'll get you twenty most of these folks wouldn't sit still long enough to learn the alphabet, anyway. There are lots of literacy programs out there, but you can't make a person learn if he doesn't want to. You see what I'm saying, Lila?"

"What you're saying is, give up," Lila countered with a frown. "But I won't." It wasn't like her to be so stubborn, so resistant to the hard facts. But damn it, she'd already given up her teaching career once. She was determined not to cave in without a fight. She wasn't going to be invisible this time.

Claudette sized her up with a long stare. "God bless you, honey," she murmured. "It's a lost cause, but God bless you. I'll talk to Reverend Munsey and see if we can wrangle an extra hour of church time a couple of days a week. Meanwhile, you'd better find out whether you've got any students willing to attend these classes of yours."

"Thank you." Lila felt strangely buoyant, rejuvenated by the very idea of doing something important, something that mattered. She knew she was facing daunting odds and innumerable hurdles, but she wasn't discouraged. She was infused with a sense of purpose, a goal, a challenge. Maybe it was a lost cause, but if it made her stop feeling so defeated, the effort would be worth it. "Thank you, Claudette," she repeated, giving her colleague a hug.

"Don't thank me," Claudette said, brushing off her gratitude. "Chances are, we're going to get shot down." She spooned out another portion of the tuna casserole, muttering, "We can't even get enough food for these clients, and now we'll have to go begging for paper and pencils." Glancing toward the door to assess how much longer the line was, she scowled. "Now who the hell is that?" she grunted. "Probably some city bureaucrat here to close down our operations."

Lila looked over to the door and froze. A tall, slim, impeccably groomed man stood just outside the doorway, peeking in. His well-tailored suit was partially hidden beneath a Burberry raincoat, and his conservatively patterned tie was knotted snugly at his neck. His thick auburn hair was damp from the drizzle and his hands were plunged into his pockets. He had a square jaw, a long, straight nose and dark, penetrating eyes set deep beneath his brow.

"He's no city bureaucrat," Lila whispered, unable to tear her gaze from him.

"He sure doesn't look like the sort who'd call a park bench home," Claudette noted. "A little too well-dressed, don't you think? Cleaner than we usually get in here, too. I bet he even smells of a fancy after-shave."

"Old Spice," Lila muttered.

"Mighty good-looking," Claudette rambled on. Then Lila's words registered on her, and she frowned. "How do you know it's Old Spice?"

"He's my husband," said Lila.

# *Chapter Four*

For the first time in his otherwise nonviolent life, Ken understood how passion could drive a man to acts of madness.

He watched Lila as she stood behind the counter dishing out salad, her hands and arms moving with natural grace and her light brown hair glinting with traces of silver and gold beneath the fluorescent ceiling lights. The oversize brown apron she wore over her woolen skirt and cardigan emphasized the delicacy of her petite build, and her vivid blue eyes shone with mercy as she met the haggard stares of the derelicts lined up across the counter from her.

Mercy for them, yes—but not for Ken. The minute she spotted him lurking in the doorway, her eyes seemed to crystallize into something hard and cold, the physical embodiment of hatred. And suddenly, after a morning spent racked with guilt and anguish and sheer dread, he found himself overwhelmed by a wrath to equal hers. His body grew unbearably taut with rage. He wanted to drag her out from behind the counter and possess her. He wanted to imprint himself on her, permanently and irrevocably. He wanted to establish beyond a doubt that she was his. He wanted to stake his claim.

Oh, God, no. He wanted to love her so sweetly she'd weep with remorse and admit that she couldn't live without him. He wanted to remind her, physically as well as emotionally, that he was good to her and good for her, that no matter what petty grievances she harbored against him, nothing was so serious that it couldn't be solved with an interlude of glorious lovemaking.

He wanted her—one way or another. And he wanted her to stop making him crazy. Because to be entertaining such wild thoughts meant he was definitely crazy at this moment.

It had been a ghastly morning. He'd wanted to get to work early, but he'd felt obliged to stay home with the boys until their school bus arrived at the stop across the street. When Danny and Michael weren't fighting over possession of the cereal box, they were crabbing about Ken's numerous shortcomings: "That's not the right orange juice glass, Dad!" "This bowl is dirty, Dad!" "Mom always gets our backpacks ready, Dad! You're supposed to put the books in first and our lunches in last!" He hadn't bothered to eat anything himself, and he'd drunk a cup of vile-tasting instant coffee because he lacked the time to brew the real stuff. What did Lila think, that he could get himself and the boys dressed and fed and on their way without any help?

He'd considered sending the boys to a neighbor's house to wait for the bus so he could leave for work sooner, but taking that tack would have required explaining that Lila had walked out on him. No way. He'd die before he'd let his marital situation become the subject of neighborhood gossip.

Gossip. He'd better warn the boys to keep their mouths shut. "Listen, guys," he'd said, breaking into their absurd debate about whether misshapen Cheerios tasted better than perfectly round ones. "I don't want you telling anyone at school about Mom, okay?"

"How come?" Danny asked.

"It's just . . ." Ken sighed. "It's the sort of thing we call a private matter, okay? You know what private is."

"Yeah," Danny said. "It's like what's inside your underpants." He collapsed into giggles.

Ken took another deep breath. "Stop laughing, Danny—this is serious. Yes, it is sort of like your private parts. There are some things we just don't share with other people. Mom's being gone is one of them."

"How come?" Michael asked.

Ken closed his eyes and prayed for an easy answer. Unable to think of one, he said, "Remember how we talked about how Mom's kind of angry about things? Well, that's not anyone else's business. As soon as she gets over being angry, she'll come back and everything will go back to normal again. It's just not something other people have to know about."

"It's like a secret, huh," Danny said, still grinning. "I can keep a secret."

Michael snorted incredulously at Danny's claim. Then he grew solemn and eyed Ken skeptically. Ken's soul withered as he read the distrust in his son's grave expression. Michael was too old to be fooled. He knew that things were bad, that everything might not go back to normal ever again.

Danny twisted in his chair to look out the window. "The bus!" he shouted, springing to his feet and dashing to the mudroom to get his jacket. Michael followed him, leaving Ken to brood about what he could have said to reassure his older son, what magic words he might have spoken to erase the fear and doubt from Michael's eyes.

There were no magic words. Ken was as racked with fear and doubt as his son.

All during the drive to Newton he'd worried. Was he burdening the boys too much by asking them to keep this domestic crisis a secret? What if the stress of it caused them to misbehave in class? He didn't want to alert their teachers, but maybe he ought to call the school nurse, just in case.

In case what? In case Michael burst into tears in the middle of lunch? In case Danny started screaming about birthday cupcakes during a class discussion on Columbus?

Ken couldn't call the school. The kids would be all right. They'd get through this. He couldn't allow himself to believe anything else.

He was steering into Allied-Tech's driveway, a good fifteen minutes behind schedule, when he remembered that, having neglected to straighten up the kitchen after breakfast, he'd left on the table a container of milk, which was undoubtedly growing warmer and more sour with each passing minute. He would have to phone Lila and tell her to stop at the grocery store to buy a fresh gallon... A short, brutal expletive leaped to his lips. He'd have to do the grocery shopping himself, damn it. In which store did Lila shop? Did he have enough cash on hand? Where the hell did Lila keep the check-cashing card, anyway? What, besides milk, should he buy? And what about the boys, stuck all alone in the house so late, while their father fought the after-work crowds at the supermarket?

He wasted his first hour as Allied-Tech's new Vice President of marketing being hailed, pounded on the back and teased by his colleagues. "Too much celebrating last night, eh?" one of his co-workers ribbed him, after commenting on his late arrival. "What's your new title, V.P. of Marketing and Hangovers?"

Ken managed a weak laugh. What alternative did he have? He couldn't very well announce to his colleagues, "I celebrated with a Pepsi on the rocks at Pizza Hut—Lila's walked out on me," or, "My new title is V.P. in Charge of Sandwich-Making and Full-Time Household Management." When Larry Talbot dropped by Ken's old office and wended his way through the stacks of empty cartons the maintenance staff had left for Ken to pack his things in, Ken couldn't bring himself to request that Larry scrap his idea for a celebratory party. "Lila thinks we may have another commitment on Saturday night," he lied, despising himself for his cowardice. "I'll have to give you a definite maybe."

One good thing about being required to pack his belongings himself for the move to his new third-floor office was that packing was mindless labor. Ken could empty his file cabinets and desk drawers into boxes while his brain skipped freely from one anxiety to the next. Would Danny blurt out the news about his mother's disappearance at recess? Would Michael crack under the strain? Would he ever forgive Lila? Would she ever forgive him?

At around noon, as he was taping down the flaps of the eighth carton of files he'd packed, he remembered that Wednesday was one of the days she worked at the soup kitchen in Roxbury. Unexpectedly, he experienced a faint ray of hope. He didn't really believe she would bother to show up at the soup kitchen after having maneuvered her disappearance so carefully, but on the slim chance that she might be there, he thumbed through the metropolitan Boston telephone directory until he found a listing for a Mt. Zion Methodist Church in Roxbury, jotted down the address and bolted from the office.

He had never visited the church before. Although the surrounding streets were seedy and grimy, the church itself was a proud granite structure sitting squarely on a corner, its oak doors carved with crosses and its spire rising staunchly into the overcast sky. He cruised into the parking lot adjacent to the church building, noticed Lila's car parked in one of the spaces and let loose with a stream of curses that, under ordinary circumstances, he would never even whisper, let alone bellow, within a stone's throw of a church.

He waited to be struck down by lightning. His windshield grew blurry beneath the raw, monotonous drizzle, but no heaven-sent electrical bolts descended upon him. Obviously God could tell that Ken was operating under severe emotional pressure.

He parked, got out of his car and entered the building through a door at the bottom of a short flight of concrete steps leading from the lot to the church's basement. Inside, he followed the sound of voices down a dimly lit hall to a spacious all-purpose room. An assortment of people sat at long, folding tables set up around the room. The air smelled of coffee, oranges and stale human sweat.

And there was Lila. His fugitive wife. Serving salad to total strangers.

He ventured into the room. She fumbled her serving spoon and let it drop into the nearly empty salad bowl, but her gaze never broke from his. He took in the nervous flutter of her eyelids, the darting of her tongue over her lips, the flexing of a muscle in her jaw. When he was within a few feet of the counter, she attempted a feeble smile. "Claudette, this is my husband, Ken," she said to the robust older woman beside her. "Ken, this is Claudette Wiley. She runs this project."

He gave Claudette a perfunctory handshake, unprepared for the woman's warm clasp. "I'm delighted to meet you, Ken," she boomed. "I've heard so much about you. I'm so glad you've finally come down here to see what good work your wife is doing for these people."

Good work? Shoveling soggy lettuce leaves onto paper plates? That was precisely the sort of "good work" she'd rejected when she'd run away from home yesterday.

Claudette didn't deserve his anger, however. "The pleasure's mine," he said politely, then turned back to Lila. "I'd like to talk to you." His voice sounded dry, almost raspy. He wondered if she could tell how close he was to choking on the words, how difficult it was for him to remain outwardly calm and courteous while he was short-circuiting inside.

Lila ran the tip of her tongue over her lips again, then glanced questioningly at Claudette. "Go on ahead," said Claudette. "I can take care of any stragglers."

Nodding, Lila moved around from behind the counter and stalked directly to the door, wiping her hands on the bottom of her apron. She didn't wait for Ken; she didn't even look at him. He had no choice but to follow.

She continued down the corridor to the parking lot exit. Opening the door, she viewed the chilly rain and let the door swing shut. She turned to face Ken.

"I'm going crazy," he said. It was the truth. Gazing down into those glacial blue eyes of hers, he felt inundated by so many conflicting desires, he was sure he'd disintegrate from the force of them. He wanted to throttle her, to kiss her, to bury his head in her lap and cry. He wanted to travel back in time, years back, to the days when he'd believed that Lila was his anchor and his mast, providing the direction and the stability in his life. His partner, his sharer. His lover.

Barring that, he wanted to flay her for being so cold-hearted.

Her silence extended beyond a minute. He struggled to regulate his breathing, his erratic pulse. All would be lost if he didn't maintain a firm grip on himself. He had to go about this properly. "We can't work out anything if you insist on staying away," he said with what he considered supreme reasonableness.

"There's nothing to work out," she countered, her tone as artificially calm as his.

"Lila—correct me if I'm wrong, but you've left me, haven't you? We're separated." He winced, his pain nearly palpable. *We're separated.* Five syllables, each one a stiletto piercing his heart.

"We aren't separated," she argued fatuously. "I mean, not like *that*. I just need to spend a little time by myself."

"By yourself?" Fury ripped through him, and his voice emerged in a growl. "You need to be by yourself and yet here you are—" he gestured down the hall toward the all-purpose room "—surrounded by hundreds of the great unwashed."

"Fewer than a hundred, probably," Lila corrected him.

Damn her. Damn her for remaining so composed when his self-control was dwindling into seething, unruly anguish. "You'll feed a hundred strangers, but not your own family!"

"My own family doesn't say thank-you," she retorted, her poise beginning to erode. "These people do."

"All right. You want thank-yous? We'll say thank you. We'll have some cards engraved. We'll practice our etiquette all you want if it means so much to you."

"The etiquette doesn't mean anything," Lila said, her tone once again muted. "It's the sentiment that matters. I'm appreciated here. These people let me know they're grateful for what I'm doing. And I leave the soup kitchen feeling that I've made a difference in someone's life."

"You make a difference in our lives, too!"

"Then why don't I feel it?" she argued, her eyes unexpectedly glistening with tears. "Why don't you ever let me feel that I do?" A sob threatened to overcome her, and she averted her face.

*Don't,* he silently implored her. If she started to cry, he would cry, too. They'd both dissolve into tears and wind up wetter than the rain-soaked steps outside the door.

He reached out to touch her, but the instant his fingertips brushed her arm, she jerked away. He watched his hand drop from hers, thinking it one of the saddest sights he'd ever seen. "Okay," he mumbled. "I forgot your birthday, and I feel lousy about it. Neglect of birthday—guilty as charged. Okay? Now come home and tell me what you want, and—"

"I want this month," she declared. "That's the only present I want. I need it. I've earned it. I'm not giving it up."

"Lila." He swallowed, absorbing her vehemence as best he could. "Lila, why didn't you tell me it was so bad? Why didn't you say something before it came to this?"

Her shoulders trembled, but still she refused to succumb to tears. "I did. I said things in my own way, but nobody ever listened to me."

"I'd listen now, if you came back."

"I'm not sure I believe you."

The accusation staggered him. How could she not believe him? He might have taken her for granted, ignored her, been lazy in their relationship. But he'd never been dishonest with her, never.

She sniffled, touched her hands to her cheeks and blinked. In a different context, her struggle to keep from crying would have moved him to compassion. But not now.

"How are the boys?" she asked.

"How do you think they are? They're scared to death."

She smiled wryly. "Nothing scares Danny."

"All right, Danny's not exactly scared. Mike is, though. He's suffering. He understands things, Lila, he—" Ken sensed he was beginning to rant. He took a breath and tried again. "How could you just leave them without even offering them an explanation?" A fresh surge of anger fueled him to add, "They're kids, Lila. And you just disappeared, without even considering how they'd take it. You let them come home from school to an empty house, and—"

"And they were probably thrilled. When I'm home, I make them eat a healthy after-school snack. When I'm not, they pig out on potato chips."

With a grimace, Ken conceded. The boys hadn't even noticed that their mother was missing, let alone seemed to care.

"I wanted to say goodbye to them," Lila admitted, fingering the apron's sash, smoothing it around her waist to give her nervous hands something to do. "I really wanted to, Ken, but I was afraid that if I did, I'd never have the fortitude to leave."

"And wouldn't that have been a tragedy," he muttered.

"For me, it would have," she snapped. "I know it's a hardship on the three of you, having to fend for yourselves for a while—"

"A hardship?" He almost laughed at her understatement.

"Well, believe it or not, Ken, it would have been even more of a hardship for me to stay. I have been a full-time, seven-days-a-week mother for ten years. I've been a full-time wife for sixteen—"

"So what? You don't want to be a full-time wife? You want to have an affair, is that it?" His caustic tone disguised the excruciating terror that tore through his soul. Good Lord, what if that was what this was all about? What if she really was involved with another man? What if she was sharing her bed with him in her very nice rooming house near the water? Ken would kill her, and the other man—and then himself.

No, he'd be civilized. He'd file for divorce. And castrate the other man.

"Of course I don't want to have an affair," she scoffed. "Don't be ridiculous."

He wished he could dismiss the idea as easily as she could. "Then what do you want?" he asked. "More help around the house? Come home and we'll talk about it. I'm not going to negotiate anything with you as long as you're off on your own somewhere, out of reach."

"I keep telling you, Ken, all I want is some time alone."

"That's not all you want."

Her eyes met his for an instant, then darted away. "It's all I'm asking for," she insisted in a hushed tone.

"Let me give you something for your birthday," he proposed. If there was even a remote possibility that she could be thinking about having an affair—even fantasizing about it, even subconsciously—he knew he wasn't going to win her back by threatening her. He'd have to present himself as superior to any other man so she would remain with him by choice. And he'd have to prove that, even if she wasn't willing to ask for more, he was willing to give more. "Just name it, Lila. We'll celebrate your birthday any way you want. I swear."

"I'm celebrating it exactly the way I want," she insisted. "I've already named what I want: a month off."

"You want to hurt me," he said bitterly.

"I want to heal myself," she corrected him. "I'm sorry if this hurts you, but for once in my life I'm putting my feelings and my needs ahead of yours. I know that's odd, it's not like me and you're not used to it. In all honesty, I'm not used to it, either. But that's what I want for my birthday—to put my feelings and my needs first for a change."

He shook his head, acknowledging the impossibility of getting her to come home today. Never before had he realized how stubborn she could be. But then, there were obviously a lot of things he'd never realized about her.

He inhaled deeply, then exhaled in a long sigh of defeat. "All right," he conceded, gazing past her, focusing on a rust-colored stain on the cinder block wall behind her. "If we can talk about practicalities for a minute..."

She waited patiently. He felt her eyes on him, the severity in them waning as she absorbed the fact that he was surrendering.

"What am I supposed to say when people ask me where you are?" he asked, chastising himself inwardly for sounding so pathetically helpless.

"Tell them this is my birthday present," she replied. "Tell them the truth. I wanted a month-long vacation for my birthday." She gave a wry laugh. "People will think you're a real prince for giving it to me."

He accepted her dig, just one more bruise on his battered psyche. "What about the boys?"

"I'll talk to them tonight," she said. "I'll call every night, Ken. I want them to understand—especially Michael. I know how intense he can be, and..." She wavered, her gaze searching the scuffed floor, as if a solution might be lying there. "I'll try to explain things to him."

"Oh, yes. Your voice on the telephone line is bound to reassure him in a way no warm, maternal hug could."

"Don't blackmail me," she shot back in a tremulous voice. "If you had any idea how hard this is for me—"

"You sure do make it look easy."

She glowered at him for a moment, then spun away and started down the hall. He chased after her, curled his fingers around her arm and pulled her to a halt.

Whatever angry thoughts he'd directed at her when he'd first seen her at the serving table, now that he was actually holding her, he felt only a deep, poignant yearning. He wanted a warm, maternal hug, or a fierce, passionate one, or even a fleeting, friendly one. Just a moment of contact, a chance for him and Lila to communicate something positive, something they seemed unable to articulate through their anger.

He stroked his thumb along her upper arm, exploring the slender muscle through the knit fabric of her sweater. He braced himself for another scathing look from her, but when she lifted her eyes to him, he saw his own agony mirrored in their beautiful blue depths. "I don't want to let you go," he confessed in a broken whisper.

He saw tears well up in her eyes again, but she bravely blinked them back. "It would be better if you did," she murmured.

She was right. He could tie her up and lock her inside the house—and she would be gone forever. The tighter he held her, the faster she would flee.

Sighing, he released her arm. His hand remained curved, aching in its emptiness. "Practicalities," he repeated, struggling to clear his head. "We've been invited to a party this Saturday night."

"Oh?"

He contemplated telling her about his promotion, then decided not to. That was news to be celebrated at a happy time, not tossed at her like bait to lure her home. If he mentioned it, she might charge him with blackmail again. She was too self-involved right now, anyway. This just didn't seem like the right moment to share something that joyous with her.

"The party is at the Talbots' house,' he told her. "You know, Larry Talbot from Allied-Tech."

"Yes."

"Well..." He chose his words carefully. "There are probably going to be a lot of people from work there, and..." *Spit it out, Kenny-boy. Tell her you're the guest of honor.* "I really don't want them knowing that we're living apart," he concluded lamely. He would not resort to manipulating her. He wouldn't make her accompany him to the party out of guilt—at least not unless nothing else worked.

"I can see how that might be a little awkward," she granted.

"Then you'll come with me?"

"Okay."

A silent cheer rose within him. He mustn't let himself become too elated, too optimistic, but damn, it felt good to hear her say *okay*. "The party starts at around seven. You could come home for the weekend, and—"

"No, wait." She held up her hand. "Why should I come home for the weekend?"

"So we can go the party together," he explained, smothering his impatience. "You just said you were willing to let the people I work with think we're together. That means we've got to arrive at the party together."

"Well..." She ruminated. "Maybe we could meet somewhere. The Talbots live in Wellesley, right? We could meet someplace not far from their house, at a shopping center or something, leave my car there and drive over together."

So much for taking her willingness to go the party as a cause for optimism. His spirit deflated like a punctured balloon, but he refused to give up. "Lila, be reasonable. I'm not going to rendezvous with you in some dark parking lot. If we're going to a party together, we're going *together*. You'll come home, and—"

"I will not come home."

"Why? Do you think I'm going to lay a trap for you?" He couldn't help himself. He could stay calm only so long before the tide changed and fury prevailed once more. "Are you afraid you might faint dead away when you see how upset you've made the boys? Or are you afraid you might actually, God forbid, enjoy being home?"

"I'm not afraid!"

"Then what is it? What's wrong with you that you won't even come home for one crummy weekend?"

"What's wrong with me?" she flared. "What's wrong with me is that if I go home I'm going to slide right back into the old routine. I'm going to see what a mess the house is and feel compelled to clean it. I'm going to hear the boys shouting that they're hungry, and you'll fade into the background and let me fix them a snack. You know that as well as I do, Ken. The minute I go home, I'm going to be right back where I started. And I'm not ready for that."

"So what am I supposed to do?" he shouted. "What the hell do you want me to do?"

Lila's eyes drifted past him, and he turned around to find a tall, silver-haired man wearing a dark suit and a beatific smile. "Reverend Munsey," Lila mumbled. "Hello."

"Good afternoon, Lila," he said in a mellifluous baritone. He turned his beaming smile on Ken, who experienced a twinge of shame. "Is this client being difficult?"

"This isn't a client," Lila informed him. "He's my husband, Kenneth Chapin. Ken, Reverend Munsey, the pastor of Mt. Zion Methodist."

The minister gathered Ken's hand in his own. "Lila's husband. How do you do?"

Ken returned the greeting and added, "Sorry about the language."

"I'm sorry about whatever it is that's making you so angry," said the minister. "We've all got to sound off sometimes, Mr. Chapin, but I'd rather you don't do it where those hungry street people might hear you. They've already got more than enough anger to deal with."

"I understand," Ken said, chastened. "I'm sorry."

The minister nodded at both of them and continued down the corridor, his rubber-soled shoes making no sound on the tiled floor. Ken gazed after him until he vanished through a door across the hall from the all-purpose room. Then he returned his attention to Lila. He felt drained, subdued, reflective.

"How about if I pick you up?" he suggested.

"Pick me up?"

"At your rooming house by the water." He wanted to hold her again, to stroke her cheek, to feel her smooth, freckled skin against his fingertips. One touch would ameliorate his fear. One touch would reassure him that she wasn't truly gone.

"In other words, you want me to tell you where I'm staying."

Her suspicion of him only fed his fear. It rose around him like water, causing the floor beneath his feet to shift, making him feel as if he were drowning. "I have no interest in chasing after you, Lila. But if we're going to attend this party together, I'm going to pick you up and bring you there with me. That's the way these things are done. I do happen to know a few things about etiquette."

She stared into his eyes. She had to tilt her head up to do so, and he was struck by how tiny she seemed. Small but feisty, like a mouse in combat with a hawk, fighting for her life, fighting all the harder because of her diminutive size. Her gaze revealed a strange blend of nerve and anxiety.

Abruptly, she turned away. "All right," she said, her voice barely above a whisper. "You can pick me up."

How much it had cost her to accept his offer. How much it had tortured her to let her husband know where she was.

And how much it tortured Ken to realize that, as long as he'd known this woman and as deeply as he'd loved her, he really didn't know where she was at all.

# Chapter Five

"You're looking pretty lively today," Jimmy called to Lila, as she neared the broad veranda extending across the front of Bayside Manor. For the first time in six days the sun was out, not just peeking between the clouds but bright and full, illuminating the crisp October afternoon. Across the street the clean white sand of the barrier beach shimmered in the sunshine. An elderly man meandered along the beach, scanning the ground with a metal detector; a young couple romped in the breeze, attempting to launch a box kite; a barefoot jogger in a windbreaker streaked along the water's edge. The bay glinted a soothing blue-green color, reflecting the blue sky.

Lila gazed wistfully at the beach for a minute, then turned and climbed the porch stairs. If she hadn't spent so long shopping, she might have had time for a stroll along the sand. She hadn't realized, when she'd packed for her month-long retreat, that she would encounter a need for dressy apparel. The tiny closet and the wicker chest of drawers in her room above the veranda held a few plain skirts and blouses, corduroy slacks, sweaters, sneakers and loafers—appropriate garb for reading and resting and putting in her stints at the soup kitchen, but not for attending parties at the elegant Wellesley residence of one of Allied Technologies' vice presidents.

If she had to show up at a soiree at the Talbots' house, then she intended to show up in the appropriate attire. After visiting her favorite restaurant in downtown Hull for a late brunch, she had wandered into a neighboring boutique, browsed among the racks and forked over eighty dollars—eight percent of her month's allotment of funds—on a long-sleeved sheath of dark blue silk with a high collar that buttoned at the nape of her neck and an enticing slit plunging along her spine from the twin pearly buttons nearly to her waist.

Once she had paid for the dress, she realized she would have to buy shoes and a bag to go with it. She could have telephoned Ken and asked him to bring her black patent leather pumps with him when he came to pick her up that evening, but if she were going to do that she could have also asked him to bring one of her old cocktail dresses. She'd already bought a new dress; she might as well go the whole way and get new shoes and a purse, too. And dangly gold-and-turquoise earrings, a couple of gold-hued combs with which to style her hair, an eye shadow the same shade of blue as the dress and a few other cosmetics besides. To preserve what money she had left, she charged everything except the dress on a credit card, enduring some qualms about spending so much money on herself. A thousand dollars seemed an extravagant enough sum to squander on her birthday without adding another sixty-eight dollars for dress sandals and a matching clutch, twenty-five dollars for costume jewelry and another twenty-five for makeup. But if she didn't put her accessories on the credit card, she would run out of money well before the month was up, and she wasn't going to cut short her vacation just so she could look spectacular hanging from Ken's arm at a social affair.

Funny what the mind could rationalize when it had to. The Talbots' party was Lila's primary justification, but she'd also bought the ensemble because it was fun to indulge herself. If she had spent too much, so be it. She would forgo any gifts for herself at Christmas.

"Shopping, huh?" Jimmy observed, surveying the monogrammed bags dangling from her hands.

Leaning against the porch railing, she nodded. She knew she ought to go inside and hang up the dress so it wouldn't get wrinkled, but she couldn't bear to leave the veranda when the sky was so clear, the sea breeze so balmy. "What are you doing?" she asked, watching Jimmy unscrew the casing from one of the porch lamps. "Changing the light bulb?"

He finished removing the screw and shook his head. "Looking for wiring problems. I told Mrs. Tarlock, either she lets me check all these ancient fixtures or I'm reporting her to the fire department. Wire insulation doesn't last forever, you know."

"Are you trying to tell me Bayside Manor is a fire trap?" Lila asked, less alarmed than she ought to be.

"Not with me around to check things," he assured her with a dimpled grin. "So, what's in all the bags?"

"You don't really want to know, do you?"

He chuckled. "It's just, you're grinning from ear to ear and I was wondering what got you in such a great mood. The last few times I've seen you— Well, it's none of my business."

She turned toward the shoreline, letting the wind toss her hair back from her face. The last few times Jimmy had seen her she had undoubtedly looked melancholy, because that was how she'd felt. But today...today she felt giddy and nervous and absurdly excited.

She hadn't purchased the new dress to dazzle Ken's associates. She'd purchased it because she was going on a date. That the date was with her husband of sixteen years didn't make her any less anxious. For the first time since she'd met Ken, she was apprehensive about the impression she would make on a man. She had no idea how the date would go, let alone how it would end. She wasn't even sure what her escort thought of her.

Her last few telephone calls had done little to enlighten her. The evening after Ken had confronted her in the basement of Mt. Zion Methodist, he'd sounded subdued on the phone, obviously working hard to keep his anger reined in. He'd erupted only once, when she'd refused to make arrangements with a baby-sitter for Saturday evening. "You can find a sitter," she'd told him. "Try Beth Parrish first—she's usually available, and you don't have to drive anywhere to pick her up. She can walk over."

"Would you call her, please?"

"Why should I call her? I haven't even got her telephone number with me."

"I'll look it up for you," Ken had offered. "Hang on a minute and I'll get it."

"No, Ken. You can set it up with her."

"It's your job," Ken had protested. "You always take care of that."

Yes, Lila always took care of hiring a baby-sitter when she and Ken were planning a night out. And when the night arrived, Ken would shower and shave while Lila would make dinner for the boys, clean the kitchen, pour the potato chips into a bowl for the sitter, write down the emergency numbers, get the boys into their pajamas and set up a tape on the VCR. If Beth Parrish was the sitter, she would walk to the Chapin house from her house down the street; otherwise, Ken would make the grand contribution of picking up one of the other sitters. Lila would rehash the rules with the sitter and the boys, then race upstairs to the bedroom to change her clothes and put on her make-up while Ken paced from one end of the room to the other, looking pointedly at his watch and muttering about how long it was taking her to get ready.

She had never complained about having to oversee all the requisite details—she'd viewed it as the price she had to pay for a night out. Yet she resented the fact that Ken didn't also have to pay a price, that he didn't also have to hustle and fuss and rush through his grooming in order to earn the blessed reward of a restaurant meal or a show. It didn't seem fair to her that she always had to take full responsibility for their outings, that she had to work so hard for a few hours off from motherhood.

"I'm not going to do it this time," she'd asserted on the phone. "If you want to bring me to this party, Ken, you're going to have to take care of things on your end."

He'd lapsed into silence for a minute—wrestling with his temper, Lila had suspected. Then: "I can't call Beth. I just can't."

"Why not?"

"Lila, I'm a forty-two-year-old man and she's a fifteen-year-old girl. I'd feel like a lecher or something, calling her up and asking her if she's free on Saturday night."

"Oh, Ken, don't be silly."

"I'm not being silly. I'm telling you, I would feel weird."

Lila had sighed. "Do you want to know something? *I* feel weird calling up fifteen-year-old girls and asking them if they're free on Saturday night, too. But I do it because it has to be done. This time, if you really want to go to this party, *you're* going to have to do it."

More silence. More wrestling with his temper. "All right, Lila," he'd finally capitulated. "But I don't like it."

"Welcome to the club."

He'd cursed under his breath, then grumbled, "Here—talk to the boys."

Tonight might turn out to be a major fiasco. She might get herself all dressed up in her new outfit and spend the evening growling at Ken and avoiding him, faking her way through lighthearted chitchat while Ken's transparent brown eyes sent poison-dart stares at her from across the enormous Talbot living room. As soon as they could leave without attracting too much attention, he might drive her back to Bayside Manor, dump her on the veranda and ask her not to bother coming home at the end of the month.

Just like a first date.

She turned back to Jimmy and raked her hands through the wind-tangled curls of her hair. He was examining the wires that connected the lamp to the shingled front wall of the building, but his eyes kept straying to her. "Go ahead, finish what you were going to say," she recklessly invited him. "What's none of your business?"

"Well..." He bent over his toolbox and pulled out a roll of black insulation tape. "You've just seemed kind of sad, that's all."

She was surprised that he'd noticed. The first time he had seen her, when he'd come to her room to fix her radiators, she had been crying. But after that first night, she had thought she'd kept her emotions pretty well hidden. "I'm not sad," she said.

"Lonely, then?" He tore a strip of tape with his teeth and methodically wound it around one of the wires. "I mean, taking a vacation all by yourself and everything..."

"I'm alone by choice," she declared.

"Oh." He smiled sheepishly.

"I don't mind your asking, Jimmy." She used his first name deliberately; she didn't want him to be uncomfortable around her.

His gaze narrowed on her. His eyelashes, she noticed, were variegated in color, some of them nearly white and others a light brown color. His eyebrows seemed particularly pale in contrast to his sun-bronzed complexion. "Well," he apologized, "it's none of my business."

"If it was none of your business," she pointed out, "I'd be the first to tell you."

He appraised her thoughtfully, turning the roll of insulation tape over and over in his hand. Then he gave her an impish grin. "It's just, well, you know how guys can be. A pretty woman tells me she's alone by choice, and I get all kinds of ideas."

"I know exactly how guys can be," Lila responded, refusing to let his playful flirting disconcert her. "A woman doesn't have to tell you anything and you still get all kinds of ideas."

Jimmy chuckled. "It's hormonal, I think. My old lady up in Portsmouth used to tell me men were the missing link between apes and women."

"She sounds smart."

"Not smart enough. She dumped a great guy like me, didn't she?" Jimmy remarked, not sounding particularly heartbroken about it. His smile lost its playful edge, becoming warm and sweet. "I'm not complaining, of course. Being unattached has its advantages, don't you think?"

Lila almost blurted out that she hardly considered herself unattached. Even if her marriage collapsed, even if it was already beyond repair, it would take her a long time to feel single—not only because of the boys but because, with or without a marriage license, Ken was an essential part of her life. If he decided not to welcome her back home once her month was up, if he cut himself off from her, if he served her with papers and signed on the bottom line, she would probably suffer from phantom pains for the rest of her life.

Not a cheering thought, especially when she would have to face Ken in three hours or so. Her watch told her it was three-thirty, and he'd said to expect him between six-thirty and a quarter to seven, depending on how much difficulty he had locating Bayside Manor. She had given him the address and directions on the phone last night, and he'd insisted he would be able to find the hotel. Usually, though, when he drove to an unfamiliar place, he had Lila seated beside him, navigating.

"Well," she said to Jimmy, "I'd better run along. I've got things to take care of." She would rather have stayed on the porch with him a while longer; thinking about the possible demise of her marriage had upset her. It was a lot more pleasant to shoot the breeze with this handsome blond man than to try to imagine what the future held for her and Ken. More pleasant and much less complicated.

"Yeah, you'd better go," Jimmy urged her. "I've got things to take care of, too, but if you keep hanging around I'm going to wind up talking to you instead of working."

"So long, Jimmy." She swung open the lobby door.

"Catch you later, Ms. Chapin."

She was momentarily taken aback by his use of her name, but then she acknowledged that, other than herself, the honeymoon couple and a trio of elderly sisters, there weren't any other long-term guests at Bayside Manor. Given his easygoing nature, Jimmy was probably on friendly terms with all of them. Yesterday, when Lila had returned from the soup kitchen and entered the parlor, she'd spotted him bantering with the Cavanagh sisters, kibitzing and joking with them while they played three-handed bridge.

"You can call me Lila," she said.

He grinned. "All right, Lila. Keep the smile—it looks foxy on you."

Her smile widened. There was no reason for her to react so strongly to flattery from a man—except that she was feeling unusually insecure today. That an attractive young man like Jimmy could use the word "foxy" in reference to a worn-out middle-aged woman like her gave her a boost she desperately needed. Jimmy had no ax to grind when it came to her, so she could almost believe the compliment was genuine.

"Thank you," she said as she opened the door and went inside.

In her room, she pulled out the dress, draped it neatly on a hanger and clipped off the tags, doing her best not to wince at how much she'd spent. Eighty dollars wasn't so astronomical a price to pay for a nice dress. If she'd purchased it under any other circumstances—if she were living at home, doing her chores and making everyone else's life run smoothly—she wouldn't have felt guilty about paying that much for it.

*You deserve it,* she tried to convince herself. But as she unpacked the purse and shoes from their bag, as she unwrapped the earrings from their nest of tissue paper, her hands trembled and her heart rattled against her ribs.

She was so nervous, so horribly nervous. What if Ken took one look at her and lambasted her for lavishing money on herself while she neglected her children? What if he started ranting that he didn't get the promotion and they could no longer afford any luxuries?

The promotion. He was supposed to have heard by yesterday whether he'd gotten it, but he'd made no mention of it on the phone last night. If he'd been promoted, surely he would have told her.

This evening was going to be a disaster.

She crossed to the window and gazed out at the brilliant sun, taking solace from the way it glittered, jewel-like, on the surface of the water. She was determined to remain composed. She would survive this night because Ken needed her to survive it. She would behave courteously with the Talbots and their other guests and engage in the required small talk. She could do that much for Ken, if he would let her—and if he didn't start the evening off by vilifying her.

She shouldn't have told him where she was staying. Allowing him to pick her up at Bayside Manor might have given him an opening to chew her out and cut her down before they were even out the door. Letting him come here had been too personal a gesture. She should have forced him to meet her somewhere near the Talbots'. She'd made a dreadful mistake—

"Stop it!" she scolded herself out loud.

Taking a deep, slow breath, she turned from the window and headed for the bathroom. She'd bought a bottle of moisturizing bubble bath on her way home from the soup kitchen last Wednesday, when she'd been overwrought about Ken's unexpected appearance at the church. By the time she'd stopped for dinner in town and then reached her room, however, she hadn't been in the mood for a bath.

Adjusting the ornate brass faucets to emit a warm spray, she recalled the bubble bath she'd taken on the afternoon of her very real first date, with Adrian Pomfret, when she was fifteen years old. Adrian had been a classmate of hers, sort of strange and odd-looking, but he'd been born to British parents and had lived in a suburb of London for the first ten years of his life, a fact that had made him seem extremely exotic in Levittown, Pennsylvania in the mid-sixties. He'd asked Lila to the Valentine's Day dance, and she'd been thrilled—and frantic.

Her mother had recommended that she take a bubble bath. "It will calm you down," she'd assured Lila, "and when you're all done, you'll feel as wonderful as you smell." While Lila had soaked beneath the bubbles, her mother had counseled her on how to make the date a success: "Ask him about himself. Be a good listener. Don't talk too much about yourself—keep turning the conversation around to him. Boys like that, Lila. They like to think they're the most important thing in your life."

Lila had spent the previous few years daydreaming about boys, getting crushes, imagining herself married to this or that rock singer and tormenting herself about the puny dimensions of her breasts, her shrimpy height, her curly hair and her freckles. At age fifteen, boys *were* the most important thing in her life.

Her mother had been right about the bath: it had helped to relax her that afternoon. As she lowered herself into the steamy bubbles in the quaint claw-foot tub at Bayside Manor twenty-five years later, she knew this bath would help, too. She sank into the scented water, watching her body vanish beneath the white froth, and closed her eyes.

This wasn't a date with a stranger, for heaven's sake. Ken was her husband. And just as her mother had advised her so long ago, Lila had spent her entire married life mastering the job of assuring Ken that, other than Michael and Danny, he was the most important thing in her life. He was probably the most important thing in his own life, too, she acknowledged with a grunt. Her mother had often warned her that when it came time for her to settle down and choose a husband, she ought to find a man with the same interests and priorities as hers. And so she had—she and Ken were both interested in Ken.

As the bubbles drifted to reveal milky, undulating glimpses of her body, she found herself worrying about the same things she'd worried about as a teenager during that long-ago bubble bath: her underendowed figure, her too-short fingernails, her unmanageable hair. She worried, as well, about the toll forty years had taken upon her. She was still slim, but her skin wasn't as soft and supple as it used to be. The heels of her feet were calloused. Her breasts were even smaller than they'd been in her youth, having shrunken like dry sponges within weeks after she'd weaned Danny. The skin around her eyes was crinkled, and what used to pass for dimples at the corners of her lips now looked suspiciously like creases. She still had those cloyingly cute freckles, and while curly hair was considered fashionable nowadays, hers contained a much-too-generous smattering of silver strands.

Here she was, a quarter of a century after her first anxiety attack over a guy, submerged beneath a layer of oiled and perfumed suds and eating herself up about whether some male would deign to consider her tolerable company for an evening. So much for maturing. So much for progress.

She kept her respiration slow and steady. She was not going to belittle herself, either for being too accommodating to Ken or for not being accommodating enough. She was going to make the best of this evening, and after it was over she would assess the damage and decide what step to take next.

She languished in the tub until the water grew cool, then stood and yanked the rubber stopper out of the drain. When the tub was empty, she pulled the curtains shut around it and turned on the shower. She shampooed her hair, rinsed the excess oil from her skin and stepped out of the tub. Wrapping herself in a towel, she strode into the bedroom to check the time.

Nearly five o'clock. What a treat, to be able to get ready for a Saturday night party in a leisurely manner. She wondered what Ken was doing right now. Feeding the boys? Ironing his shirt? Dashing to the bank's cash machine for money with which to pay the sitter? Damning Lila to hell for not being home to do those things for him?

More slow, deep breaths. She rubbed the towel through her hair, donned her bathrobe and rummaged through the bag containing her new cosmetic purchases until she found the bottle of nail polish. So what if her nails were too short? She was going to fix herself up so ravishingly that, even if Ken decided he never wanted to see her again after tonight, at least he'd be haunted by memories of how beautiful she'd looked the last time he saw her.

Once her fingernails were dry, she polished her toenails. Then she dug the old hair dryer out of her suitcase—she'd considerately left the new hair dryer at home for Ken—and blow-dried her hair into soft, shiny ringlets. She put on her stockings and slip, returned to the bathroom and spent an unconscionable amount of time applying her makeup. The sparkling blue shadow on her lids accentuated the color of her eyes, and the clear mascara added a luster to her already dark lashes. A dusting of golden blusher downplayed her freckles, and a patina of dark lip gloss gave her lips an alluring shine. Nothing too heavy or obvious; just enough to let Ken know she'd put forth some effort to look good for him.

Quarter to six. In less than an hour he would be here. She picked up the paperback she'd been reading, settled into the easy chair by the window and pretended to read.

Perhaps he would be showering now, she thought. No bubble bath for Ken. He would be standing beneath the spray and closing his eyes as the stinging droplets of water bounced off his smooth, well-toned skin. He would be rinsing his hair, which would lie as sleek as an otter's fur along the contours of his skull. The muscles in his back would flex as he shifted beneath the spout, and water would break from the brown wisps of hair adorning his chest and skitter in rivulets down the flat, hard surface of his stomach and lower, into a denser, darker nest of hair...

What if this date ended with sex?

She cleared her head with a brisk shake. How much easier life had been when all she'd had to think about were the right questions to ask Adrian Pomfret so he would feel free to chatter about himself in that charming British accent of his. How much easier life had been when kissing a boy was about as torrid an activity as her imagination could conjure up.

Tossing her book onto the night table, she rose from her chair and finished getting dressed. The only mirrors available to her were a framed dresser-top mirror in the bedroom and the medicine cabinet door in the bathroom, neither of which provided her with a full-length view of herself. Posing before the dresser-top mirror, she studied her reflection from the waist up. Somehow, the dress didn't look quite as becoming now as it had a couple of hours ago at the boutique. The high neck in front made her chin look too pointy, and without a bra—she couldn't wear one because of the slit in back—her breasts looked even smaller than usual. Although she couldn't tell whether the hem was too long, she assumed it was.

Eighty dollars down the drain, she concluded grimly. Eighty dollars and a bubble bath wasted. Sixteen years of marriage up in smoke.

With a bleak sigh, she lifted her wedding band from the top of the dresser and slid it onto her finger.

# *Chapter Six*

It was a plot, Ken decided—a diabolical plot on her part. As she descended the broad, arching stairway, he saw first her feet, strapped into dainty black sandals with narrow heels, and then her slender ankles, her calves and the dress, a deceptively modest design with a high neck and long sleeves. The fabric draped her body in a subtly seductive way, hinting at the feminine curves beneath. It was a remarkable shade of blue, a dark echo of her stunning blue eyes.

Then he saw her eyes themselves, discreetly made up to enhance their heavenly color, and dangling gold earrings imbedded with polished turquoise. She had her hair swept back from her face and fastened with combs, revealing not only the flirtatious earrings but also a span of smooth, pale skin behind each ear. A few soft tendrils framed her face, and behind the combs her hair tumbled loose in a shoulder-length cascade of golden-brown ripples.

She reached the bottom step and smiled shyly at him. He realized that the heels of her sandals weren't as high as he'd thought; the top of her head was even with his lips. He also realized, as he glanced down at her feet, that she'd polished her toenails.

Definitely a plot. She had gotten herself up in this gorgeous manner to taunt him. Her dress, her makeup, that tantalizing sliver of skin behind the curve of her earlobe—it all seemed to be screaming at him: "Eat your heart out, Kenny-boy! Feast your eyes but don't get too close. Men who forget their wives' birthdays aren't allowed to touch."

Oh, Lord, how he wanted to touch her. He caught a whiff of some unfamiliar perfume and it took all his willpower to keep from gathering her to himself and nuzzling that damnable earlobe of hers.

As a self-protective measure, he took a cautious step backward and scanned the small hotel lobby. Like the exterior of the hotel, it bore an atmosphere of faded gentility. The marble floor tiles were laid in a diagonal checkerboard pattern, the wall moldings were painted with an antique white enamel and the front desk featured a countertop of scratched mahogany. A long-bladed fan hung idle from the high ceiling; he imagined that it wouldn't do much good on a humid July day, but it was a nice touch.

"Did you have any trouble finding this place?" she asked.

"No." A few missed turns, but nothing remotely as troublesome as surviving the next few hours in her company was bound to be.

He'd been working himself into a state of irascibility all afternoon, even though the preparations for his night out had gone more smoothly than he'd thought they would. The boys had been satisfied to dine on a pizza from the freezer—the third pizza dinner they'd had since Lila's departure last Tuesday—and they'd cleared the table and stacked their dishes in the dishwasher afterward while Ken went upstairs to shower and dress. They'd gotten into their pajamas and brushed their teeth without coaching, raided the master bedroom and taken turns splashing each other with Ken's after-shave. They'd told him to tell their mother they were feeling perfectly healthy in spite of the fact that they hadn't eaten any vegetables since she'd left, so she ought to stop lecturing them on the importance of spinach and broccoli in their diets. The baby-sitter had arrived on time, and Ken had concocted a feasible explanation for Lila's absence.

The unexpected tranquility at home allowed Ken to redirect his energy into such productive activities as resenting Lila and anticipating a dreadful evening with her. Too much was riding on tonight. All he had to do was slip up once, make some trivial mistake and he would destroy everything—his marriage, his future, everything. Even if he didn't make any mistakes, he might discover that her decision to run out on the family had dealt a fatal blow to his love for her.

What he hadn't predicted was that she was going to look so utterly bewitching. He hadn't counted on being overwhelmed by desire.

It was more than her dress that turned him on, more than the delicate sandals and the earrings and that absurdly tiny purse she had clasped within her manicured fingers. There was something in her enigmatic smile, in the unfamiliar sparkle in her eyes, something in her scent, exotic yet teasingly faint. She seemed wary of him—he could understand that. But she also seemed...serene. Well-rested. Focused.

"You look good," he said inanely.

"Thank you."

"New dress?"

"Yes."

"I like it." Jeez. Were all their conversations tonight going to be this stilted? "The boys say hello," he went on, not wishing to torture himself by dwelling on how fantastic she looked.

"I take it you found a baby-sitter?"

"Beth Parrish." He scanned the lobby once more, then gestured toward the door. He and Lila had a vital issue to discuss, but he didn't want to broach the subject inside the hotel. As quaint as Bayside Manor was, he considered it enemy territory. He had to prepare Lila, to fill her in on what had happened at Allied-Tech, but the chances were too great that when he did, she would laugh in his face and declare that at this point she no longer gave a hoot about his career. If she reacted that way, he'd rather nurse his wounded ego in the privacy of his car, not in this brightly lit lobby.

They strolled together to the front door, and he held it open for her. As she passed in front of him, he glimpsed a strip of bare skin along her spine. The dress had a slit in back, a narrow, wickedly subtle one. He swallowed hard, and swallowed again when it dawned on him that his fleeting view of that enticing stretch of skin had been uninterrupted by the white elastic of a brassiere.

He considered taking Lila's hand as they headed down the porch steps, but because she held her purse so tightly in both hands and avoided looking at him, he didn't offer his arm. He also considered placing his hand at the small of her back, but if he did that his fingers would likely stray inside the delectable opening in her dress, and he couldn't risk letting that happen.

Fortunately, the chilly breeze rising from the water cooled him off. By the time he and Lila arrived at his car, he felt secure in his decision not to be distracted by her beauty. It helped to remember that she hadn't fixed herself up for him—she'd done it for Larry and Joyce Talbot and their other guests. The only compliment Ken might derive from it was that she obviously had been willing to make an effort so that he wouldn't be humiliated in front of his business associates.

Which reminded him that he'd better get with it and inform her of the situation at Allied-Tech. He opened the passenger door for her, closed it once she was settled in her seat and walked around the car to the driver's side. Once he was seated behind the wheel, he inserted the key in the ignition, then let his hand drop to his knee and twisted to face her. "We've got to—" He cleared his throat and organized his thoughts. How weird it was to feel so awkward around his wife, so utterly unsure of himself. "Lila, there's something I've got to tell you before we go."

She gazed at him expectantly.

Damn, but her eyes were dazzling, even in the dark interior of the car. Had her lashes always been that long? Had her brows always arched so alluringly? And her lips—had they always been that pink, that glistening? "It's about my work," he said, buttressing himself against her probable indifference. He couldn't expect her to care. It had been his uncertainty about his job, after all, that had distracted him to the point where he'd forgotten her birthday.

"The promotion," she supplied, her tone surprisingly gentle. "You've heard?"

"Yes."

Her eyes met his, and he was aware of more than just their beauty. He saw empathy in them, and something akin to remorse. "I should have asked you about it when we talked on the phone yesterday," she murmured. "It was so important to you, and I didn't even ask. I'm sorry."

Her apology astonished him—and moved him deeply. "Actually, I've known for a few days," he announced. "Maybe I'm the one who should say I'm sorry for not mentioning it sooner, but..." He sighed. "I guess, when we talked on the phone I was usually angry, or the boys were making noise or something. Anyway, I wanted to tell you calmly, in person."

"I'm sorry, Ken," she said again, lowering her eyes to the gear stick between them.

It dawned on him that she thought he hadn't succeeded in getting the promotion. He wished he had the guts to cup his hand under her chin and tilt her face up, so he could witness her reaction when he told her how ridiculously wrong she was. But to touch her would be too intimate a gesture. She might shove him away, and he didn't think he could bear that.

"I was named Vice President of Marketing," he said.

Her head jerked up without any assistance from him. "What?"

"Vice President of Marketing."

"But—" She shook her head, bewildered. "I thought you were up for Ed Healey's old job."

"So did I. Instead, here I am, in charge of hiring Ed Healey's replacement."

"Oh, Ken." She searched his face as if looking for a sign that he was joking. "Wasn't that woman, Cecile Something—"

"Cecile Patterson," he told her with a nod. "She's Head of West Coast Operations now. She's out in California."

"But isn't that a step down for her?"

"Her husband landed a hot job with Wells Fargo, and she asked Allied-Tech to find her something in the Bay Area." He bit his lip, wondering whether Lila would sense a subtle reproach in his words, an implied message about how even high-powered women executives sometimes stifled their own ambitions in order to conform to their husbands' professional needs. He didn't intend to send Lila any such message. He himself had been flabbergasted by Cecile's decision to relinquish her V.P. status. At the time, he'd thought Cecile's husband had to have been pretty selfish to have placed that sort of demand on her.

Cecile's husband probably hadn't forgotten her birthday, though.

"And they gave you her job?"

"Her job, her office, her secretary...her headaches, too, if I want them."

Lila's eyes widened and her mouth spread in a genuine smile. "Oh, Ken—that's wonderful!" she exclaimed, looping her arms around him and planting an exuberant kiss on his lips.

Almost immediately she fell back into her own seat, withdrawing her hands and inhaling sharply. Her smile faded and she glanced away. "That's wonderful," she repeated, this time demurely.

Ken studied her. Her mouth had tightened into a straight line and her eyes had become evasive. Her fingers curled and uncurled in her lap. *You're my wife,* he nearly shouted, *you're allowed to kiss me.* But he held his words, running his tongue over his lips, reliving the sensation of her mouth on his.

"There's more," he continued, fingering the car key. He ignited the engine and pulled away from the curb. "This party tonight...well, it's sort of supposed to be in my honor."

"'Sort of supposed to be'?" Lila asked.

He took heart in the humor implicit in her words. "I'm a new vice president," he pointed out. "I've just been moved to the third floor. This is my coming-out party."

"Oh, my." Lila chuckled. "Thanks for warning me."

He pointed the car south and they traveled in silence. Lila stared at the road ahead, meditating. He shot her brief looks whenever he could. Her eyes were so vivid, yet so inscrutable, and her fingers continued to fidget against the soft blue skirt of her dress, which was pulled just taut enough across her lap to remind him of how smooth and shapely her legs were. At one red light, when he glanced her way, he saw her run the tip of her tongue over her lips, just as he'd done a few minutes ago. Was she also trying to recapture the flavor of that impetuous kiss? Or was she trying to remove all traces of him?

Crazy. God, she was making him crazy.

"So, this vice presidency," she finally said as he steered up the ramp onto the highway. "What does it entail?"

"A forty percent raise and a bunch of perks," he answered.

She digested the news, then paused meditatively. "Actually, I was curious about whether you're going to have to do a lot of traveling, like you did when we lived in Phoenix."

He should have known. Lila had never been overly interested in money. As long as there was enough to cover the bills and a few extras every once in a while, she was content. Indeed, she often complained that she felt guilty for having so much when the people she served in the soup kitchen had so little.

That she would care about the frequency of his business trips was flattering, even though he suspected that her concern was based less on how much she missed him when he was away than on how much he took her for granted while he was on the road. He never had to worry about spending time away from home; he knew Lila would keep the house running smoothly and the boys on track. He knew there would be food in the fridge while he was gone, and gas in the cars. His shirts would be picked up from the cleaners without his having to remind her, Danny and Michael would get to their after-school activities, the floors would be vacuumed and the lawn watered. If any minor crises cropped up during his absence, Lila would handle them. She freed Ken from the need to think about domestic hassles. She was dependable, competent, always there.

Until last Tuesday.

"I won't have to travel much at all, just an occasional conference or trade show, that sort of thing," he said. Impulsively, he added, "Maybe you could come with me."

"To a trade show?"

Her incredulous tone alerted him to back off. Furthermore, he wasn't going to take her to any trade shows unless she brought this little birthday trip of hers to a conclusion. She would have to come home and swear to him not only that she forgave him for every thoughtless thing he'd ever done to her but that she wanted *his* forgiveness for the things she'd done to him—like walking out on him and his sons one rainy day while their backs were turned. Yes, he ought to retract the invitation altogether. Why should he prostrate himself before her? Why should he grovel, present her with peace offerings, buy her fidelity with the promise of a trip? She'd gotten the birthday gift she'd wanted, even if technically he hadn't given it to her. He didn't owe her a damned thing.

He shot another quick look at her and his mood swung back to contrition. She didn't appear defiant or pleased by the prospect of accompanying him on a business trip. Her gaze darted from the dashboard to the road to her hands, still fluttering restlessly above her knees. She was edgy, he realized. Edgy and frightened.

If he genuinely loved her, he would tell her she had nothing to be afraid of. Yet, the words stuck in his throat. She *did* have something to be afraid of. They both did. And all the love in the world might not be enough to overcome it.

Somehow, though, her obvious apprehension endeared her to him. Leaving home had been such a strong, bold move on her part. Knowing she'd scared herself as much as she'd scared him was somewhat reassuring.

Neither of them spoke during the balance of the drive. Ken cruised along the winding, tree-lined streets of Wellesley until he reached the Talbots' circular driveway, which was already lined with cars. The front windows of the stately brick Colonial glowed with amber light, and drifting through an open window somewhere the buoyant sounds of chattering voices, clinking glasses and bouncy music could be heard.

Ken parked behind a Lincoln and shut off the engine. Then he turned to Lila and presented her with a brave smile. "Ready?"

She reached across the gear stick and touched his arm. Her lips twitched in an uncertain smile that jolted him with a flash of déjà vu. He'd seen that smile before, years ago, aeons. He'd seen it when she'd been standing next to the beer keg on the porch of Dean Howard's house in Bolinas. It expressed confusion and hope; it resonated with both invitation and panic. It was a smile that asked questions, questions neither she nor Ken could answer.

"What do you want me to say to people?" she whispered. "I mean, about your promotion. When was I supposed to have found out? And what did we do to celebrate? Shouldn't we get our stories straight before we face your fans?"

He appreciated her foresight, even though he felt disturbed by the thought of having to concoct an elaborate story to feed his colleagues. "I told the baby-sitter you were staying with a cousin of yours who'd just had surgery," he revealed.

Lila's eyebrows rose as if in amazement at his skill at lying. "I suppose we can tell these people the same thing," she suggested.

"Or we can tell them nothing," he declared. He preferred not to lie if they could manage it. "I got the news on Tuesday. People can assume I told you about it that night."

"And what did we do?" she asked timidly. "Did we go out for dinner or something?"

"I brought you roses and champagne," he told her, wondering whether she realized he was no longer lying. He wanted to embellish his story, to let it evolve into a suitable fantasy celebration: *After the boys were asleep, we polished off the champagne and went to bed and...*

No, that hadn't been part of his plan for Tuesday evening. It was a thought that belonged squarely in the present, an inchoate longing to do something mindlessly passionate tonight with this breathtaking woman who may or may not still be his wife. That mystifying smile lingered on her lips, the smile he'd seen all the way from the far side of the volleyball net some eighteen years ago, a smile that had made him realize that, even though he didn't know who she was, he wanted her.

He was even less sure now that he knew who she was—and he wanted her even more.

"We'll be fine," he said, referring to the party.

"I don't want to mess things up," she explained. "I didn't know you were going to be in the spotlight tonight."

Ken was tempted to counter that she, not he, was going to be in the spotlight, looking as beautiful as she did. Eyes were going to follow her throughout the house; people who'd last seen her in denim shorts and an Allied-Tech T-shirt at the company picnic in July were going to do double takes. He doubted many people would pay much attention to him. Most of them saw him every day at work, and he looked now as he generally looked there, clad in a nicely tailored but unremarkable navy wool suit. He hadn't had time to buff his loafers that afternoon, his hair was in need of a trim and he had mixed feelings about the salmon-pink necktie he'd chosen. Lila had given it to him, insisting that it wasn't really a *pink* pink and that it looked wonderful with his auburn hair, but he still wasn't convinced.

He had worn it to please her. He had worn it because it had been a gift from her. Would it really be such a drastic leap from the truth for him to believe she'd made herself look lovely to please him?

"You won't mess up," he assured her. "Thank you for caring."

She smiled, but her eyes appeared unnaturally shiny. He couldn't figure out why she seemed to be on the verge of tears. All he'd said was thank-you.

To her, the two most precious words, he realized. The words she'd complained she heard more often from hungry strangers at the soup kitchen in Roxbury than from her loved ones.

"I guess it's time," he said, reaching for the handle and opening his door. She withdrew her hand from his wrist, and he acknowledged how natural it had felt there, how cold he felt now without that gentle contact.

They ambled side by side up the front walk to the porch. Ken rang the bell and the door swung open. "Well, if it isn't the man of the hour!" Larry Talbot bellowed. As usual he had on red suspenders, but in honor of the festivities he was also wearing a bright red, comically foppish bow tie.

Ken and Lila exchanged a swift glance—part amusement, part wariness, total understanding. Ken realized it would take more than a five-day estrangement for them to lose the ability to communicate with their eyes, and he took heart. As long as they could still speak to each other without words, their marriage might survive.

Larry swept Lila and Ken through the crowded living room, pausing a few times to allow his other guests to greet the Chapins and then hastening onward with them to the kitchen, where, he promised, drinks awaited. Lila did an admirable job of smiling and nodding and recollecting the names of people she'd met only at the company's summer picnics and Christmas parties. She beamed appropriately as Ken accepted congratulations from the Buonos, and again from the Abramses, and from Frank Coolidge and his startlingly young second wife. Pulsing below the din of voices was the cheerful sound of Dixieland jazz. Ken would have felt more at ease hearing music of his own generation—some wailing acid rock, perhaps.

They reached the kitchen, where Larry's wife Joyce was busy arranging fresh trays of hors d'oeuvres at the center island. With Larry's hand clamped firmly on his shoulder, Ken was propelled to an array of liquor bottles, soft drinks, glasses and a sterling silver ice bucket that stood in formation on the counter at the far end of the room.

At their arrival, Joyce looked up and let out a hoot. "Hello, Ken—Lila, you look fabulous! It's so good to see you! How have you been?"

Ken smiled politely at his hostess, but before he could return her greeting Larry ordered him to name his poison.

He mumbled something about a gin and tonic, but his gaze strayed to the two women at the center island. Joyce's outfit—a beaded satin top over swirling satin trousers—was arguably more high fashion than Lila's dress, but in Ken's mind Lila looked infinitely more glamorous.

"I'll tell you what looks fabulous," she said modestly. "This food. What's on these crackers, caviar?"

"Here, eat one," Joyce urged her. Leaning back, Joyce gave her a long appraisal. "You've lost weight," she guessed, then contradicted herself with a shake of her head. "No—you never had a weight problem to begin with. What is it? A new hairstyle? A face-lift?"

Lila laughed. "No, but I could probably use one of each," she admitted. "I just turned forty this week."

"On you, forty looks great. Come on, tell me—what have you been up to? Did you go to one of those spas or something?"

Ken could tell from Lila's grin that she thought Joyce was overdoing the compliments. But Joyce *wasn't* overdoing it. Lila really looked fantastic.

"Actually," Lila revealed, reflexively helping Joyce to arrange the sprigs of parsley in a decorative pattern around the tray, "I've been taking it kind of easy lately. And Ken took care of the boys tonight so I could get ready without having to rush."

Ken's eyes narrowed as he analyzed her casually tossed-off remark. Maybe that was it. She'd lavished time on herself before the party. She'd pampered herself. Not just the elegant hairdo and the manicure, but she'd taken time with her body, her mind and her soul. She'd indulged herself, taken care of herself.

And it showed. Oh, how it showed.

He accepted his drink from Larry, along with a goblet of white wine for Lila, and crossed the kitchen to her.

"Here," he murmured, pressing the glass into her hand and slipping his arm around her waist. People were supposed to assume that their relationship was normal. Putting an arm around her was the proper husbandly thing to do.

"Thanks," she said, glancing at him and then at his hand where it came to rest above her hip. With a rueful smile, he withdrew his arm. His fingers brushed against the exposed skin of her back and he sighed.

He wasn't sure, but he thought he heard her sigh, too.

# *Chapter Seven*

"Your husband is a lucky guy," said the man—Tim or Tom, she wasn't sure. A short, mustachioed fellow, he had introduced himself as a designer at Wang Laboratories. He'd had a fair amount of contact with Ken over the years, he informed her, and he considered Ken a great human being. "I mean, really, at his age—a veep. Doesn't happen every day, Lily."

"Lila," she corrected him, feeling a bit less embarrassed about her failure to remember his name.

"Sorry." He raised his scotch in a silent toast, then drained the glass. "So, I understand you're a full-time mom, is that right?"

She suffered a pang of indignation but recovered quickly. Now was not the time to start raging about her limited horizons. "I also work part-time outside the house," she replied, stressing the word "also" to let him know that she was holding down the equivalent of more than one job.

"Oh? Ken never mentioned it."

Another pang, which she combatted with her full supply of willpower. She wasn't going to give in to her anger. She had promised Ken she would be his smiling wife tonight, and she had every intention of keeping that promise. "Perhaps he never mentioned it because it's not a happy subject," she explained, fixing her companion with a steely stare. "I help to run a soup kitchen for the homeless in Roxbury. It's the sort of job Ken and I both wish no one had to do. The world would be a much nicer place if everyone had enough food to eat."

"Oh, so, you do volunteer work," said Tim/Tom.

As if that were less valuable than paid work. "Yes, it's volunteer. Try as I might, I just can't seem to bring myself to charge the homeless a fee for my services," Lila said, unable to stifle her sarcasm.

She felt a hand on her shoulder, warm and strong and mollifying. Ken's hand. "Tom," he said, greeting the fellow with the mustache. "You've met Lila?"

Evidently, Tom had detected her growing irritation, because he appeared greatly relieved to see him. "Hey, Ken—or do I have to call you Lord Chapin now?" he joked, shaking Ken's hand. "Your wife has just been telling me about the soup kitchen."

Ken's hand lingered on Lila's shoulder. It wasn't the first time he'd touched her that evening. There was nothing suggestive in his touch, nothing possessive. His hand was just there, his long fingers arched slightly to fit around the curve of her shoulder. It was a friendly, comfortable gesture, and she could accept that.

What she couldn't accept was the way her blood heated up at the light pressure of his palm, the way her pulse raced, her cheeks colored and her body grew warm with a heavy, sensual yearning.

It was true she was biased, but in her eyes Ken was the handsomest man in this house teeming with handsome people. Without any apparent effort, he looked gorgeous. His hair was thick and lustrous with red highlights, his eyes bright and alert, his smile good-humored even though she knew he was as much on edge as she was. His physique was trim and athletic, the sort of build that carried a conservative cashmere suit as appealingly as it might a ratty sweatshirt and a pair of old dungarees. She wondered whether it had been a mere coincidence that he'd chosen to wear his navy blue suit—the color complemented her dress so well. She doubted that his choice in a necktie had been coincidence, however. He'd worn the salmon-pink tie to tell her something.

That he trusted her? That he cared? That he wasn't about to throw away what was good between them?

She wanted to believe she was here at the Talbots' with him for more than window dressing. She knew he was angry with her. She knew he was bitter. Every conversation they'd had since her departure five days ago had been steeped in acrimony. And yet . . .

And yet, she couldn't shake the feeling that if he truly despised her he would have removed his hand from her shoulder long ago—or more likely, he wouldn't have put his hand there in the first place. If preventing gossip had been his only concern, he wouldn't have sent her long, meaningful looks time and time again during the evening, searching for her through the swarms of guests, stalking her movements with his gaze even when he was engaged in a discussion with someone else.

The only justification for his solicitousness was that he'd simply wanted a valid excuse to check up on her frequently, to seek her out in the crowd and wander over and place his hand on her shoulder again. She was flattered by his attentiveness, and disturbed by the fact that she was flattered. It could all be an act for his colleagues or a sop he was throwing her to keep her satisfied for this one evening. She couldn't take any of it to heart. He still resented her—probably hated her.

But if she hated him, she wouldn't have experienced a hot shiver down her spine whenever he did catch her eye, a corresponding awareness, a consciousness that even as they chatted casually with the other guests their souls were circling, approaching and retreating, testing each other, sizing each other up like boxers in a ring.

"He's a jerk," Ken muttered, once he and Lila had taken their leave of Tom.

She grinned and nodded.

"I thought you might need another drink," he said, eyeing her half-empty wineglass.

"You keep asking me if I want another drink," she remarked. "Are you trying to get me drunk or something?"

"Of course not." He gave her a wounded look.

"Ken!" A silver-haired man worked his way over to them. "Don't tell me this lovely lady is your wife!"

Under ordinary circumstances, Lila would have found such gushing obnoxious but harmless. Tonight, however, when her status as Ken's wife was in doubt, the man's words jolted her.

Ken handled the question tactfully. "All right, I won't tell you," he joked, presenting her to the man. "Lila, this is Frank Coolidge. He's the head of the legal department at Allied-Tech."

"How do you do?" she said, shaking his hand.

As soon as he'd released her, he extricated a young woman from her conversation with someone else and introduced her into their little group. "Ken, I don't know if you've ever met my wife, Denise. Denise, this is Ken Chapin, our new Head Honcho in Marketing, and his wife Lila."

More how-do-you-dos, and then Frank snagged Ken's arm and hauled him off, claiming that he wanted to talk shop with him for a few minutes. Ken shot Lila a helpless look before Frank swept him out of sight.

Lila shaped a polite smile for Denise. "Your husband certainly is assertive, isn't he?"

Denise tossed back her head and laughed. In her razor-cut hair and her haute couture jumpsuit with its off-the-shoulder sleeves, she looked awfully cosmopolitan for someone so young. "He can be bossy as hell," she admitted, "but he's cute, so I forgive him."

Cute? Lila thought that adjective applied more to Denise than to Frank.

"You must be real proud of your husband," said Denise, "getting this big promotion and all."

"Well, it's something he deserves," Lila said diplomatically. "And I know he'll do well in the new position."

"It's a real big jump for him, isn't it?" Denise lifted a glass of sparkling wine to her lips and sipped. "I mean, Vice President. Frank tells me your husband has been with Allied-Tech forever."

"Ten years," said Lila.

Denise laughed. "That sounds like forever to me. Well, you're right—the man deserves it. *You* probably deserve it even more. Ten years. Wow."

Lila wasn't sure how to interpret Denise's statement. On the one hand, she agreed that she deserved Ken's promotion as much as he did, but on the other she distrusted the hint of cynicism coloring Denise's words. "They've been ten productive years," Lila told her, realizing as soon as she spoke how true that was. The past decade had brought her Michael and Danny, Phoenix and Massachusetts, unemployment and Claudette Wiley's soup kitchen, a few wrinkles and too many silver hairs to count. And now this: an exalted husband. A vice presidential spouse. "Ken and I have both worked hard," she continued, hearing herself verbalize his sentiments. "You're right—we both deserve this. As he likes to say, we're a team."

"I guess that kind of teamwork is one way to get where you're going," Denise said, smiling knowingly. It occurred to Lila that Denise *hadn't* worked hard for the privilege of basking in her husband's professional glory. Frank Coolidge had undoubtedly already been well on his way to becoming a high muckamuck in the legal department before Denise was even born.

Then again, Denise was obviously a woman who knew exactly where she was going. At the moment, Lila had no idea where she was going at all.

"I've got to find some more of those miniature crepes," Denise announced, applying her sophisticated sense of direction to plotting a course to the kitchen through the crowd. "Nice meeting you."

"Nice meeting you, too," Lila said, forcing another artificial smile. She felt alone all of a sudden, abandoned and insecure. She was forty years old in a world full of beautiful young women like Denise Coolidge, women who felt no particular desire either to help their mates struggle up the ladder or to struggle up the ladder themselves. A woman like Denise would forge a very different partnership with someone like Ken. She would ask for nothing but the privilege of marrying a high-powered executive and in return would provide whatever he needed, no questions asked, no demands made.

So many women knew what they wanted—and were years away from their first wrinkle. If Ken wasn't a fool, he'd dump Lila and find himself a breezy new wife like Denise.

Ken wasn't a fool.

A frisson of dread tore through her. She had known the risks when she'd fled from her house last Tuesday. She had known that Ken might refuse to accept her back, might despise her forever, might even—God forbid—try to interfere with her relationship with the boys. She had known he might change the locks and hire a lawyer. But for some stupid reason, it had never occurred to her that he might find himself a spectacular-looking twenty-five-year-old lover with nary a crow's-foot nor stretch mark, someone who would worship him and pamper him and be grateful to bask in his reflected glory.

The anger she'd felt when she'd talked to Tom dissipated, replaced by a sense of hopeless inevitability. She had made her move and given herself a month off; now she would have to suffer the consequences. She'd done what she believed she had to do, and Ken would do what he had to do. If what he had to do entailed leaving her for a younger woman, well, at least he'd have no legal grounds to deny her custody of the boys.

She would have them, and her independence, and—who knew?—maybe she'd find a younger man for herself. She didn't want anyone else, but still, if Ken could do it why not Lila? Fair was fair. Hadn't Jimmy said, just that afternoon, that she looked foxy when she smiled?

She didn't feel the least bit foxy at the moment, though. She felt more like a mole. She wanted to burrow underground and hide. She wanted to race to Wayland, grab her sons and run away with them, leaving Ken to seek comfort with whatever sweet young thing would have him.

"Lila."

She heard his voice behind her and spun around. He was inching his way through the crowd to reach her. As soon as he did, he cupped his hands around her elbows and held her in place facing him. "I'm sorry."

Peering up into his face and reading the sincerity in his eyes, she very nearly apologized, as well. She had no right to convict him of crimes he hadn't committed. But she kept her thoughts to herself and asked, "Sorry about what?"

"Letting Frank drag me off like that."

She smiled. It was his job tonight to let people drag him off. "You couldn't help it. You're the guest of honor, after all," she reassured him.

"He has this way of commandeering people," Ken explained vaguely, then shook his head. His fingertips moved against her arms. "Actually, that's not what I have to apologize for."

Whatever he thought he *did* have to apologize for, she didn't want to discuss it, not now. She wanted to gaze up into his luminous brown eyes, inhale the bracing, familiar scent of his after-shave and memorize every precious detail of him. He could decide never to forgive her for having taken a month in Hull. He could leave her whenever he wanted. He could catch himself a Denise Coolidge lookalike and start all over again. Lila wanted to remember this moment so she would know exactly what it was she'd sacrificed in her effort to gain an identity.

Strange shadows danced across his eyes as he wrestled with his thoughts. He was not usually an emotional person—at least not the sort who revealed his deepest emotions to just anyone. Lila wasn't sure what emotions he was experiencing right now, but she felt their thundering force. That he could hide them from everyone else in the room was impressive; that he refused to hide them from Lila was extraordinary.

"You don't have to apologize for anything," she argued, unable to break his steady gaze.

He let out a tentative laugh. "Everybody keeps telling me how great you look—"

"Oh, Ken, don't be silly." Empty flattery was the last thing she needed to hear.

"It's true. I mean, it's true that you look great, and it's true that everyone's mentioned it, and..." He took a deep breath and steered her toward the window, away from a knot of people boisterously arguing about property taxes. "I've always thought you looked wonderful, Lila, but maybe... maybe I haven't told you often enough."

For heaven's sake—did he think she'd left home because he didn't dish out compliments on a regular basis? Did he think she was that shallow?

Clearly sensing her dismay, he plowed ahead. "I finally figured it out, Lila. It's not just your dress and the earrings and the way you fixed your hair. It's that you don't look... I don't know, tired. Rushed. Frazzled. You always look frazzled when we go out—or at least you always have in the past. That was my fault, and I'm sorry."

"Oh." She lowered her eyes, no longer able to look directly at him. She honestly didn't want to have this conversation in the middle of the Talbots' living room in Wellesley, with inappropriately lively music from the Preservation Jazz Band blaring out of the stereo speaker a few feet away. Tonight was Ken's night, an occasion to celebrate his professional achievement, not a night for him to perform hara-kiri over his past neglect of her. What he'd said had been nothing less than the truth, but tonight, when she was beginning to recognize precisely how much she'd risked by leaving him, how much she stood to lose and how likely she was to lose it...

"Don't say that. It's not your fault," she refuted him.

He ran his hands slowly up her arms, tracing the delicate ridges and hollows of her shoulders. "I don't know whose fault anything is anymore. I don't know—"

"We can talk later," she gently interrupted. His face was just inches from hers, his sculpted jaw close enough to touch, his mouth close enough to kiss. She recalled the spontaneous kiss she'd given him in his car outside the hotel, and her cheeks warmed with color.

This wasn't how they were supposed to reconcile. Ken wasn't supposed to toss her an offhanded apology in the middle of a cocktail party, surrounded by his elegantly appointed colleagues and their equally elegant spouses—and he wasn't supposed to look so wonderful, so desirable while he did it. She wasn't supposed to capitulate under the threat of losing him forever.

Abruptly she broke away from him.

"Lila—"

"Later," she whispered shakily, wishing she could tune him out—or else crush her lips to his and kiss him until her fear melted away. She was trembling with anger and confusion and an inarticulate yearning that echoed hollowly within her. She wanted Ken to belong to her, to love her, to respect her. She wanted him to devote his life to her as she'd devoted hers to him. She wanted to have a purpose, a goal, a sense of her own significance in the world. She wanted to be young and full of illusions again.

Perhaps he sensed her anguish. Without a word, he tucked her hand around the bend in his elbow and guided her deftly through the milling guests. When he found Larry Talbot, he invented a believable yarn about how Michael had been running a fever that afternoon and he and Lila wanted to get home early, just in case. He delivered heartful expressions of gratitude to his many well-wishers. And then they were outside, striding down the circular driveway to his car. He helped her into her seat, got in on the driver's side and slammed the door.

"What happened?" he asked.

She eyed him circumspectly. "You railroaded me out of the party," she answered under her breath. "What do you think happened?"

"You looked like you were on the verge of tears. It seemed like a good time to leave." He ran his palms along the leather-wrapped steering wheel, mulling over his thoughts, avoiding eye contact with her. "Are you feeling all right?"

"Yes. I don't know." She studied the purse, which sat in her lap. "It's all been a bit much," she admitted.

"It has, hasn't it?" He fondled the steering wheel for a minute longer, lost in thought. Sighing, he started the engine, released the parking brake and drove around the arcing driveway to the street.

What now? Lila took a deep breath and turned to look at him. She saw only his rugged profile intermittently lit by the headlights of passing cars. She couldn't begin to guess what he was thinking.

He broke the silence when they reached the highway. "It was a nice party."

"Yes." She fingered her purse, tracing its clasp with the edge of her polished thumbnail. "Joyce made such incredible hors d'oeuvres." Why were they wasting time with this? Now, when they were finally alone, why couldn't they talk about what really mattered? "Those cheese puff pastries were delicious, weren't they?"

"Yeah. They were good."

"She made all the food herself, from scratch." Lila slid another nail over the gold-tone clip. "I think she ought to go into the catering business."

"Mmm." His expression remained impassive, with only a flicker of annoyance crossing his face when a car cut in front of him without signaling.

"She told me she'd like to," Lila pressed on, awaiting a reaction from Ken. "She's talked to Larry about it and he thinks she's nuts."

Ken shot a glance at her. Then he turned back to the road. His fingers tightened around the steering wheel. The night cast oblique shadows across his face. "Maybe he's afraid that if she tries to turn a hobby into a money-making venture, it'll stop being fun," he said.

Lila would be willing to bet that wasn't Larry's reason for objecting to the idea, but she couldn't bring herself to argue with Ken, at least not about something so peripheral to their own situation. She ought to save her strength for her own more immediate battles—if she or Ken ever got up enough nerve to fire the first shot.

"Maybe," he went on without prompting, "Larry's an idiot. Or maybe they've found their own special balance in their marriage. Every marriage is different, Lila. Every marriage is a never-ending struggle to strike a balance."

She hadn't expected philosophy from him, especially not when he seemed so wired, so deeply engaged in a struggle for his own inner balance. She could feel the tension emanating from him in waves. She could see it in the twitching of a muscle in his jaw and in his rigid grip on the steering wheel. She could sense it in the way his foot pressed hard on the gas pedal, pushing the engine to perform, trying to drive back to Hull in as short a time as possible.

To get rid of her? Was he that eager to bring this awkward evening to an end? She shouldn't have mentioned Joyce's griping about Larry. She should have obeyed her mother's advice and said only the things Ken would want to hear. If this was in fact a date, she had blown it.

"What did you think of Frank Coolidge's wife?" he asked.

She didn't dare to tell him the truth: that Frank Coolidge's wife was too painful a reminder of how old Lila was, how old and demanding and easily replaceable. "I only talked to her for a few minutes," she said carefully, "but she seemed pleasant."

"She's closer in age to Michael than to us," Ken remarked. "It's mind-boggling to think she was in diapers during the Age of Aquarius."

"She's very pretty."

"She's a child."

Lila swallowed and stared out the window. Either Ken wasn't interested in courting a younger woman, or he was deliberately trying to mislead Lila into thinking he wasn't. Either her fears were totally justified, or she was paranoid.

Why, after sixteen years of marriage, did she feel so anxious around Ken? Was it possible for one week of separation to undo all those years of togetherness? Or had the doubt and insecurity been there all along in her marriage, and she simply hadn't addressed them until now? Had she left him, perhaps, because deep inside she believed that a man who forgot his wife's birthday couldn't possibly love her?

The rest of the drive passed in silence. The air inside the car seemed to crackle with invisible currents of tension. She wanted to get out. She wanted to scream. She wanted to grab Ken and beg him not to let her ever feel this unloved again.

She wanted him. But even more, she wanted not to want him so much.

The porch lights flanking the front door of Bayside Manor glowed brightly through the coastal fog. Lila recollected her conversation with Jimmy that afternoon, when he'd been repairing the wiring in the lamps. She had been keyed up then, too—nervous but optimistic, the way she always used to be before a date. Jimmy had told her she looked cheerful.

What a joke.

Ken parked the car and turned off the engine. She peered at him, bracing herself for the possibility that as soon as she unfastened her seat belt, he'd reach across her lap to open her door and then give her a firm shove. The reflected light from the porch illuminated his face, however, and in his eyes she saw something entirely different: not antipathy, not malice, but uncertainty and something else, something she couldn't identify.

She started to speak, but she lacked the courage to say what was on her mind—that she, too, was beset with uncertainty. That even though she felt buffeted by fear and confusion and years of built-up resentments, she didn't want to live the rest of her life without him. That when he looked at her that way, his eyes so clear and direct, she stopped feeling invisible.

He turned from her and got out of the car. By the time he reached her door she had it open. He took her hand and helped her to her feet. Then he shut the door and locked it. She shot him an inquiring look, but he refused to meet her gaze. Continuing to hold her hand, he ushered her up to the porch stairs and into the hotel lobby.

Lila squinted against the glaring light. Behind the counter sat Mrs. Tarlock, muttering imprecations at her computer. No wonder the woman was always in a foul mood, Lila thought vaguely—she was behind the desk by seven-thirty every morning, and still there at eleven o'clock on a Saturday night. When Mrs. Tarlock glanced up and frowned, Lila responded with a sympathetic smile. Running a hotel must be something like being a mother, she thought—you were always on duty.

Oblivious to the scowling woman behind the counter, Ken continued toward the stairway, still holding Lila's hand. His decision to escort her upstairs to her room was nothing but an act of courtesy, she told herself, and his having locked the car door was simply the standard precaution when parking in an unfamiliar neighborhood.

At the top of the stairs he paused, awaiting a cue from her. She turned right and he turned with her, their footsteps muffled by the faded runner that covered the hardwood floor of the hallway. She halted at her door and pulled the key from her purse. Her fingers trembled, and she couldn't get the key into the lock.

Gently, Ken took the key from her and inserted it. Why was his hand so steady, his demeanor so calm? Why were men better than women at hiding their emotions?

The latch gave and he pushed the door open. The room was visible through the shadows, diffuse moonlight entering through the waterfront windows. Bracing herself for the derision he was bound to give vent to when he saw the archaic radiators, the airy furnishings and crooked floor, she reached for the light switch.

Ken grabbed her hand before she could flip it on. His fingers closed around her wrist and he urged her into his arms. Bending down, he covered her mouth with his.

She had kissed him before, countless times, kissed him with joy and sadness and occasionally boredom, kissed him sometimes without thinking and sometimes without feeling. But this kiss was different. It was hard, urgent, fierce with a passion she had thought had been completely eroded by time.

His lips moved greedily against hers, nipping and sucking. His tongue probed and pressured her; his teeth were smooth and dangerous and his hands clamped down around her shoulders, refusing her the opportunity to escape. She was visited by a vague memory of a nature special she'd recently watched on television with the boys, in which a brown bear held a doomed salmon immobile between its paws, pondering it and playing with it before he killed it.

If Lila were doomed, though, she felt exhilaration along with her fright. Ken's kiss was as exciting as it was alarming. She was afraid—yet she couldn't keep herself from kissing him back, kissing him with the same crazy, desperate passion.

Was this tall, strong man actually her husband? She knew his face, his build, the shape of his hands gripping her. But she no longer knew what her relationship with him entailed. "Husband" seemed too basic a term, too definitive, too absolute.

His hands skimmed up into her hair, tugging at the combs until they came free and the liberated curls spilled down against his knuckles. A low groan filled his throat as he edged back and fumbled with her earring. "You'd better do this," he murmured. "I might hurt you."

His voice, though thick with desire, was recognizable. Ken. This was Ken, her husband. Her estranged husband.

"No," she protested, pulling back.

He ran his fingertips along the curve of her earlobe and then behind it, exploring the sensitive crease and causing a dark shiver to seize her. She didn't want him to arouse her this way. She didn't want him to be able to break through her defenses with a few well-placed caresses.

"Don't," she whispered, even as her body defied her, her flesh melting in the pulsing warmth he'd unleashed with his gentle stroking.

He sighed and let his hand fall away. "You smell so good," he whispered. "Is it perfume?"

"Bubble bath." Why couldn't he have tried to seduce her not because she smelled good but because he loved her, loved her so much he was ready to change his attitudes toward her, toward marriage, toward their future together?

Why couldn't he have dropped to his knees, begged her for forgiveness and pledged to try harder for her?

He was too busy chuckling, that was why. "You're kidding. You took a bubble bath?"

"Yes, I took a bubble bath," she snapped. "What's so funny about that?"

"A bubble bath . . . I don't know, it makes me think of toy tugboats and rubber duckies."

"I didn't have any toys," she muttered. "It was just me and the bubbles."

Her words evidently evoked an image in his mind—an extremely erotic one. He closed his eyes for a moment, and when he opened them again he was no longer grinning. "I want you," he said, his tone devoid of humor. "Please, Lila. I want you."

He extended his arms to her. They looked so inviting. She wanted him, too. And damn him, he knew she did.

"I can't," she said forlornly, pivoting and stalking to the window, putting more distance between them.

He cursed under his breath. "Lila—I'm not . . ." He inhaled, then started again. "I'm not saying we're going to work out all our problems here tonight, but . . . whatever is wrong between us, I still love you."

Unbidden, she heard the weak echo of her mother's voice warning her teenage daughter, "Don't ever let a boy kiss you on the first date. They'll say anything, you know—they'll swear they love you. Don't fall for it."

*But, Mom,* she silently responded to the admonition, *he's not a boy—he's my husband.*

She heard him moving behind her, approaching her. She felt his breath ruffling through the loose curls of her hair. "I miss you," he said quietly. "I can hardly sleep at night when you aren't there."

"You're just horny," she grunted, even though she knew that wasn't the whole truth.

"If I am, it's for you," he whispered, hovering close, so close she could feel the radiant warmth of his body against her back. "Only for you, Lila. I want to make love to you. I've wanted you all evening, ever since you first came down those stairs. I've been watching you and wanting you."

She almost pressed her hands against her ears to shut out the tantalizing sound of his voice. He had never talked this way before, and his words had never had such a provocative effect on her. When his hands came to rest on her shoulders, she flinched as if burned.

"I want to make it good for you," he went on in a hypnotic purr. He urged her back against him, and she could feel his arousal through the layers of their clothing. "I want to make it so good you'll know how much I love you. I've made mistakes, Lila—we both have. But making love with you now wouldn't be a mistake. It would be the best thing in the world."

She closed her eyes and shuddered. His breath continued to warm her scalp, and his lips grazed through the silky curls of her hair as he bowed to kiss the top of her head. Slowly, subtly, his hips rocked against the small of her back.

"I can't," she argued weakly, even as she leaned into him, increasing the contact between them. "Ken, don't do this. I'm not going to make love with you. I'm not."

"Why? You want to torture us both?"

Using all her reserves of strength, she pulled away and turned to face him. "How could you possibly want to make love with me when you don't even know who I am?" she charged, as exasperated with herself as with him.

His expression hardened into a bitter frown—but not before she glimpsed the vulnerability in it. "I know damned well who you are, Lila."

"I'm not some fantasy object you can take to a party and then bring home and—"

"I didn't bring you home," he cut her off, his voice taut with anger. "I brought you *here*. And right, you're not a fantasy object. You're a woman who's driving me crazy, who thinks it's all right to make me beg just because your birthday slipped my mind."

"Forgetting my birthday was just the catalyst. That's not why I left. I left because *I've* slipped your mind, Ken, because you've forgotten *me*."

"Bull."

"It's the truth. You don't see me anymore. You don't listen to me. Sure, you could make love to me and it would be great, and then I'd just blend into the background once more while you went off to be an exalted vice president. That's the way it's been for the past sixteen years, Ken. And it's not good enough. It's not good enough." She felt a sob filling the back of her throat, and she covered her face with her hands and tried to will away her tears before they broke free.

He didn't say anything for a minute. Then: "What would be good enough, Lila? Tell me. I'm seeing you and I'm hearing you, so now's your chance to tell me."

Swallowing the lump in her throat, she opened her eyes and gave him a long, hard stare. "All right," she said, her tone soft but resolute. "I will."

# *Chapter Eight*

What the hell was she talking about?

He sat in the armchair by the window, his head rolled back against the upholstery so he could gaze up into the shapeless gloom of the ceiling. Despite having loosened his tie and opened the collar button of his shirt, he felt as if he was choking. Lila was on the bed, her legs drawn up underneath her, her shoes off and her dress smoothed neatly over her knees. Her voice rolled through the room, low and earnest, expounding on subjects he couldn't begin to make sense of. She was only a few feet from him, but she seemed miles away, off in some other world where he didn't understand the language and where he didn't belong.

He still desired her. His body had cooled off but his mind continued to burn with hunger—and it had nothing to do with the fact that he hadn't had sex in nearly a week. He'd gone without it for longer stretches more than a few times in his life. He wasn't a maniac, for crying out loud. Lila was his wife and he wanted to make love with her, but she was way off base if she honestly believed the only reason he had tried to seduce her was that he was horny.

Regardless of what she thought of him, he did love her. And tonight, the way she'd looked at the party, the way everyone had looked at her, the way that tantalizing sliver of her back had beckoned to him through the slit in her dress, the way her unconfined breasts had moved beneath the blue cloth and her earrings had winked in the light, the way she'd smelled, the way she'd kept glancing over her shoulder and catching him in the act of spying on her...

All he wanted to do was give her his heart and his soul—and she was babbling about some stupid literacy program. "There's such a need for something like this," she was saying, her tone soft but fervent. "I can't ignore that need, Ken. I really feel I could contribute something."

"Fine. Contribute something," he snapped, wishing he could sound more agreeable. Wishing he could *feel* more agreeable. "Do whatever you want. I don't see what the problem is."

"Ken." Her voice held a warning, and he forced himself to look at her. Her eyes communicated not so much reproach as despair. "You've just proved exactly what the problem is," she said sadly. "It's that you don't really listen to me."

"I do so listen to you," he objected, not bothering to add that he would listen much more diligently if she said anything that pertained to reality.

"You don't..." She sighed and looked away. "You don't take me seriously, Ken," she mumbled into her lap.

"I *do* take you seriously!" Damn. Why was she doing this, feeding his anger until he could no longer contain it? "I take you very seriously, Lila. What in God's name does that have to do with our sex life? What does it have to do with your staying here in this hotel instead of being at home?"

"If you were really listening to me you'd know the answers to those questions."

A man could take only so much of this before he blew up. "All right, Lila," he said, clinging to what little was left of his patience. "Walk me through it one more time and I swear I'll listen to every breath you take. Explain to me how you could kiss me the way you just did a few minutes ago and then turn it off like a light switch. Explain that to me, Lila."

She gave him an incredulous stare. "The problem isn't sex, Ken."

"At the moment it sure feels like it is," he grumbled, then succumbed to an unexpected laugh. Lila laughed, too. It defused his tension a bit, both physically and emotionally. Maybe if they could laugh together, they could somehow manage to avert disaster. He gazed at her and his heart seemed to swell at the sight of her, her eyes so bright, her smile so lovely, so *familiar*. This was his wife, the woman he loved. He wasn't crazy to long for her.

"I love you," he said, not to lead her on or to manipulate her, but simply because it was the truth. "Lord knows I'm not perfect, but I love you. I want you back, Lila. If we could just cut through the garbage here—"

She held his gaze for a pregnant moment, then turned away. "The problem isn't love, Ken. It's..." Her finger traced an abstract pattern on the floral bedspread as she pondered her words, choosing them with exquisite care. "It's our relationship."

"What relationship? We love each other. *That's* our relationship."

"No. That's our love," she said slowly, quietly. "Our relationship is that you go out each day and contribute brilliant ideas and strategies to your firm, and you get all the glory, and meanwhile, I'm at home making life easier for you and the boys. Your job changes and grows but my job stays the same. We're supposed to be a team, Ken, but your life keeps evolving and mine doesn't."

He listened this time, really listened. "Do you want a job?" he asked, the epitome of tolerance. "No problem. Get a job. I have no argument with that."

"I already *have* a job," she retorted, anger flaring in her wide blue eyes. Then her anger subsided, and her voice was once again deceptively soft and gentle. "My job—which you're obviously not even aware of—is to cook and clean, to take care of the boys, to make sure there's a hot meal on the table every evening and clean dishes to serve it on. My job begins at six-thirty in the morning and ends at around nine or ten at night, seven days a week, twelve months a year. I don't do it because I enjoy it, Ken. I don't do it because I get ego gratification or mental stimulation from it. I do it because I'm your wife. And I'm not sure that's a good enough reason anymore."

"So what do you want?" he muttered, wishing he could ignore the sinking feeling in his gut. "A raise? Better hours?"

"I want appreciation," she whispered, her gaze oddly diffident.

He wondered why she had so much trouble asking for something so simple. Perhaps it was because her spirit had been broken from so many years of feeling unappreciated. Or perhaps it was because giving appreciation wasn't at all simple.

"Would it be better if you got a job outside the house?" Ken had no problem with that. His mother and his sister both had careers. In fact, it was something of a joke in his family that Ken had wound up in such a traditional marriage. "We can deal with that. We'll make adjustments."

"Would dinner be waiting for me when I got home at the end of the day, the way it's always waiting for you?" she asked, in a tone not accusatory so much as wistful.

He shrugged. "We would eat take-out, or frozen dinners, or something."

"And the house? Would it be tidy?"

"Not as tidy as you'd like," he conceded. "But you could get used to that if you had to. I'm not the only one who would have to adjust."

She seemed to wrestle with her thoughts for a minute. Then she busied herself pulling one of the pillows out from under the spread and propping it against the white wicker headboard. She leaned back against it and sighed. "The job I want is what I was just telling you about: to teach reading skills to some of the clients at Mt. Zion Methodist. I've been thinking about it for a while. I can't get a teaching job in any of the public schools around here, not without going back to college for a year and getting a new certification. But that's okay—I don't want to teach in some nice suburban school. You know I've wanted to work with the underprivileged, ever since I entered graduate school."

Is that what she had wanted? The idea sounded vaguely familiar to him, but he couldn't recall her ever having discussed it with him. *Terrific, Kenny-Boy,* he grumbled inwardly, acknowledging that she'd probably discussed it with him on dozens of occasions, and he'd failed to listen to her. Even back then, when they were first starting out, he wasn't listening to her. "Is there a position available for you at the church?" he asked, attempting to overcome the crushing sense of guilt he felt at having been deaf to her ambitions for so long.

She shook her head, but her eyes glowed with a determination he couldn't recall having noticed in them before. "I would have to create the position myself. There's no money, other than what we might be able to beg and borrow for books and paper. I have to talk to Reverend

Munsey at Mt. Zion to see if I can use the basement, and Claudette said she might know of some other people who'd be willing to help. She isn't optimistic, Ken. But the need is so great—I'm not going to give up."

"Why Mt. Zion? There must be plenty of established social agencies that would be glad to have you on board."

She shook her head again, this time wrinkling her nose. "Anything within the existing programs would require me to have an up-to-date state certification, plus I'd have to deal with the bureaucracy and all that red tape. In the meantime, these people are losing years of their lives. They have to learn how to read. The sooner they learn, the sooner they'll be able to develop some marketable skills. I want to help them. I've known some of these people for two years, Ken. They're not just hungry mouths—they're human beings. I'm not doing this for money or glory. I just want to help them."

*Because they say thank-you, and I don't.* He remembered what she had said in that musty, dank hallway in the church basement a few days ago. Those people thanked her and her own family didn't.

For one irrational moment he felt jealous of the hungry street people in Roxbury. Helping them infused Lila with a purpose in a way that helping her husband and her sons didn't. Had he and the boys beaten her down that badly? Had their indifference snuffed out the flame of her enthusiasm so completely that she had to count on strangers to rekindle it?

"This is my dream, Ken," she murmured, sounding almost plaintive. "I've given you all the support you needed to achieve your dream. Now I'd like to give some of that support to myself."

"You don't have to support yourself," he protested. "I'll support you. The boys and I will."

She gave him another incredulous look.

*Guilt, guilt, guilt.*. Okay, so he hadn't been terribly supportive over the years. He didn't even like the word "supportive"—although, in retrospect, he had to admit that he'd gotten used to receiving plenty of support from Lila. It was long past time to return the favor. "Lila, I love you," he repeated. "I'll help you. I'll support you any way I can, I promise."

Her eyes glowed. "Will you?"

"Absolutely. You have my word." He held up his hand as if swearing an oath. "Now please, honey, come home."

"Come home?" she echoed, then gave her head a nearly violent shake. "No."

He should have asked some other way. He shouldn't have let it slip out as if it were an afterthought. He should have wooed her, or lured her, or found a way to dump some of his guilt on her. Or not asked at all.

But it was too late. The statement hung in the air, along with her vehement reply. "Why not?" he asked, although he already knew it was a futile cause. "We agree that you should take a job outside the house. We agree that we love each other. We're on a roll here, Lila. So come on home, and—"

"I can't," she declared, sounding mournful, as if she almost wished she *could*. "If I do, the minute I step through the door I'll be back where I began. I need more time, Ken. If I go back now... it's like quicksand. I'll get sucked right in." Her voice wavered and she pressed her lips together in an effort to silence herself.

He couldn't deny the truth in what she'd said. If she came back home with him now, her return would make things awfully simple for him. She would vacuum all those crumbs and clods of dirt that had been accumulating on the floor for nearly a week—was it his fault that she'd never taught him how the vacuum cleaner worked?—and scrub the dried crust of toothpaste from the boys' bathroom sink—could he be blamed for not knowing where she kept the scouring powder? She would put a dent in the mountain of dirty clothing heaped on top of the washing machine and find the laundry ticket he'd misplaced so he could retrieve a half-dozen shirts from the cleaners. Of course he would support her in her effort to set up a literacy class among the soup kitchen's patrons—but it would be a hell of a lot easier to support her if he didn't have to eat pizza three nights a week.

He gazed at her. She'd drawn her knees up to her chin and was hugging her ankles. There was something little-girlish about the position, something vulnerable yet self-protective. Her distrustful stare cut into him, daring him to refute what she'd said.

He couldn't refute it.

When had he turned into such a jerk? Had it been gradual, each step up the professional ladder carrying him that much further from the nice guy he'd once been? Why hadn't Lila complained before now? Why had she let it continue for so long? What if he was too far-gone to change?

"If you won't come home," he said, "I guess I'd better leave." He rose to his feet, taking his time, waiting to hear her invite him to stay, even though logic told him she wouldn't.

She cleared her throat and he nearly cheered at the thought that wishes could overcome logic. "Ken—" she sounded curiously meek, and he silently urged her to continue "—I'd like to see the boys."

The boys. Well, of course she'd like to see them. Right now she loved them more than she loved him. They may have taken her for granted as much as Ken did, but they got tried for their crimes as juveniles, not adults. "You want to see them? Come home," he replied churlishly.

"I was hoping maybe you could bring them here," she said, her voice rising questioningly.

He didn't look at her. Why should he bring her the boys? They were his last hope for getting her back to Wayland. But if he insisted that she had to come home if she wanted to see them, she still might refuse to come home, and then the boys wouldn't get to see their mother. He couldn't use them as pawns. He couldn't dangle them in front of her like bait. They'd survived this week with courage and confidence, but he couldn't deprive them of their mother so he could achieve some Machiavellian end.

"Please, Ken." Obviously she could sense his ambivalence.

"All right," he yielded. His muscles strained from the effort of remaining standing; his back hurt and his head drummed with pain and fury. "I'll bring them for lunch."

"Thank you," she said quickly, springing from the bed and approaching him. "Thank you."

He looked at her then, pivoted and looked at her, and saw tears of grief and gratitude running down her cheeks. He wanted to gather her into his arms, to comfort her and take comfort from her. He wanted to prove, to both her and himself, that he loved her.

He wanted, most of all, to prove that true love conquered all. But he knew better than to try, so he only patted her shoulder and headed for the door.

"REALLY? She lives right by the beach?" Danny exclaimed, knocking over his glass of milk in his excitement. "And we're going? Awesome!"

"The beach is different in the fall—don't expect to go swimming or anything," Ken reminded his sons as he ripped several squares from the roll of paper towel. He spread them flat across the table and let them absorb the spilled milk. "Settle down and finish your breakfast, Danny."

"Mom always makes whole wheat pancakes on Sundays," Michael said, tapping his spoon listlessly against the Frosted Flakes in his bowl. Ken knew Lila wouldn't approve of the boys eating sugary cereals for breakfast, but if she didn't like it she could come home and do the grocery shopping herself. He'd had to run that particular errand Thursday night, after an exhausting day at the office, and he'd had to bring the boys with him. They had besieged him with requests for nonnutritious items on every shelf. He thought he'd withstood their pestering rather well, buying only the Frosted Flakes, some overpriced sandwich cookies that looked like little chocolate jack-o'-lanterns, a box of cupcakes with colored sprinkles on top, Fiddle-Faddle and a six-pack of bubble gum apiece. At least the bubble gum was sugarless.

"So, like, can we build sand castles and stuff?" Danny asked.

"I don't know," Ken said as he finished the coffee in his mug and grimaced. He was sick of instant coffee. "Mike, you wouldn't happen to know where Mom keeps the coffee filters, would you?"

"Uh-uh," Michael answered before making an explosive torpedo noise and sinking a cereal flake under the surface of the milk with the tip of his spoon.

Ken rose and crossed the kitchen to begin a search. If Lila was going to force him to be more self-sufficient, the best way to begin would be with a cup of real coffee in his system. Before he reached the cabinet most likely to contain the filters, however, the telephone rang. He answered.

"Kenneth! Good morning," said his mother-in-law.

Cripes. Did she know about the stunt her daughter had pulled? Had Lila bothered to apprise her? If not, should he tell her?

"Hello, Margaret," he mumbled. His need for a strong, black cup of real coffee grew exponentially. No one should have to contend with their in-laws without the benefit of caffeine, he thought.

"I'm sorry I'm phoning so early."

It wasn't that early—nearly nine-thirty. "No problem," he assured her.

"Well, it's just that after church we're taking a drive up to Florence and Bill's place in the Poconos for the day. The leaves aren't supposed to peak for another couple of weeks, but we figured it's such a nice day for a drive. The leaves must be in full color where you are, aren't they?"

Ken hadn't even noticed. "They're beautiful," he lied. "Can I talk to Lila?"

The Moores didn't know about Lila's vanishing act, then. "Um, I'm sorry but she isn't available right now," he stammered, praying that Margaret wouldn't press him for details.

"Oh, that's too bad. I've been waiting to hear from her for several days. I'm just dying to hear what you got her for her birthday. Forty! I can't believe my little girl is forty! How did you celebrate? What did you get her?"

He smothered the groan that filled his throat. He'd always liked his mother-in-law, but at the moment he would have welcomed the opportunity to strangle her. "Lila got exactly what she wanted for her birthday," he said, providing about as honest an answer as possible.

"Oh, come on, don't be so secretive. Tell me, Kenneth—I'm dying of curiosity."

"I think it would be better if Lila told you herself. It's kind of hectic right now, Margaret. Can I have her get back to you?"

"Of course," his mother-in-law conceded reluctantly. She was probably trying to decide whether it was worth the effort to grill Ken some more, but luckily for him she decided not to. "She got the card we sent, didn't she?"

Who knew? "Sure," Ken replied. "She liked it."

"I'm so glad. Well, tell Lila to give us a call later this evening. We should be home about eight o'clock or so."

"I'll tell her," Ken promised. "Take care. Have a good trip." He hung up and wrestled with the urge to pound his fist through a wall. Coffee filters, he remembered, focusing on something practical to allow his rage to dissipate.

He rummaged through one cabinet and then another, nudging aside boxes of pasta and bags of rice, crackers, jars of apple sauce and tins of spices. "Come on, guys," he called to his sons. "Haven't either of you ever seen Mom make coffee?"

"I don't know, Dad," Danny replied. "She's always down here getting breakfast ready before any of us are dressed."

"If I can't have pancakes, I'm not hungry," Michael announced sullenly. "I'm gonna read the comics."

"Me, too!" Danny shouted, bolting from the table and racing his brother to the doorway. "I call *Spiderman*!"

"You can't call *Spiderman*," Michael argued. "I called the comics, so I get them first—including *Spiderman*."

"Well, you can't read them all at the same time," Danny rationalized as he and Michael raced each other into the family room.

Ken's gaze traveled from the family room doorway to the table, now covered with soggy wads of paper towel along with the remains of the boys' abandoned breakfast.

Frosted Flakes were strewn across the floor, Danny's milk glass remained poised on its side, a few sections of the Sunday *Globe* had wound up under the table, and a full-color circular for one of the area department stores lay near Michael's chair, suspiciously open to an advertisement featuring nubile young models in lacey underwear.

Ken simply couldn't do it. He couldn't get breakfast made, brew himself a cup of coffee, talk to his mother-in-law on the phone, psyche himself up for a new round of facts-of-life lectures with Michael and read the sports section. Most Sunday mornings in the past, he got to read the paper without any interruptions; Lila took care of the rest.

Again that sinking feeling, that crushing influx of self-hatred. He was finding it harder and harder to keep his resentment of Lila alive. If he felt at all angry toward her, it was only because she'd done such a thorough job of forcing him to acknowledge his failings as a husband.

At eleven o'clock, he rounded up the boys. Danny had won possession of the comics, but he was too engrossed in watching cartoons on television to read. Michael was out in the mudroom fussing with his collection of moldy bread slices. Two of the slices were on the verge of turning a spectacular turquoise shade and a third had sprouted cottony puffs of white along the crust. Ken was starting to worry about how much time Michael was spending alone in the mudroom. He'd almost prefer the kid to be inside drooling over the models in the lingerie ads. Perhaps communing with moldy bread was Michael's way of dealing with Lila's absence, just as wanting to punch walls was Ken's.

"Come on, boys," he said with more enthusiasm than he felt. "Time to go visit Mom."

"Yay!" Danny hooted, flinging on his jacket and running through the mudroom to the car.

Ken envied Danny's imperturbability, even though he wasn't blind to the possibility that all that cheerful energy may be masking some deep-seated fear about his mother's absence. Michael's angst was more understandable. "Are you sure Mom wants to see us?" the older boy asked as Ken started the engine.

"Positive," he reassured Michael. "This visit was her idea."

"Is she going to yell at us?"

"No."

"Not even for forgetting her birthday?" Michael pressed him.

"No. She really wants to see you boys very badly."

"So you think she's not sick of us anymore?"

"I don't think she's ever been sick of you," Ken said, unable to include himself in that benign assessment. He was thrilled to be able to give the boys the reassurance they craved. They needed their mother, and Lila... She needed them, too.

"Where are we going for lunch?" Michael asked.

"I don't know. Mom must know of some restaurant close to where she's staying."

"A real restaurant?" Danny called out. "Like, with cloth napkins and stuff?"

"Maybe. Think you can handle it?"

"Nah," Michael answered for him. "He'll probably just knock over his milk or something."

"Yeah? I'll knock over *your* milk," Danny threatened.

"Yeah? I'll dump your milk on your head."

"Yeah? I'll—"

"Pipe down," Ken shouted over his shoulder. "Button your lips and enjoy the scenery."

For most of the ride, the scenery was nothing but highway. Contrary to his mother-in-law's expectations, the trees weren't at all colorful. The rain of the previous week had knocked too many of the leaves off their branches before they could dress up in their autumn hues.

The boys grew more animated as they got closer to the seaside communities. Ken rolled down his window and the car filled with the briny scent of the bay. He had memorized the route last night, and he had no trouble finding his way onto Hull's narrow peninsula, which curled into the Massachusetts Bay north of Plymouth. By the time he'd reached the block on which Bayside Manor was located, the boys were jabbering with excitement: "Look! The beach!" "Hey, get a load of that kite!" "Check out that remote-control airplane, Danny!" "Look at that dog! Is he ugly or what?"

Not until Ken braked to a stop at the curb did the boys seem to remember that their mother was the primary reason they'd driven all this way. They tumbled out of the car and raced toward the hotel's veranda, where Lila stood waiting for them. "Mom! Mom! Wow, this place is neat!"

Ken lingered by the car, spending an inordinate amount of time making sure all the doors were locked. He wanted to give Lila a few minutes alone with the boys. Even more, he wanted to build up his courage to face her.

Finally, having run out of doors to check, he started toward the worn concrete stairs that led up to the veranda. Lila was squatting down between the boys, with an arm wrapped tightly around each one. She peered past them at Ken, and her smile lost a bit of its force. Her eyes glistened with tears.

"Thank you," she whispered. "Thank you for coming." Not "thank you for bringing the boys," or "thank you for not keeping my children from me."

Did he dare to hope that she was glad to see him, too? Had she spent an endless, restless night as he had, recalling every word that had passed between them yesterday, every look, every touch? Had she relived their kiss? Had she wondered how it was possible for two people to kiss like that, to want each other so much, when in every other respect they were traveling on two different planes, in different directions, at high speed?

Had she stared into the darkness as he had, long after the moon had disappeared, riddled with doubt and racked with dread?

Before he could speak, she had returned her gaze to the boys. She released them and straightened up. "Who's ready for lunch?" she asked with feigned cheer.

"We are! We are! Daddy says we're going to a restaurant!" Danny bellowed, grabbing Lila's hand and dragging her down the porch steps.

The restaurant was just a few short blocks away, she announced; they could walk. The boys flanked her on the narrow sidewalk, Michael chivalrously strolling on the strip of sand-choked grass separating the sidewalk from the street, so there would be enough room on the pavement for his mother and brother. Ken lagged behind, watching the three of them. Michael informed her of how his bread experiment was progressing, describing in intricate detail the growth of the fuzzy white mold. Whenever he paused for breath, Danny interjected, "It's real yucky, Mom! You wouldn't believe how yucky it is!"

Ken observed the gentle sway of her hips as she walked, the confidence in her strides, the way the midday sun got trapped in the gold-edged curls of her hair. Viewing her objectively made him keenly aware of how attractive she was. Viewing her subjectively was even worse.

The restaurant had a homey charm to it: large curtained windows, ladder-back chairs, red checkered tablecloths and white enamel ceiling fans. "I made a reservation for four. The name is Chapin," Lila informed the hostess, who greeted them.

Ken was surprised. More than half the tables were empty, so a reservation hadn't really been necessary. Obviously Lila had been concerned about making sure everything went smoothly today.

The hostess led them to a table, and everything stopped going smoothly. The arrangement of the table—like the other four-person tables in the room, Ken quickly determined—made provision for two seats on either side. Both boys wanted to sit with Lila.

"I get Mom," Michael declared imperiously. "I'm older."

"Yeah, but you're stupid," Danny argued.

"That's the stupidest thing you ever said."

"Yeah? Well, you're the stupidest thing I ever saw."

"Hush," Lila silenced them, raising her hand. Quieting down, they eyed her warily. She took a moment to make sure the peace would last, then said, "You two sit there, and I'll sit facing you. It's the only fair thing to do. And this way I'll get to see you both, and you can see me."

A supremely masterful solution, Ken thought, except for one thing: it meant he had to sit next to Lila. As soon as he took his seat beside her, he regretted it. She exuded that same hypnotic fragrance that had stirred his senses last night. He wondered whether she'd taken another bubble bath, or whether the perfume had clung to her skin all this time.

Then there was her ear. That she was wearing a modest gold hoop earring instead of a coquettish gold-and-turquoise dangly thing didn't matter. Her fisherman's sweater and corduroy slacks weren't the least bit seductive, but he was uncomfortably aware of what lurked underneath the comfortable weekend clothes. He knew how she'd felt in his arms last night, how her lips had tasted, how her face had glowed with uncalculated delight when he'd told her about his promotion. He knew how much he'd desired her last night. Today, the feeling was even stronger.

And here she was, seated beside him, just inches from him, ignoring him. Danny was laboring over the particulars of a knock-knock joke, and she was laughing as if she'd never been happier in her life.

"Do they have peanut butter here?" Danny asked, once he'd stopped giggling. "I want a peanut butter sandwich."

"I don't think they do," Lila said, skimming one of the menus the hostess had left for them. "This is a fancy restaurant, Danny."

He perused the menu and curled his lip. "Chopped sirloin is a hamburger, right? That's what I'll have. You know what, Mom? We've been making our own lunches for school. Dad lets us do it all ourselves—the sandwiches, the dessert, everything."

"Really?" Lila shot Ken an inquiring look. He confirmed Danny's assertion with a nod.

"Yeah, 'cuz you know why? The first day, he made my sandwich and he forgot to trim the crust the way I like it, and I complained to him about it and he said, 'If you don't like the way I do it, you can do it yourself.' And so that's what we're doing. It's fun, Mom."

Lila looked bemused. Ken wondered if it had ever occurred to her that the boys were old enough to make their own lunches. To him, the issue had been a matter of necessity. He was a firm believer in delegating responsibility. Whatever tasks the boys could manage he assigned to them.

"The sirloin tips look good to me," he said with deliberate nonchalance. He liked the notion that Lila had been thrown off balance by Danny's news about the school lunches.

Michael laid down his menu and declared, "I'll have the stuffed shrimp."

Lila looked even more bemused. "Michael, you don't like shrimp."

"That's what I want," he insisted.

"Michael," Ken interjected sternly. "Order something you'll eat." He wasn't going to blow fourteen dollars on an entrée that that would wind up in the garbage.

"I want stuffed shrimp," he said. "I bet it's what Mom's going to get."

"We-ell..." Lila scanned the menu again. Stuffed shrimp happened to be one of her favorite dishes. She frequently ordered it when they went out for dinner.

"I want what Mom's having," said Michael.

Ken bristled. He'd been knocking himself out, putting in a full workday at Allied-Tech and taking care of the boys at home. Why didn't they want to order what *he* was having? Why didn't they fight over who got to sit next to *him*? They always used to, when Lila had been home and life had been normal. Even if the family was only going out for pizza, the boys used to argue over who would have the privilege of sitting next to Dad, and if he said he wanted mushrooms on his pizza, they both swore they wanted mushrooms, too, even though they despised mushrooms.

Now, all of a sudden, it was Mom they were fighting over, Mom they were emulating. Talk about feeling invisible...

"Here's the deal, Michael," Lila said evenly. "You order stuffed shrimp and I'll order a hamburger, and we can share. How does that sound?"

"Okay," Michael said.

"The wisdom of Solomon," Ken muttered under his breath. He knew Lila would end up eating most of Michael's shrimp and very little of her hamburger.

Over lunch the boys continued to regale her with news of happenings at home. Danny related the plots of all the cartoons he'd watched that morning, and Michael quoted a few lines from a Beastie Boys rap song he'd memorized. Michael told Lila about how Ken had let the boys stay up late Friday night to watch a Red Sox game on television, and Danny had waxed hyperbolic over the thrill of staying up till ten o'clock.

Ken listened only superficially to their chatter, most of his attention focused on Lila. She listened raptly to everything the boys said, asking the right questions and smiling at the right moments. That she had the patience to sit through their long-winded stories, to empathize and to encourage them was the true source of her beauty, he realized. He was always so tired by the time he got home from work, and then he had to cook—even if cooking amounted to tossing a frozen pizza into the oven—and set the table—even if *that* amounted to tearing a few sheets from the paper towel roll and distributing it one to a seat…

Who was he kidding? Even when he didn't have to cook and set the table, he had never listened as intently to the boys as Lila did. He'd never had to. He had always known she was there, doing the listening for both of them, and he'd relied on her to let him know if something important was being said.

He relied on her for so much. He took so much for granted.

When would he stop feeling so horribly guilty? When would he start hating her again?

The boys couldn't finish their generous-sized hamburgers, but they protested loudly when Lila suggested that they skip dessert. "Maybe you can have ice cream later," she offered.

They left the restaurant and ambled back toward Bayside Manor in the brisk, sunny afternoon. At least a dozen people, and twice as many sea gulls, were enjoying the beach. Danny and Michael gazed longingly at the clean stretch of sand. "Can we go play?" Danny asked, gesturing across the street.

Lila glanced at Ken and then grinned at the boys. "It's okay with me," she said.

"Wow!" Danny hooted. "The beach in October!" He darted across the street, Michael at his heels. They paused on the sidewalk to remove their high-tops and socks, then plowed through the dune grass to the sand.

Ken dared to take Lila's hand as they crossed the street. She glanced at him in surprise, but he refused to release her. Her hand felt small and dainty within his. He shouldn't have touched her; it would be agony to let her go.

Once they'd reached the beach side of the street, her hand moved against his palm. Uncurling his fingers and freeing her, he confronted that expected agony. She flexed her hand, then shoved it into her pocket. *Fine,* he almost shouted. *You're coming through loud and clear. I won't touch you again.* Not that he had to touch her to feel her imprint on him, the delicate ridge of her knuckles, the familiar silkiness of the skin on the back of her hand. It was there on his palm like a brand. He was permanently marked, eternally scarred.

They spotted the boys standing side by side, the legs of their dungarees rolled up to their knees and their feet buried in the sand. They appeared transfixed by the sight of a sturdy-looking blond fellow in a UMass sweatshirt and blue jeans, who was kneeling on the beach, painstakingly untangling a snarl of kite string. His kite was shaped like a stingray, its wings and tail striped with the colors of the rainbow. Catching the sea breezes, it flopped about on the sand like a dying fish.

The young man glanced up at the boys and gave them a broad smile. "Hey, guys—what's happening?" he asked.

Michael and Danny exchanged a look.

"You ever see a knot this bad before?"

"Uh-uh," Danny said solemnly.

Ken felt his adrenaline begin to pump. The boys should know better than to talk to a stranger, even a friendly, harmless-looking one. *Especially* a friendly, harmless-looking one. "Mike, Danny," he called to them, not too loudly, not to embarrass the stranger or the boys, just to draw them away.

Lila slid her hand from her pocket and patted his arm. "It's all right, Ken," she whispered. "He's a friend of mine." She started across the beach in surefooted steps, her hair streaming back from her cheeks as the wind snagged in its dense waves. "Hi, Jimmy!" she shouted, waving at the blond fellow. "What have you got there, a kite?"

Jimmy. Ken stared at the blond man, stared at him as he raised his eyes to Lila and returned her wave, as Lila introduced him to the boys and he shook each one's hand and then explained to them the aerodynamics of his kite. Ken stared at the man, much too blond, too young, too athletic. All that energy, all that virility, all that damn male charm.

His adrenaline began to pump even harder. *Kenny-boy,* he thought grimly, *this isn't good. This isn't good at all.*

# *Chapter Nine*

"Ken?" Lila called to him. He had remained behind when she'd gone over to say hello to Jimmy, and his gaze revealed distrust if not outright hostility. At her summons he trudged reluctantly across the sand in her direction. "This is my husband, Ken," she said, presenting him to Jimmy.

Jimmy stood, dusted his hand on the seat of his jeans and gave Ken a robust handshake. "Jimmy Peele," he said, introducing himself with an amiable grin. Ken returned the handshake and smiled coldly. "I hope you don't mind if I borrow your kids for a little while," Jimmy said. "I could sure use their help getting this kite into the sky."

"Yeah!" Danny crowed ebulliently, lifting the kite and sprinting down the beach.

"Hey, slow down, sport!" Jimmy picked up the spool of string and nudged Michael to join him in pursuit of Danny. They chased him along the sand, laughing and shouting when Danny let go of the kite. It made a promising swoop before plummeting to the earth.

Lila watched them for a minute, savoring the keen pleasure of seeing her sons, seeing them enjoying themselves and knowing that, far from either rejecting her or clinging neurotically to her, they felt comfortable with her despite the unusual circumstances of this visit. A satisfied smile curved her lips as she glanced up at Ken, but it vanished when she read the suspicion in his transparent stare.

"It's all right," she assured him. "The boys are perfectly safe with Jimmy."

"Are they?" he grunted.

What was bothering him? Did he resent Lila for having made a friend in Hull? Or did he resent her for having made a *male* friend? "He works at Bayside manor," she said, even though she didn't owe Ken an explanation. "He's been in Hull only a few months, and—"

"Sure. Fine." Ken dug his hands into the pockets of his trousers and continued to follow Jimmy and the boys with his gaze. Compared to Jimmy's casual attire, Ken looked as if he'd stepped out of an L.L. Bean catalogue: cuffed and pleated khaki trousers, an oxford shirt under a crew-neck sweater, moccasin-stitched loafers and argyle socks. When Lila had first met him, he'd been dressed like Jimmy—his jeans had been cut off above the knees and instead of a sweatshirt he'd had on a cotton T-shirt, but the basic style had been the same. It was, she supposed, what athletic men in their mid-twenties wore.

Maybe he was too old to dress like that anymore, too mature, too much the successful executive. Maybe she was too old to appreciate that sort of adorably scruffy look. She would choose L.L. Bean over grungy-dude any day.

She missed Ken. Even though her anger was directed more toward him than the boys, she missed him just as much as she missed them. Last night after he'd left her room, she'd gazed out through the window at the misty moonlight and thought not only about their argument but also about the way he'd kissed her. She'd thought about the unexpected, almost embarrassing twinges of longing he'd ignited within her every time she'd felt his gaze on her at the Talbot house, and about the way his body had hardened against hers when he'd gathered her to himself in her room.

What if they had made love last night? Would the world have come to an end?

Now, of course, it was too late. The boys were here and Ken was in a grim mood. She'd lost her chance, and while her brain told her she had done the right thing in refusing him last night, her body was tense with frustration.

"Your mother phoned," he said abruptly.

Lila grimaced. "When?"

"This morning." He sauntered slowly along the beach, as if not wanting to leave too much distance between himself and his sons. Lila fell into step beside him.

Her mother. She should have called her mother on Tuesday and explained... but she still hadn't figured out a simple explanation for what she was doing, and she couldn't stomach the notion of talking to her mother when she was not prepared to justify her actions. "What did you tell her?" she asked nervously.

"I told her you'd call her back."

Then he'd revealed nothing about her departure. Well, she supposed, that was better than if he'd spilled his guts to her mother, told her she had gone off the deep end and abandoned her children and the family was on the brink of collapse.

"She and your father were going to visit your Aunt Florence in the Poconos for the day," he continued. "She said they should be home by eight, so you should call then."

Lila nodded. What would she say? How should she handle this? Why couldn't a woman's search for meaning in her life be a private matter? Why did so many people have to be dragged into it?

Most of all, why did her mother have to be right? Margaret Moore had issued a dire warning to her daughter years ago, when Ken had been offered the job in Dallas and Lila had given up her teaching position in San Jose to accompany him to Texas. "Teaching jobs are hard to come by," her mother had reminded her. "Are you sure you want to give yours up?"

"I don't have a choice, Mom," Lila had asserted. "Ken has such a fine opportunity in Dallas—"

"You know I like Ken very much," her mother had said. "And I want you to be happy with him. But Lila—*you* have a fine opportunity in San Jose. If you give it up, you may find yourself resenting him sometime down the road."

"Mom," Lila had said with unfounded confidence, "if I give up my job for him this time, he'll give up his job for me next time. That's the way marriages work these days."

"I hope you're right, Lila. I just hope you aren't giving up too much."

How prophetic her mother had been. If Lila told her the truth now, she might resort to smug I-told-you-sos. Lila didn't think she could stand that.

"She wanted to know what I gave you for your birthday," Ken went on, his voice gravelly.

Lila turned to him, surprised. "What did you tell her?"

"I said you got exactly what you wanted."

His dark eyes were still riveted to Jimmy and the boys, who had finally launched the kite. Its rainbow-hued wings quivered vibrantly against the clear blue sky. Jimmy handed the spool of string to Michael and bent over to instruct him on how to maneuver it to make the kite dance. Danny's clarion voice reached them on a breeze as he hollered, "My turn's next! I want a turn, too!"

"They seem..." She sighed. "They seem to be doing well."

"The boys?" Ken shrugged. "I've made sure they kept eating and sleeping while you've been gone."

"That's not what I meant," she countered, unsure of whether she should reveal her inner turmoil to him. "They accept me, Ken," she said carefully. "They seem to have accepted my absence."

"Would you prefer it if they were having a nervous breakdown over the situation? What do you think is going on at home? They hit me with a million questions every night. 'When is she coming home, Dad? When are we going to be back to normal?' They're sparing you today, Lila, because they're happy right now. As soon as you're out of the picture it's going to be more 'When is she coming back? Why isn't she home?' "

"I wish I could just explain to them—"

"Explain what? That you wanted a break from the day-in-day-out of it? They don't need you to explain that."

"You know it's more than my just wanting a break."

He gazed down at her. The breeze ruffled his hair, blowing it across his brow. His eyes seemed infinitely sad. "It's that you're not sure you want to be my wife anymore," he guessed, his voice heavy with emotion.

She ached to assure him that he was wrong, that she wanted nothing more in the entire universe than to be his wife. But he wouldn't believe her—and he'd be right not to. She did want to be his wife, but not the way she'd been his wife for the past sixteen years.

"Maybe we should see a counselor," he mumbled.

Lila returned his penetrating stare. "A counselor?"

"You know," he said, obviously having trouble spitting out the words. A muscle in his jaw twitched and he glanced away, gazing first at the boys and then at the water—anywhere but at her. "A marriage counselor."

Even if he'd made the suggestion enthusiastically, she would have been stunned by it. She couldn't imagine sitting in some office and describing the details of her marriage to a total stranger. She had difficulty enough trying to talk about her feelings with Ken himself. She didn't have to go to a marriage counselor to learn that if she felt invisible in the relationship, something was going to have to change. She and Ken both knew that already.

Anyway, people didn't go to marriage counselors unless their marriages were on the verge of disintegration. In Lila's mind, marriage counseling was something people sampled on their way to a divorce.

Maybe Ken thought they were on their way to a divorce. If he did, it may well be true.

"Is that what you want?" she asked evenly, struggling as hard as Ken was to keep her voice level.

He shot her a poignant look, then sighed and swung his gaze back to Jimmy and the boys. "I want you home, Lila. I'm willing to try anything if it'll get you to come home."

"It sounds as if you're faring quite well at home without me," she noted, remembering what the boys had talked about at the restaurant. Their self-reliance and maturity should have reassured her, but instead she had felt dismayed. She was delighted, but also unsettled, by the realization that they were doing so well without her. Their ability to cope made her feel unimportant, even expendable. "I think it's great that the boys are fixing their own school lunches," she said, trying to convince herself. "It's great that they're learning to help out—"

"There's nothing great about it," Ken retorted. "I got them to make their own lunches so there'd be one less thing for me to do. I told them if they weren't going to straighten up their rooms, they could leave their doors shut so I wouldn't have to see the mess. I told them if they spill food on their clothes, they can rinse out the stains themselves or else put on a different shirt. They're eight-and-a-half and ten-and-a-half. There are plenty of things they can do for themselves, if only you'd stop knocking yourself out trying to do everything for them."

She pressed her lips together to keep from responding defensively. She'd knocked herself out trying to do things for them because that had been her role. "Well," she said tightly, "I'm glad everything's going smoothly at home."

Ken shrugged again, squinting into the sunlight. "It isn't smooth," he admitted. "Where do you keep the coffee filters, anyway? I've been living on instant coffee for days, now."

How ironic, she thought, that the children were fixing their own lunches and Ken—the adult of the household—couldn't figure out how to make a pot of coffee. "They're where they've always been," she answered. "In the drawer to the right of the silverware drawer."

"Why do you keep them in a drawer?" he railed. "I looked in every damned cabinet—"

"I keep them in a drawer because that's a convenient place for me to keep them. I've kept them in that drawer ever since we moved to Wayland. That's where they've always been." *Don't lose your temper,* she admonished herself. *Don't lose control just because Ken hasn't made a single pot of coffee since you settled in Massachusetts.* But she couldn't help herself. All the pent-up emotions that had been simmering inside her coalesced into a hot rage—rage at the thought that her sons were too independent and her husband too dependent, that she was both essential and unnecessary—both a coffee-maker and a former sandwich-maker and, in either case, a set of functions rather than a human being.

How was it that a kiss from Ken in a darkened hotel room overlooking the water could persuade her that she loved him, and yet a question about coffee filters could make her despise everything her life with him represented? Was it possible they were so far down the road toward divorce that they'd already passed the point where marriage counseling could do them any good?

Coffee filters, she thought bleakly. When they hammered out their settlement in court, would she wind up blaming coffee filters for the ultimate dissolution of her marriage?

Above her a jubilant breeze lifted the stingray kite in a whirling, giddy ballet. *Coffee filters,* she fumed, biting her lip to keep from crying.

AT EIGHT-THIRTY THAT EVENING she descended from her room, feeling like a fraud.

She had lied to her mother. Just as Ken had fabricated a story about a recuperating cousin for the baby-sitter's sake, and had escorted Lila to the Talbot party so no one would think anything was amiss in his personal life, so Lila had lied about her situation to her mother. "What Ken gave me for my birthday," she'd claimed, "was the use of a room in a little hotel by the sea whenever I want to get away. Isn't that sweet? . . . Well, no, I wasn't at the seaside resort when you called this morning—of course I wouldn't go on a Sunday morning. I'd only been across the street at Irene McCormick's, returning a pie plate I'd borrowed. So, how are Aunt Flo and Uncle Bill? Did you have a good time at their cottage?"

When had she developed such a flair for lying? If her sons lied to her the way she'd just lied to her mother, she'd be shattered.

On the other hand, she knew her mother would have been shattered by the truth. She would have assumed that Lila's marriage was over—a painfully reasonable assumption, considering the disheartening few hours she and Ken had spent together that afternoon.

Too miserable to remain cooped up in her room, rehashing in her mind the mess her life had become, she wandered down the hall to the stairs. The solitude she had relished during the past few days felt more like loneliness tonight. Seeing how cheerful and self-sufficient the boys were made her miss them all the more. She could no longer remember how often they used to drive her crazy with their petty squabbles and their self-centeredness.

As for Ken—she had no difficulty remembering. All she had to do was whisper the words "coffee filters," and a strange, chilly despair overtook her.

Arriving on the first floor, Lila discovered the Cavanagh sisters in the parlor playing three-handed bridge. They reminded Lila of birds, all three of them slight in build, with beaklike noses and twittering voices. They chirped a chorus of hellos at Lila, who manufactured a smile for them before she donned her cardigan and exited onto the veranda. The sky was a dull purplish gray and the air was heavy with a saltwater aroma. Lila leaned on the railing and faced the water, which was scarcely visible as the murky evening fog rolled in.

"Hey there, how's it going?" came a familiar voice.

She glanced behind her to see Jimmy bounding through the door to join her on the veranda. She hadn't seen him since he'd bade her family farewell on the beach a few hours ago, after his successful effort to launch his kite. He was still wearing his faded jeans, sweatshirt and leather sneakers; his face glowed from the afternoon he'd spent in the sun and his hair was streaked with platinum.

"Hi, Jimmy," she said, turning back to the water and clasping her hands together, as though she were trying to maintain a tight hold on herself.

"I really liked your kids," he said. "It was fun playing with them on the beach today."

"They liked you, too," she murmured, willing her eyes to remain dry.

He scrutinized her for several seconds. "So now they're gone and you're in the pits."

She opened her mouth to refute his statement, then closed it without speaking. She'd done enough lying for one night. "I'm in the pits," she confirmed with a glum laugh.

"How about a drink?" he asked. "I could sure use one. You think you've got troubles? I just spent the last half hour in the cellar with Mrs. Tarlock, trying to explain the problem with the water pressure on the third floor. I swear, if that woman ever tried to smile, her cheeks would probably crack."

Lila laughed again.

"So, how about it? You wanna go get a beer and listen to me complain about my boss?"

Why not? Jimmy was her friend—at the moment, her only friend close enough to have a drink with. She couldn't discuss her marital crisis with Claudette Wiley—Claudette would consider Lila's problems trivial when compared to the anguish endured by the soup kitchen's clients. As for her other friends—Irene McCormick or Naomi Parrish or Karen Schiller—they all lived in her neighborhood in Wayland. She wondered whether they were aware that she was gone, and if so, whether they had questioned Ken about her absence. He would probably lie to them as Lila had lied to her mother.

If they ever found out what Lila had done, they would be flabbergasted. Whenever Lila coffee-klatsched with her neighborhood friends, the other women invariably tore their husbands to shreds while Lila sat quietly, saying little. To admit publicly that Ken wasn't perfect was to admit that she'd made a mistake in choosing him as her husband. Furthermore, she would feel disloyal criticizing him behind his back.

Besides, she loved him, and for a long time she'd believed that loving him meant being willing to overlook his flaws and her own dissatisfactions. If, all of a sudden, she announced to her friends that she'd exploded from pent-up frustration, they would certainly conclude she'd gone insane.

Which might very well be an accurate appraisal of her condition.

"A person's got to let it all out sometimes," Jimmy said gently. His eyes glowed in the light from the porch lamps; his expression was welcoming. "Come on, let's get a beer and you can listen to me rant and rave."

She could tell from his sympathetic smile that he thought she was the person who needed to rant and rave. She appreciated his diplomatic way of pretending otherwise, and his sweet persistence in dragging a dreary old lady out of her doldrums. "All right, Jimmy," she said, returning his grin and accompanying him down the steps to the sidewalk. "Let's get a beer."

They strolled around the corner and down the block, heading toward downtown Hull. Neither of them spoke. Jimmy walked with a slightly swaggering gait, she noticed, his legs bowed and his arms swinging free. There was something blatantly male about it, something appealingly youthful. Once men became accustomed to wearing tailored suits and conservative loafers or wing tip oxfords, they tended to walk in a less overtly sexual manner.

The tavern Jimmy led her to was moderately crowded but not too noisy. They found a booth against a side wall, with a corny painting of a lighthouse hanging above them on the weathered pine paneling. Within a minute a waitress arrived at their table. "I'll have a Bud," Jimmy ordered, then eyed Lila questioningly.

"I'll have the same," she said.

The waitress nodded and left. Jimmy leaned into the seat and gave Lila a congenial smile. It occurred to her that she hadn't gone out for a drink with a man other than Ken in nearly two decades. Jimmy was so much younger than she, she almost couldn't think of him as a man... Nonsense, she corrected herself. His voice was deep, his chin shadowed with stubble. He had to be in his early twenties, at least.

At the moment, he seemed more sensitive to her moods than her husband was. She didn't care how young he was; she was pleased to be in his company, even if she felt a little like his maiden aunt. "So," she said, returning his compassionate smile, "what horrors did Mrs. Tarlock inflict upon you?"

He groaned, although his eyes sparkled with humor. "I swear, someone ought to put her out of her misery. She's such a witch. Nobody seems to know what did her husband in, but I wouldn't be surprised if she growled him to death."

"*Growled* him to death?"

"Yeah, like, she growled so much he went loony-tunes and died. I mean, there I was, Lila, down in the cellar with her, and I said, 'Look, Mrs. Tarlock, you need a bigger water tank.' People visiting the beach like to shower a lot, right?"

Lila nodded.

"And she said, 'Don't you tell me how to run my affairs!' Affairs—I mean, give me a break! Like anyone would want to touch her without wearing surgical gloves. She said, 'I've been in the hotel business a darned long time, young man, and I know we can get by with a hundred-fifty gallon tank, so don't you tell me otherwise!' And all the while she was wagging her finger at me like I was a naughty dog who peed on the carpet, or something. Sheesh!" He fell silent as the waitress delivered their beer, then took a long drink directly from the bottle.

Lila poured her beer into the glass the waitress had provided and took a sip. "Why do you work for her, then?" she asked. "I assume you've been to UMass—" she gestured toward his sweatshirt "—so you must have some education. You could get a better job elsewhere, couldn't you?"

"Elsewhere, meaning outside Hull," he clarified, then shrugged. "Sure, there are openings in Boston. Hey, it's not like I've got a really marketable degree or anything. I majored in American Studies—an interdepartmental major, good for nothing but going to law school, which I don't want to do. I like working with my hands, you know? Up in Portsmouth, I was a member of a crew restoring an old church, and I really enjoyed it. I could probably get work like that in Boston. There's sure a lot of crumbling old historical buildings up there."

"Maybe you could commute to Boston," Lila suggested. "You could stay on in Hull and commute up there to work."

He pulled a face. "We're talking over an hour each way, with traffic. Uh-uh. My father did that for twenty years, and now he's got high blood pressure and heart problems."

"How is he doing?" Lila asked.

Jimmy shrugged. "He's okay, really," he said. "But he's lonely. It was a real scare last spring, chest pains and dizzy spells, the whole bit. The poor guy lives alone and he's scared."

"Oh." She traced a line through the frosty condensation on her glass, thinking about Jimmy's lonely father and wondering where Jimmy's mother was.

He answered her unvoiced question. "My mother walked out on my father about ten years ago, when I was in high school."

"Oh," she said again, suffering a mixture of pity and guilt. Would her boys someday be telling someone in a bar that their mother walked out on their father?

Jimmy leaned forward, appraising her thoughtfully. "Look, Lila, it's none of my business, but hey, I survived one of these trips. If you're having trouble with your children, maybe I could talk to them, or something."

It took her a minute to adjust to the abrupt change in direction their conversation had taken. Jimmy was apparently done ranting and raving; now he seemed to be saying it was her turn. She usually kept her feelings well hidden, but he obviously had no difficulty reading her mind.

"You think I've walked out on my family," she said, then smiled faintly and shook her head.

He continued to scrutinize her, his gaze probing. "I'm sorry if I've got it wrong."

"Don't be sorry. I mean...you aren't completely wrong. I'm not about to get a divorce or anything, but..." *A person's got to let it all out sometimes,* she recalled him saying, and it was true. Keeping things locked up inside her had led to her current state of misery. If he was willing to listen, she ought to talk. "I needed some time away, that was all."

"So you're separated."

"That sounds so—so formal." She sighed. "But I guess I *am* separated from Ken. We're working some things out. Actually, I'm the one working everything out."

"Did something precipitate it?" he asked. "With my mother, it was another guy."

"Oh, no," Lila said vehemently. "It's nothing like that."

"Hey, it isn't a crime. People fall in and out of love. It happens. One thing I really admired about my mother was that she was up-front about the whole thing. She didn't sneak around. She met this guy, the sparks flew and she told my father. She asked me who I wanted to live with, and since she and her new husband moved to Quincy they were close enough that I could go back and forth. It was rough for a while, but then I got used to it. If your sons are getting antsy, Lila, maybe I could reassure them. I've been there."

"And you've survived."

He spread his arms outward as if to display himself. "More than survived, Lila. I've turned out terrific, right?" He let out a self-mocking laugh.

"You have," Lila asserted, refusing to let him ridicule himself. She ran her finger around the rim of her glass, pondering her words. "I'm not involved with anyone else," she explained. "If anything precipitated my situation, I guess it was my fortieth birthday." She nearly added that turning forty was arguably as traumatic as having an extramarital affair, but given how young Jimmy was she doubted he would believe her.

"You're forty?" Jimmy appeared shocked.

Lila nodded.

"No kidding? I never would have known."

"You thought I was fifty," she joked modestly, trying to deflect his flattery.

"No, really. You look much younger. Wow. If you're forty, forty isn't half bad." He drank some more beer and studied her intently. "So, you're going through a mid-life crisis or something?"

"Oh, my." She chuckled. "Words of wisdom from one who's been there."

He joined her laughter. "Hey, it's just that forty is supposed to be one of those times of self-evaluation. I went through one at twenty-one. I imagine I'll go through another one at thirty, forty, sixty-five... They're kind of like power surges. Everything gets scrambled and you've got to rewire yourself. My mother was forty when she met my stepfather. She wanted her second forty years to have some excitement in them."

Lila could understand that—although her own idea of excitement lay in finding a new purpose for her existence, a new significance, an opportunity to contribute to the world something more important than dinner and clean laundry. "I'm looking for something different," she told him. "You might say I need a job change, just like you."

"What kind of job have you got now?"

Lila rolled her eyes. "I'm a homemaker," she said, hating how unliberated that sounded. "I gave up my career years ago to raise the kids and all. But I've been doing volunteer work at a soup kitchen. I want to do more to help the homeless, maybe teach them to read."

"Whoa. Heavy-duty." Jimmy whistled, his admiration obvious. "That would be really decent of you, Lila. Go for it."

"Well, if I can raise the money to get a literacy project off the ground..."

"Go for it," Jimmy repeated. "Go where the need is. If your husband doesn't like it, he's got problems, Lila. You want to do something for the human race. Don't let your old man stand in your way."

"He isn't standing in the way," Lila said quickly. Then she took a long, slow sip of beer and reconsidered her answer. Maybe Ken *was* standing in her way...or maybe it had nothing to do with him at all. Maybe she was standing in her own way. Maybe she'd been standing in her own way all along and blaming him for it. Maybe if she'd proclaimed her wishes years ago he would have said the same things Jimmy was saying: "Go for it. Go where the need is."

Maybe he and the boys were no longer where the need was. Maybe her family didn't really need her anymore.

The possibility shook her, but she couldn't retreat from it. She lifted her gaze to Jimmy, whose eyes never left her even as he tipped his bottle of beer back against his lips and drank. "It's good talking to you," she said, grateful to him for forcing her to confront such troubling thoughts.

He lowered his bottle to the table and covered her hand with his. He gave her a brief, comforting squeeze, then spread his hands in another comical self-display. "I told you I'm terrific," he boasted, then grew serious. "And so are you, Lila. We're a couple of winners here. Don't you forget it."

Smiling, wishing she could believe him, she raised her glass to him in a toast and took a drink.

# Chapter Ten

"Ken?"

Theresa tapped on the door to his office and then inched it open. Nearing thirty, she was always beautifully groomed. In the days since he'd moved up to the third floor, Ken had often found himself puzzling over the fact that Theresa could be the mother of a two-year-old and still manage to put herself together with immaculate style. He already knew that she, and not her husband, delivered their daughter to the day-care center before work and picked the child up at night; Theresa had informed Ken of this so he would be sensitive to her schedule. How, he wondered, had she trained a two-year-old not to spill her cereal on her mother's impeccable outfits? How was Theresa able to arrive at the office promptly at eight forty-five, with her lipstick perfect, her shoes polished and nary a hair out of place? Ken himself had lately taken to knotting his tie and combing his hair in the Allied-Tech parking lot, using the rearview mirror to check the results. He couldn't seem to get himself completely dressed along with everything else he had to do to get the boys fed and off to school on time.

He glanced up from his desk, saw Theresa peeking around the edge of the door and beckoned her inside. Then he leaned back in his chair, resting his head against the high back and propping his elbows on the polished teak arms. Someday, he assumed, he would start to feel comfortable in this exalted environment. He would feel he wasn't just a little kid who'd sneaked into his father's office, climbed into this oversize leather swivel throne and embarked on a game of let's-pretend-I'm-the-boss.

"Yes, Theresa," he said, marveling at his ability to inflect his voice with an authority he didn't yet feel.

Theresa opened the door wider, and he saw she was holding her spiral-bound appointment notebook as well as a file folder and some loose papers. "Here's what's on your calendar for today," she announced, reading from the notebook. "At one-thirty you've got an interview with the final candidate for Ed Healey's position. His name is Gerald Heffernan—personel sent up his file." She crossed the spacious room, the sound of her footsteps muffled by the plush carpeting, and presented Ken with the folder. Then she placed the loose papers on the desk. "This is a preliminary report Sue DiLetto faxed up from Sematech. Read it when you've got a minute. She would like some feedback by midweek." Theresa glanced at her notebook again. "At four o'clock, Diane Suralik would like to meet with you and Herman to rank all three candidates for Ed Healey's position and maybe formulate an offer to one of them. Also, Cecile Patterson would like to do a conference call some time this afternoon to discuss some thoughts she has on collaborating with Perkin-Elmer on their new circuit board design. If it's all right with you, I'll try to arrange the call for about two-thirty. And of course," she concluded, folding her notebook shut, "you've got the Monday morning powwow."

"What Monday morning powwow?" he asked.

"Oh, that's right—this is your first Monday as a vice president. Every Monday at nine-thirty all the top executive people meet in the conference room to discuss strategy for the week."

"Strategy?" He grimaced. "I'm still trying to work out a strategy for getting my old telephone extension transferred to this office."

"Don't worry. It's basically an informal coordinating session. People toss ideas around. It's supposed to be casual. Nobody's going to expect anything structured from you—certainly not this week."

"Good."

She examined him for a moment, tilting her head slightly. "Are you feeling okay?"

"Sure," he said, once again with more authority than he felt.

Theresa clearly didn't believe him. "You look exhausted."

"Well—it's been a hectic few days."

"More like a hectic few nights, from the looks of it. Haven't you been getting any sleep?"

He frowned. Theresa's efficiency pleased, even awed, him, but he didn't want her to apply her abundant administrative skills to his personal life. "Not as much as I need," he conceded, adding vaguely, "The excitement of the promotion and all..."

"You've got bags under your eyes."

"And in time, when I catch up on my sleep, they'll go away." He made a futile attempt to stifle a yawn, then asked, "What I could use right now is a cup of real coffee. Is there a place up here where I can get some?" He knew where the second-floor coffee machine was, but he didn't want to waste his dwindling supply of energy trekking up and down the stairs. That morning he had actually located the coffee filters at home, but just as he was about to prepare a pot Michael shouted down the stairs that Danny was throwing up.

As it turned out, Danny was only suffering from dry heaves. He had no fever and after he was done retching he wolfed down two heaping bowls of Frosted Flakes, so Ken sent him off to school and tried not to feel guilty about it.

Ken, on the other hand, hadn't even had time for a cup of instant coffee. He was certain a shot of caffeine would eradicate at least some of the bags under his eyes.

"Do you want me to get you some coffee?" Theresa asked.

"No, I can get it myself," Ken answered quickly. He wasn't a sexist; he wouldn't ask his new secretary to serve him as if she was a waitress. He knew treating professional women in a professional manner was correct behavior.

She gave him a patient smile. "If you want to wait until the meeting, you can get your own coffee there. There's always a big urn in the conference room. Dr. Karsch won't start the meeting without it. If you want some coffee now, though, you'll have to let me get it for you. The secretaries up here don't allow executives into our kitchenette. You men always leave the place a mess."

"I see," he backed down, properly chastised. "Fine, then, you can bring me a cup." If she was bigoted enough to think all men were messy, he could match her bias by treating her like a waitress.

She nodded and left his office, closing the door behind her. Groaning, he folded his arms on his blotter and rested his head on them. He had never considered himself messy before Lila had left. He liked living in a house where the kitchen floor shone and the counters were sponged clean. He was meticulous about hanging up his clothes, making sure his trousers were properly pleated and his jackets straight and symmetrical on the hanger. But after a week without Lila he was coming to the realization that his neatness extended only as far as someone else's willingness to neaten things for him. Without Lila to sponge the counters, mop the floors and hold the hanger for him so he could drape his slacks smoothly across the horizontal bar, he'd developed a startling tolerance for slovenliness.

*Lila, come back,* he whispered into the pinstriped sleeves of his jacket. *I promise I'll help you clean, if only you'll show me what you want me to do.*

He closed his eyes, wishing there was some telepathic way he could communicate to her his vow to reform. But when he tried to picture her in his mind, he pictured instead that big blond stud she'd introduced as her "friend."

Oh, God. Ken was losing her. He knew it. Even if she and the kite-flyer were only friends, he couldn't dismiss the tormenting knowledge that he was losing her.

It would serve him right if he did. Try as he might to rearrange his perspective and mend his ways, his true sentiments kept slipping out. Just now, wasn't he thinking about how *he* was willing to help *her* clean the house? Why shouldn't he instead be willing to let *her* help *him*?

Because he didn't want to, that was why. He wanted everything to go back to the way it had been before. And it never would, never.

"Ken?"

At the sound of Theresa's voice he bolted upright and smiled sheepishly. His eyes gradually came into focus on her as she carried a mug of steaming coffee across the room to his desk. The mug was a graceful streamlined shape, made of white porcelain with little pink hearts all over it.

"This really isn't a good time to catch up on your sleep," she chided him. "If you aren't busy, you ought to take a look at Sue DiLetto's report."

"Once I have some coffee I'll be able to climb mountains and swim oceans," he said, attempting a smile. "Right now, my primary goal in life is to keep my eyes open."

"I forgot to ask if you take sugar or cream."

"Black is fine." He took a sip of the coffee and smiled, ignoring its scalding temperature. "This is great, Theresa. You've saved my life." She hovered beside his desk like a doting mother, and he felt obliged to take another sip. "It's delicious," he told her. "The valentine motif is a little corny, though, don't you think?"

She smiled. "Those of us with access to the kitchenette tend to be a romantic bunch," she said simply. "You've got fifteen minutes till the powwow." She pivoted on her heel and strode out of the office.

Continuing to sip his coffee, Ken went through the motions of reading the faxed report Theresa had placed on his desk, but he absorbed none of the typed words. His mind stubbornly returned to Lila, to the way her blue eyes had lit up with joy when she'd seen the boys yesterday, to the way the shore breezes had tossed the untamed curls of her hair, to the profound contentment he occasionally glimpsed within her, a contentment that would have seemed utterly alien to her a week or two ago. Other than to see the boys, what reason did she have to return home? As long as Ken brought them to Hull on a regular basis, and as long as her money lasted, she was no doubt perfectly happy where she was. As far as sex went . . .

As far as sex went, she had young Jimmy with his surfer-deluxe face and his manly muscles to keep her company.

The only way Ken could hope to win her back was if he met her halfway, if he changed for her, if he listened to her and accommodated her and—curse the word—was *supportive* of her. No wonder she didn't want to see a marriage counselor. She knew exactly what was wrong with their life together, and so did he. They didn't have to turn to a detached professional to learn the truth.

What they needed—what *Ken* needed, anyway—was the strength and selflessness to meet Lila's needs.

By the time his mug was empty he began to feel a little more alert. He shrugged his shoulders to straighten his jacket, fidgeted unnecessarily with his tie, sucked in a deep breath and stood. He had no illusions about overwhelming anyone at this executive meeting with his accomplishments as a new vice president, but he didn't want to underwhelm anyone, either. Grabbing a blank legal pad so he'd have something on which to take notes, he locked his desk and left his office.

Theresa glanced up from her word processor as he passed her neat L-shaped desk, and gave him a wave. Plastering an unjustifiably confident smile on his face, he waved back and stalked out into the hall, where he came within inches of bumping into Larry Talbot. "Hi, Ken," the balding older man greeted him. "I was just coming to get you. You know about the powwow?"

"Theresa warned me. I'm not going to be put in the spotlight, am I?"

Larry laughed and headed down the hall with him. "Just long enough to humiliate you," Larry teased.

"Hey, I thought I did my time in the spotlight at your house Saturday night."

"Stardom has its price." Larry relented with a smile. "Don't sweat it, Ken. These Monday morning meetings are a time when we all let down our hair and say what's on our minds without fear of recrimination. Aaron Karsch has been running these meetings for years now. They're great for getting everyone in gear for the week, making sure no one's stepping on anyone's toes and laying everything out on the table. We toss ideas around, that's all. It's a mixture of brainstorming and b.s. You'll see."

The conference room was redolent of the aroma of coffee. Ken made a beeline to the urn and filled a mug for himself. This mug, he was pleased to note, was decorated not with cute pink hearts but with the Allied-Tech logo—a green "A" and "T" separated by a jagged black line that was supposed to resemble a bolt of electricity. The executives might be too messy for the secretarial staff's taste, but at least they weren't romantic fools.

Armed with his coffee, Ken took a seat next to Larry at the broad oval table. He placed his pad in front of him, pulled a pen from an inner pocket of his jacket and smiled expectantly at the others converging around the table. He was once again visited by that strange image of himself as an imposter, a little kid who had gotten mixed up in this lofty grown-up world by mistake.

If only it were true, if only he were still a little kid, if only he could live his life over again... What would he do differently? Would he forgo the Dallas job, so Lila could keep teaching in San Jose? Would he forgo the Phoenix job, with its extensive traveling, so he could be at home more often when the boys were infants? Would he sacrifice all his career advancements for her?

Of course not. Yet she'd done that for him, every step of the way. And what had her reward been? To be taken for granted.

*Powwow,* he muttered. He couldn't go back to the past and change things. He was here, now, and the only place to change things would be in the future. The only way to reach the future was through the present, which at the moment consisted of this confab of the high and mighty of Allied-Tech.

The first thing that happened, once the meeting came to order, was that Ken was put in the spotlight. Aaron Karsch, Allied-Tech's Chief Executive Officer, rose to his feet and waved a beefy hand at Ken. "Let's start by giving a warm welcome to Kenneth Chapin, our newest addition to corporate. Ken, welcome aboard."

Everyone else at the table burst into applause. Ken sank in his chair and managed a modest smile. He wanted to stand and announce to everyone, "As proud as I am to be in your elite ranks, the truth is I don't belong here. My wife has worked harder than I have over the years. She's sacrificed much more than I have, yet I'm the one who's reached this pinnacle. We're a team—only she's done all the planting and I've done all the reaping, and I feel like a hypocrite."

He kept his mouth shut.

As Larry and Theresa had predicted, the tone of the meeting was informal. Larry spoke for a while on the subject of unstable interest rates and their impact on the company's investments. Jack Stearns described a psychologist who ran motivational seminars for sales people on the weekends, and said he was looking into the possibility of sending some of Allied-Tech's sales staff to one of the seminars. Diane Suralik mentioned that she'd been contacted by an organizer from one of the clerical workers' unions, seeking a meeting with representatives from the secretarial staff.

Ken scribbled notes on his pad, thinking that if he wrote about the meeting he would be able to keep his mind on it. But his thoughts kept returning doggedly to Lila, to how much she'd contributed to their life together and how little credit she'd received, how much she'd had to say and how little he'd listened over the years. How much he wanted to do for her now, how desperately he wanted to make it up to her—if it wasn't too late.

As soon as the discussion reached a lull when all the vital issues had been disposed of, he tossed down his pen and addressed his associates: "Can we talk about corporate donations?"

Aaron Karsch circled the table with his gaze. When nobody objected, he nodded benevolently at Ken. "No subject is off-limits at these meetings," he said. "So go right ahead—tell us what's on your mind."

"Well..." Ken lifted his pen again and tapped it against his palm, taking the time to collect his thoughts. "Allied-Tech has a fund from which we give corporate donations to various programs and so on. I know we're corporate sponsors of the Boston Symphony Orchestra."

"That's right," murmured Frank Coolidge.

"We give to the Museum of Science, too, right?"

"Right," said Aaron Karsch. "Who else do we give to, Larry?"

"We offer National Merit Scholarships for the children of Allied-Tech employees," Larry enumerated, "and we've participated in sponsorship of specific exhibits at the Museum of Fine Arts. We used to give regularly to the American Repertory Theater, too, but there was some flak about one of their productions a few years ago—some people considered it racist or something. I don't remember the particulars."

"With or without the American Repertory Theater, these are all basically cultural forums," Ken summarized, gazing about the room, feeling his anxiety drop away and self-assurance take its place. "I know I'm a rookie here, but I'm wondering whether we might give some consideration to donating something more to the Boston community itself."

"What did you have in mind?" Aaron asked.

"A literacy project," said Ken. "A program that would teach illiterate adults to read."

Silence for a minute, and then Aaron inquired, "Do you have a specific program in mind, Ken?"

"As a matter of fact, yes. I'll admit right off the bat that there's a personal connection here—the program is being organized by my wife. She's been doing volunteer work for two years at a soup kitchen at the Mt. Zion Methodist Church in Roxbury, and apparently a number of the unemployed and homeless people who come there to eat need to be taught how to read."

More silence.

"The actual outlay of funds would be minimal," he went on. "A reasonable rental fee for a room in the church basement and a small fund for books, papers and pens. We could bankroll the entire project for about a thousand dollars a year, by my estimate. As corporate sponsors of the B.S.O., what do we give, ten or fifteen thousand?"

"Ken..." Frank Coolidge gave him a hesitant smile. "The B.S.O. is glamorous. Forgive me for being a little blunt here, but a reading project in the slums is kind of depressing."

"We're in the information systems business," Ken persevered, refusing to be discouraged by the fact that his proposal hadn't been greeted with a standing ovation. "What could be more relevant to what we do than teaching illiterate people how to read? I'll grant you, it's not glamorous—but it *is* important. Illiteracy threatens our very industry, Frank."

"Uh—Ken," Aaron interjected, "I have one minor problem with this whole idea, and that's your wife's participation. I mean, the thing smells of nepotism."

"So what?" Ken returned Aaron's steady stare. Being in the spotlight no longer bothered him. Running the risk of making a fool of himself seemed irrelevant. He felt inspired, motivated, ready to fight. "Your wife's on the Board of Directors of the Museum of Fine Arts and we give money to them. The issue isn't my wife, Aaron. She happens to be a teacher, and the people she works with in Roxbury need to be taught. She doesn't expect a salary from her work with them. All she needs are some books and paper and a room with a few tables and chairs in it."

"You're supposed to be our marketing person, Ken. What on earth does this have to do with marketing?" Diane Suralik asked.

He shrugged. "Other than the fact that we can't market our computer systems to an illiterate population, nothing. I thought this meeting was for talking about anything that concerned us."

"Yes, and we're all concerned about illiteracy in our society," Aaron Karsch said in a conciliatory tone. "Ken, I don't know what to tell you at this point. You've got an interesting idea, but I'm just not sure it's right for us."

"What's not right about it?"

Seated at Ken's side, Larry shook his head and erupted in a low chuckle. "You've met Ken's wife, haven't you?" he addressed the others. "Most of you probably saw her at my house last Saturday. Hell, I'd jump through hoops of fire for that woman. She's smart, she's tough and yet she's as sweet as maple syrup. I can see why Ken's all worked up about this concept. If Lila Chapin had my ear, I'd be all worked up about it, too."

Ken was tempted to inform Larry that Lila hadn't been behind his proposal—that she was completely unaware of it. But he thought it best to press his case without getting sidetracked into an inventory of his wife's numerous assets. "I'm worked up about the project because I think it's a valid place to target our charitable dollars. I think we could earn a lot of respect in the community—"

"What community?" Frank snorted. "Roxbury?"

"Yes, Roxbury, which is a part of Greater Boston. This happens to be where we're located, Frank. This is the region we serve. Why not give something to the people who need it most?"

Frank laughed. "Gee, if I'd known you were such a flaming radical, Chapin, I might not have supported you for V.P."

"Of course you would have," Aaron said. "One reason we all supported Ken was so we'd have a fresh perspective. So far, Ken, you've served us well in that capacity."

"Meaning, we're going to fund a reading project at Mt. Zion Methodist?"

"Meaning," Aaron corrected him, "that you can investigate the idea a bit further and report to us on it when you've got something a bit more substantial. We need numbers, for one thing. We need to know whether this thing is going to be church-sponsored, because if it is I can tell you right now Allied-Tech won't touch it. If we did, every employee of every religious denomination in this company would be banging on the door, demanding to know why we're willing to fund this particular Methodist project and not their church's rummage sale or their synagogue's preschool."

"I understand."

"We need to know whether your wife's program would be duplicating programs already in existence. And most importantly—if I may be a touch crass here—we need to know what Allied-Tech is going to get out of it. In all honesty, I don't see much benefit accruing to us if our name gets bandied about in the public housing projects of Roxbury."

Ken decided to quit while he was ahead. Aaron was right; he would have to present something more concrete to the company if he expected to garner any support. He had to think it through dispassionately, get a budget worked out on paper and formulate some arguments for the project based on logic rather than righteous indignation.

At least he hadn't gotten shut down unconditionally. Aaron was giving him a chance to explore the concept. For that he was grateful.

Would Lila be grateful? he wondered. Or would she think he was trying to pay her off?

It wasn't a payoff. It was her chance to reap the rewards of his promotion, her chance to become an equal member of the team, to get something more from her years of labor than a VIP for a husband. She'd worked hard; she deserved to be compensated for her efforts. If Ken could do this for her, he would.

At last, eighteen years after he'd met her, he was truly listening to her.

"YO—MIKE AND DANNY!" he called from the kitchen.

The boys materialized in the doorway to the family room, each one armed with a video game control. Seeing the broom and dustpan their father was brandishing, they exchanged a skeptical look.

"I need your help cleaning the kitchen," he told them. Let Theresa think executives were slobs. He'd prove her wrong, even if he earned his sons' enmity in the process.

Danny sulked. "Aw, come on, Dad. We've only got an hour left till bedtime, and we just loaded Teenage Mutant Ninja Turtles into the Nintendo."

"Sweeping won't take an hour. Look at the floor. It's disgusting."

"You're suppose' ta use the vacuum cleaner," Michael informed him.

"Yeah, well, I turned it on and it didn't work."

"Did you try plugging it in?" Michael asked with a condescending smirk.

"Yes, I tried plugging it in," Ken returned. "The little red light went on, but the motor wouldn't start. So we're going to have to rely on these archaic tools." He was in too good a mood to lose his temper over the boys' back talk. He handed the broom to Michael and the dustpan to Danny. "Hop to it, guys. There's a week's worth of crud on this floor, and the sooner you can get it off the linoleum and into the garbage pail the sooner you can go play Nintendo. As a matter of fact, get this floor clean and I'll challenge you both to a game of Nintendo. Losers have to take out the garbage."

Grumbling and scowling, the boys headed for the table, beneath which most of the dirt was located. In less than a minute they were bickering, Danny complaining that Michael was deliberately sweeping crumbs into his face and Michael complaining that instead of kneeling on the floor with the dustpan, Danny ought to be moving the chairs out of the way.

Ken tuned them out. Wiping the counters with a soapy sponge, he whistled to himself. What had started out as a ghastly day had turned out rather nicely, and once the kitchen was clean he would be feeling even better.

It had been his first genuine full day at his new job—the previous few days at work had been consumed by the details of settling in, adjusting, filling out forms, searching for a couple of cartons that had somehow gotten misplaced in transit from his old office to his new one, and reviewing with Theresa the way he did things as compared to the way Cecile Patterson used to do them. But today he'd gone to his first powwow, helped the personnel department to reach a decision on a replacement for Ed Healey and commissioned Cecile—his erstwhile superior—to meet with the people at Perkin-Elmer, learn their needs and send him a feasibility study. He'd talked to some engineers at Sematech, the computer-science consortium based in the southwest, about a new system the army wanted designed to assess topographical conditions. And he'd started putting together his ideas for a reading program in Roxbury.

What excited him about the literacy project wasn't so much the flexing of his long-unexercised social conscience. Lila was the do-gooder of their family, not Ken. But he was thrilled by the fact that he would wield his new executive power to achieve something special, something that mattered to her. That his vague proposal at the powwow had been met with less than monumental enthusiasm didn't faze him. Once he had a solid proposal worked out, he'd be able to get the third floor squarely behind him.

A couple thousand dollars—no more than that, and probably less. He was sure his colleagues would come around eventually. He would win Lila's project the funding it merited—and that was something her blond beachcomber pal from UMass could never do for her.

Not that Ken wanted to get hung up on the notion that Jimmy was an actual rival for Lila's affection. She was living alone in Hull; she deserved a friend, and Jimmy was the friend she'd happened to find. Ken only wished she had happened to find a female friend—preferably, a happily married one who could persuade her to return to her husband.

Ken knew he was no spring chicken. While women were alleged to reach their sexual prime at forty, a man of forty-two had kissed his glory days goodbye a good twenty years ago. Ken couldn't hope to compete with some strapping young kite-flying buck—except professionally. As a new denizen of the third floor, he could, with luck and perseverance, provide the financial backing for Lila's dream. That was something young Jimmy Peele, with his sun-bleached hair and boyish dimples, couldn't do.

You went with what you had. Ken had a few wrinkles, a few gray hairs and a whole lot of reprehensible behavior to atone for. But he also had corporate power. Whatever Jimmy could give her, Ken had to have faith that it wouldn't come close to fulfilling her dreams. If he lost that faith, he'd lose everything.

The phone rang. Danny dropped the dustpan, scattering the pile of crumbs Michael had carefully amassed with the broom, and grabbed the receiver. "Hello! Hi, Mom! It's Mom," he unnecessarily informed his brother and father.

"Yeah? I wanna talk to her," Michael shouted, tossing down the broom.

"Take turns," Ken admonished them. He listened to the cheerfully competitive babble of his sons' voices as he scrubbed the sink. Once it was clean, he crossed to the phone and nudged the boys back to the table, saying, "It's my turn now, guys. Finish up the sweeping and then you can go warm up the Nintendo."

"Sweeping?" Lila said before he could greet her.

"Yeah, they're sweeping the kitchen."

"What's wrong with the vacuum cleaner?"

"I don't know. I plugged it in and it didn't start."

"Did the little red light go on?"

"Yes."

She laughed. "That means you need to change the bag. If the bag gets too full, the motor automatically shuts down and the red warning light goes on. Do you know how to change the bag?"

"I'm not sure. I could probably figure it out," he said. "You'd better tell me where you keep the bags, though."

"On the shelf in the broom closet. Listen, Ken, if you can't do it—"

"Hey, I've got a Ph.D. and an M.B.A. I think I can manage it," he said good-naturedly. "So, how are you?"

If she was able to detect his upbeat mood, she didn't comment on it. She seemed remarkably chipper herself. "I had the most wonderful experience at the soup kitchen today," she told him. "Just as we were finishing up serving everybody, Claudette made an announcement that anyone who wanted to take a special class to improve their reading skills could stick around after they were done eating. The woman is so tactful, Ken—she explained to me that most of them would be too embarrassed to admit they couldn't read at all, so she phrased the question so they could pretend it wasn't directed at illiterates. And letting them simply linger over their lunch, instead of making them march forward in front of everyone to sign up, also preserved their pride. But here's the best part, Ken—*twelve* people stayed after lunch, and two of them said they had some friends who might want to participate. Twelve, Ken! Even Mitzie stayed."

Ken was happy for her, and for himself. If he knocked himself out to get corporate funding for the project and then no one wanted to participate in it, he would have expended a great deal of personal energy and company capital for no good reason.

"Who's Mitzie?" he asked.

"I've told you about her lots of times."

Lots of times when he hadn't been listening, obviously. "The name rings a bell," he fibbed. "Refresh my memory."

"She's a woman who's been coming to the soup kitchen for as long as I have. She's kind of withdrawn, but I've always thought of her as a friend. She seems basically healthy and intelligent, and I think she could get herself out of the poverty she lives in if she only cleaned herself up and learned some skills."

"And now she wants to take your class," he said.

"Yes. I'm so glad, Ken—I really want to help her. I mean, I want to help all of them, but her in particular. She's my friend." Lila drifted off, as if embarrassed by her effusiveness.

"Well, that's great," he said.

"That part is," she agreed, then sighed. "Unfortunately, the other part—getting funding—isn't so great at all. Claudette talked to Reverend Munsey and he said the church wants to use the basement room for bingo every afternoon. The way he explained it, they need to raise money if they're going to be able to afford to let the soup kitchen continue. Adding another charity program without any income to pay for it will drain them dry."

"I can understand that," Ken said noncommittally.

"Claudette said she'd look into some other locations for us. I just don't know where the funding is going to come from. We could apply for a grant, I suppose, but that's going to take forever."

He opened his mouth and then closed it. He wanted to tell her about his effort to extract some money for her project from Allied-Tech. He wanted to swear to her that he intended to move heaven and earth to get her the financial backing she needed.

But he held his tongue. For one thing, he might fail in his effort; he might move heaven and earth and come up empty-handed, and then he would have gotten her hopes up for nothing. More importantly, he didn't want her to think he was doing this to win her back. He didn't want her to view it as a bribe.

It wasn't. It was, in part, his own little exercise in noblesse oblige, using his power on behalf of the powerless. It was also his attempt to make Lila happy. He wanted her to be as satisfied in her work as he was in his. He wanted her dreams to come true. If they did, if she was happy again, perhaps his own dream would come true and she'd come home.

This literacy project, more than a thousand dollars and a month by herself in a hotel at the shore, was what he wanted to give her.

"Well," she was saying, "at least we know there's a demand for a program like this. I'll just have to keep my fingers crossed and hope we can work something out in the money department."

"I'm sure you'll find the money somewhere," Ken responded. The sound of a door slamming behind him prompted him to turn around. Michael had just shut the broom closet, and he and Danny darted into the family room. Ken surveyed the floor. Not spotless, but not bad.

"I've got to go play a video game with the boys," he informed her. "The outcome determines who has to take out the garbage."

Lila didn't say anything. Ken could guess what she was thinking—that taking the garbage out was no longer her chore. The boys were supposed to do it, but they tended to forget, and Monday nights at ten o'clock frequently found Lila tying the bulging plastic bags and lugging them to the garage so Ken could drag them down to the curbside in the morning.

In her place, he would have awakened the boys and made them go downstairs to do it. When Lila came home—*if* she came home—he was going to have to teach her something about delegating responsibility.

When—if—she came home, he was going to start his own educational project: training Lila in the art of occasionally putting her own needs first.

# *Chapter Eleven*

He didn't care.

She stared at the telephone in her lap, reviewing the conversation she'd just had with Ken and reaching the inescapable conclusion that he wasn't even remotely interested in what she was trying to accomplish with the soup kitchen clients at Mt. Zion Methodist.

He'd made all the right noises, of course, wishing her luck, being polite and properly sympathetic. But how could he get all worked up about it? He had too many other things going on in his life: people hosting parties in his honor, people promoting him, answering to him and lionizing him. His life was centered in a universe utterly unrelated to hers: the marketing department of a small but growing computer company versus the uneducated homeless of Greater Roxbury.

That wasn't quite fair, she contradicted herself. He'd spent less time talking about his job than grilling her on the workings of the vacuum cleaner. Back when his life revolved around his job, though, and hers had revolved around the vacuum cleaner, she hadn't been as unreceptive to him as he was to her now. She'd kept her concerns to herself and let him ramble on about whatever was happening at Allied-Tech.

Either way, it seemed as if they were missing each other, operating on different wavelengths.

She sighed and replaced the phone on the night table. Then she settled back in the armchair and gazed out the window, trying to make out the line dividing the sky and the water, as the mauve fog of night drifted onto the shore. She wanted Ken to be as excited about her aspirations as she was. Apparently that was too much to want.

Pushing aside the fresh memory of her phone conversation with Ken, she reached back for a previous memory, of her stint at Mt. Zion Methodist that day. She'd pulled into the church parking lot, raring to go, at ten-fifteen—earlier than Claudette, for once. The sky was clear but the wind was brisk and chilly, and she'd waited for Claudette outside the basement door, huddled inside her jacket and trying not to think about how cold she was. At last Claudette arrived, the back of her station wagon filled with crates of food. "We're in luck today," Claudette shouted to her. "We've got fish sticks."

Along with the fish sticks were boxes of whipped potato mix, envelopes of dehydrated gravy, some pathetic-looking iceberg lettuce, cucumbers and a case of Pillsbury Golden Cake mix. Lila and Claudette lugged the food down the stairs and into the kitchen, then propped the basement door open so they would hear when the trucker from Star Market arrived with a promised delivery of milk and oranges.

As she and Claudette bustled about the kitchen fixing lunch, Lila found herself wondering why she enjoyed this work in a way she rarely enjoyed preparing meals for her family. Fish sticks, salad and whipped potatoes were such bland fare. There was no room for exotic flourishes or creativity. She and Claudette didn't even have any parsley with which to garnish the food. Not that Lila was a gourmet chef at home—but she had more to work with there, newer equipment and a greater selection of spices. Why should this be more fun?

No doubt it was partly because she knew that every last morsel of food would be devoured and appreciated by the soup kitchen's clients. It was also partly because she enjoyed Claudette's company so much. But most of all, she was beginning to understand, her pleasure came from her sense of purpose. She liked doing actual work during working hours, escaping into the real world and interacting with other people instead of remaining shut up inside her house, defining herself by her domesticity.

Only about seventy-five clients showed up for lunch. The closer it got to winter, the smaller the number of people who took advantage of the free meals offered to Mt. Zion Methodist. Claudette had explained to Lila that clients who were homeless but mobile tended to head south in the colder weather. A bench on Boston Common was not the most hospitable place to curl up on a December night.

Mitzie was among the soup kitchen's clients today. She hadn't fled south for the winter in the two years Lila had worked at the church. Last winter, she'd told Lila she had a bed at a woman's shelter in Dorchester permanently reserved for her because she'd volunteered to clean the lavatory every morning. If Mitzie could clean bathrooms for a free bed, she could, with a little training, hold down a real job. Lila was certain of that.

"Cold out today, isn't it," Lila commiserated as Mitzie slid her tray along the counter.

"Yeah."

"Have you got a place to stay tonight?"

"Yeah."

Lila studied Mitzie's downturned face. Her wan cheeks were smudged with dirt, and it took a minute for Lila to notice the dark blue bruise beneath her left eye. "What happened to you, Mitzie?"

Mitzie glanced up and shaped a fleeting smile. "Nothing, Mrs. Chapin."

"Did somebody hit you?"

Mitzie shrugged and muttered something unintelligible.

Lila reached across the table and cupped her hand around Mitzie's wrist. Her skin felt leathery, in need of soap and moisturizing lotion. Grime seemed to be permanently ingrained along her knuckles, which were rough and cracked.

Lila shouldn't have touched her—Claudette had warned her not to get personally involved with the clients—but honestly, a bit of human contact was as important to these people as the food being served. Mitzie flinched slightly, but she didn't shrink from Lila. She clearly knew that Lila wasn't her enemy. "Did you get hit anywhere else?" Lila asked.

"I'm okay, Mrs. Chapin."

Not wanting to press her luck, Lila released her and slid her serving spatula under a couple of fish sticks. "If you ever get hurt like that, Mitzie, you can go to the emergency room of a hospital. Boston City Hospital isn't too far away, and they aren't going to charge you any money. All they'll do is look at you and make sure you're all right."

"I don't need them to tell me I'm all right," Mitzie said. Her usually timid smile grew more defiant. "I may o' got hit, but the other guy got hit worse, you know? Word is out, and nobody's gonna mess with me for a while now.

Thanks for the fish sticks, Mrs. Chapin. They look real good."

Claudette had obviously overheard the exchange. She waited until Mitzie had left the counter to find a seat at one of the tables, and then muttered, "All sorts of things happen to these people on the weekends, when they've got to look after themselves. If I know Mitzie, the fight was over a bottle of vodka."

"Whatever it was over, it sounds like she won," Lila said, refusing to be pessimistic. "She's tough, Claudette. You've got to give her that much."

"I'll give her more than that," Claudette whispered. "If she could direct that toughness of hers into something worthwhile, she could pull herself out of this down-and-out routine. Speaking of which..." She banged a steel serving spoon against an empty metal tray until she had the clients' attention, then made her announcement requesting that anyone who might want to participate in a free reading enrichment program should stay on at the church after they were through eating.

Mitzie stayed on. Bruised cheekbone, dirty fingernails, ratty clothes and all, Mitzie stayed on. "If you're doin' it," she said to Lila, "I could be interested."

Lila wanted to extract something in return from Mitzie—a pledge not to get into any more fights, a promise to go to the Boston City Hospital and have a doctor check her out, a vow of sobriety. But it wasn't Lila's role to place conditions on her potential reading students. The best way to get Mitzie to stay sober and out of trouble was to give her an alternative, and that was what Lila hoped her reading classes would be. "I'm doing it," she said with conviction.

Mitzie gave her a lopsided smile. "Then I guess I'm interested."

If only Lila knew of an appropriate room where she could meet with the twelve brave souls who remained in the church basement after lunch. If only she could get her hands on some pencils and paper, a blackboard, some simple story books geared to adult readers. If only she could raise some money.

"Don't hold your breath," Claudette told the clients—and Lila, as well. "At this point, we haven't got the dollars to put anything together. But if we do, you'll be the first to know. We just want to make sure the interest is there. I want to be able to go to the service agencies and say that this many people will benefit from the program."

"Listen, Mrs. Wiley," said an emaciated young man whose sallow skin was festooned with tattoos, "I ain't gonna give you my name or nothin'. I mean, you can't put it down anywhere, you know what I'm sayin'?"

"I understand," Claudette assured him. Lila had been working at the soup kitchen long enough to understand, too. Some of the clients had had run-ins with the law, or had fled from halfway houses, drug rehabilitation programs, or foster care. They had their reasons for dropping out of the system, and, as Claudette had long ago explained to Lila, the function of the soup kitchen was not to force them back into the system, but to get some hot food inside their bellies five days a week. "All we want to do is give you folks the chance to get your skills up to snuff," she told them. "It'll help make life a little easier for you."

A petite teenager with an infant perched on her hip and an incongruous Georgia drawl said she knew a couple of other girls who might want to participate. "This girl, I'm living with her in a project, well, she says she still can't read and her havin' finished through tenth grade an' all. I'd like to talk to her about this if that's all right with you-all."

"That would be fine," said Claudette. "Does your friend get enough to eat? She can come here for lunch with you."

"Naw, she gets enough. Her old man don't like me, though, so he don't bring food for me an' my baby. Sometimes I think he's just tryin' to starve me out."

"Well, you keep coming here, then, honey," Claudette urged her. "We'll keep you and your baby fed. And once you've brushed up on your reading and writing skills, maybe you'll be able to get a job or some A.F.D.C. and move into your own place."

The girl broke into a beatific smile, and Lila knew, just knew, she had to help these people.

Driving back to Hull that afternoon, she tried to calculate how much she could afford to donate to the project from her family's savings. If she cut short her stay in Hull, told the boys they'd have to give up junk food, canceled the cable TV subscription and ordered Ken to cash in his Celtics season tickets... A few hundred dollars, maybe, and that would only be for this year. Where else could she squeeze out some money? Their mortgage was a major drain on the budget, and she wouldn't even consider touching the boys' college fund.

Maybe she could set her students up on busy street corners in Copley Square and have them panhandle to raise the balance, she thought grimly.

Giving of her own money was a bad idea, anyway. It would set a dangerous precedent. If she not only did the teaching but also funded the project, people would see her as a bourgeois dilettante buying her way to a clear conscience. In addition, if she supplied the money she would somehow be implying that her time and effort weren't a worthy enough contribution.

No, the funding would have to come from somewhere else. She was going to give herself; that was plenty.

She was eager to call Ken and discuss the developments with him. How frustrating it was to have important matters to talk about and no one to talk to. It took all her patience to wait until the evening to telephone him. And when she finally got through to him, he didn't sound the least bit enthusiastic about her project.

The hell with him. She wasn't going to let his indifference put a damper on her mood. As it was, she could hardly wait until Wednesday.

But why wait? Where was it etched in stone that she could work at the soup kitchen only three days a week? According to Claudette, Mrs. Galt from the Mt. Zion congregation sometimes helped out on Tuesdays and Thursdays, donating an hour of her time along with the paper plates, but she had health problems and couldn't always be counted on. Now, especially when Lila didn't have any household obligations, she could put in time on Tuesdays and Thursdays. Why not?

Invigorated by the idea, she marched across the room to the dresser and pulled her private phone book from the top drawer. She flipped it to the "W" page and found the number for "Wiley." She didn't like disturbing Claudette at home, but she believed Claudette would be pleased enough by her offer not to mind.

She carried the phone book back to the night table and dialed her number. Claudette's husband answered, and Lila asked to speak to Claudette. After a moment Claudette got on the line. "Hi, it's Lila Chapin."

"Lila! What a surprise. Don't tell me—you found yourself a Rockefeller who wants to support the literacy project."

"I wish," Lila grunted, though she was grinning. "I'm calling to see if I can come and work at the soup kitchen on Tuesday and Thursday this week."

Claudette didn't answer right away. "Why?" she asked. "Is something wrong?"

"Of course not. What could be wrong?"

"I don't know, maybe some plans fell through or something. I mean, it's awfully kind of you to offer, but you know I've got Mrs. Galt coming in, and we usually keep things simple on Tuesdays and Thursdays, anyway—soup and grilled cheese, mostly. I don't know that I really need you there."

Lila felt her spirits sink. If she wasn't needed, there wasn't much she could do about it except swallow her disappointment and count the minutes until Wednesday.

No. She wouldn't cave in so easily. She had called not because she thought the soup kitchen needed her, but because she needed the soup kitchen. If she wanted to work there tomorrow, she would simply have to ask again, more firmly. "It's something I want to do, Claudette," she claimed, surprising herself with her assertiveness.

"Do you?"

"Very much."

"Well...it's okay by me. I'm not stupid enough to turn down an offer like that."

Lila suppressed a joyous laugh. "Great. I'll see you tomorrow." She said goodbye, then hung up and punched her fist jubilantly into the air.

Restless in her room, she laced on her sneakers and headed downstairs. As usual, the Cavanagh sisters were playing cards in the parlor. They twittered a cheerful hello to Lila, who returned the greeting before she stepped outside onto the veranda. A white-haired man was helping an attractive older woman out of a luxury sedan parked at the curb. They were dressed stylishly; the man had an elegant silk handkerchief wedged into the breast pocket of his tailored blazer and the woman had a cashmere wrap draped around her shoulders. After the man locked the car, he tucked the woman's hand securely into the crook of his elbow and escorted her up the stairs to the veranda. They smiled briefly at Lila, but it was clear to her that they'd scarcely seen her. They were much too absorbed in each other.

Lovers, she thought, her eyes reflexively dropping to the woman's left hand. A diamond band encircled her ring finger.

Not lovers, a husband and wife. Married and still lovers.

She watched them vanish inside the hotel and let out a long breath. Where would she and Ken be in twenty years? With the boys grown and gone, would they indulge in a romantic night at a hotel every now and then? Would they want to? Would they even be married twenty years from now? To each other?

She checked the urge to chase after the couple, to collar them and demand that they tell her how their relationship had survived, how they had gotten through the rough times, how, at their age, they could still look at each other with such sheer adoration, how they'd kept their marriage alive. But what if the woman answered, "Oh, I just gave up everything and devoted myself to making him happy. I never wanted anything but to see him succeed in life. That's what a good wife does, isn't it?"

Lila swallowed the lump in her throat. She was a lousy wife, because she wanted more than just to watch Ken's success from the sidelines. She was a lousy wife, and she wound up spending her nights alone, away from her children and her husband, the man who used to be her lover.

She spent her nights alone, dreaming of the kiss Ken had given her Saturday night in her room, remembering the heat that swept through her body. She'd wanted Ken that night more than she could believe possible—and yet she'd wanted something more, and so she'd driven him away.

Why was she here? The solitude and shapelessness of her existence were depressing. She didn't like this new life any better than she'd liked her old one.

So what if Ken wasn't enraptured with her idea of teaching reading to illiterate poor people? He had never been thrilled with her volunteer work in Roxbury. He had always worried about her safety in that neighborhood. Until she'd walked out on him, he had never even bothered to visit the church where she worked.

But she and Ken were two distinct individuals, each with their own dreams and ambitions. Maybe she didn't have to have his wholehearted endorsement of the literacy project. She was doing it not for him and not even for her potential students, but for herself, because she needed to do it.

Sixteen years after she'd married Ken, it was high time for her to learn to listen to herself, to seek approval for her choices from within herself, to find her own satisfactions. To answer her own needs.

"HOW DO YOU DO IT?" she asked Claudette the next day.

Claudette glanced over from the stove, where she had two huge pots of vegetable soup simmering, to the center table where Lila was unloading a huge plastic bag filled with borderline-stale hamburger rolls, which had been donated by a local burger chain. "Do what?" she asked.

"How do you get people to donate all this food?"

Claudette chuckled and turned back to her soup. "Easy, Lila: I ask."

"You just ask?"

"I ask nicely," Claudette elaborated. "With something like the hamburger rolls it's a snap. They aren't fresh—McDonald's would have just thrown them out. But they're edible, so it's almost like we're doing McDonald's a favor by taking them off their hands. With the fruit, well, it's also not the freshest. Star Market gives us produce that's been sitting on the shelves for a few days, that in another day or so would wind up in the trash. All it costs them is the expense of running a truck over to deliver the stuff."

"The milk is fresh," Lila pointed out. "That must cost Star something."

"Well...to get things like milk," Claudette confided, "I resort to different tactics—guilt and greed. When I first set up this program, I went to the executive offices of the supermarket chain and persuaded the folks there that they had certain obligations to the community. Made 'em feel real guilty, you know? Then I pointed out to them that they'd get a tax break for donating the milk. It gave them a solid bottom-line excuse to relieve themselves of all that guilt I'd just laid on them."

Lila gazed admiringly at Claudette. "You're so good at getting things done. I don't think I could pull it off."

"Of course you could. The one thing you've always got to remember is that it never hurts to ask. Nobody's going to hate you for asking. Nobody's going to shoot you. The worst that can happen is they'll say no."

She made it sound so simple, a lot simpler than Lila suspected it would actually be if she tried it. She had no talent for making demands or asking for things. She had taken her solo vacation without asking Ken because she hadn't known how to ask for it. He accused her of having failed to verbalize her dissatisfactions firmly enough so he could hear her, and he was right. She wasn't good at stamping her feet and issuing orders.

It was one thing to make demands on one's own behalf, however, and quite another to make demands on behalf of other people. Difficult as it was for Lila to ask for things, at least she did have a voice—which was more than she could say for her potential students in the literacy program.

A few hours later, as she drove back to Hull from Roxbury, she rehearsed her speech. She could have asked Claudette to make the call for her, but that would have been cowardly. If Lila wanted her next forty years to be different from the first forty, she would have to begin right now, by speaking for herself and speaking loudly.

She arrived at her room, shut the door, took a few deep breaths and marched resolutely to the telephone. From the drawer in the night table she pulled a stubby pencil and a sheet of Bayside Manor stationery. Then she dialed Directory Assistance and requested the telephone number of the Wayland school system's administration office. The operator provided the number and Lila dialed it.

Listening to the rhythmic purr of the telephone ringing on the other end of the line, Lila silently repeated Claudette's words: *Nobody's going to hate you for asking. The worst that can happen is they'll say no.*

A clerk answered, and Lila's tenuous confidence flagged. Even knowing that if they did say no, that her project would be no worse off than it was now, it was still hard for her to push herself and make her request. She added her own mental pep talk to Claudette's: *You're doing this for someone else, not yourself,* and that made it easier. "May I speak to whomever is in charge of ordering textbooks for the primary schools?" she asked in a deceptively calm voice.

She heard a few clicks and then a woman said, "Marilyn Campbell speaking. Can I help you?"

"Hello. Is this the office where primary school readers are ordered?" Lila asked, jotting down the woman's name next to the phone number.

"Yes."

"My name is Lila Chapin and I've got two children in the Wayland school system," she began, reciting the speech she'd practiced in the car.

Before she could continue, the woman interrupted. "Chapin? As in Michael Chapin?"

"Yes, that's my older son. Do you know him?"

"I sure do. I used to be the librarian over at the Claypit School. What a bright little boy. You had another one in kindergarten, as I recall—that was my last year there before I moved over here to central administration."

Lila's chest swelled with pride. "Danny's my younger son."

"Danny. I confess I don't really remember him as well—the kindergarteners didn't take books out of the library very often, but the older children did. Michael was always taking out books designated for fourth and fifth graders," she recollected. "I would tell him I thought they were too advanced for him, but he never listened to me."

Lila laughed. "I remember having to read all those books to him, because he couldn't read them himself. I learned an awful lot about minerals and aerodynamics when he was in second grade." Talking about Michael relaxed her. If this former librarian had such fond memories of Lila's son, perhaps she'd take kindly to Lila, too. "I was wondering if I could ask you a question," she said, then shook her head at how humble she sounded. "I'm trying to organize a class to teach reading to illiterate adults in Roxbury. Funding is a real problem, Ms. Campbell, and I'm looking for donations."

"Oh," the woman said, the warmth fleeing from her voice. "I'm sorry—I give to the United Way, but—"

"No—no, I'm not calling to ask for money," Lila broke in, desperate not to lose her audience before she'd made her pitch. "I'm looking for books. I was thinking, if the school system is going to be ordering new readers, well, there might be older readers you're planning to dispose of, and well, I'm sure you've already earmarked them for something else..." *Don't be so wishy-washy! Assert yourself!* "But if you haven't, I could really use them for my literacy project," she concluded with as much of a flourish as she could manage.

A brief silence, and then Marilyn Campbell said, "Basal readers, you mean?"

"Large print, simple vocabulary. Whatever you've got." *Don't beg,* she cautioned herself, but she couldn't stop herself from adding, "I'll take anything you can give us, anything at all."

"You say this is a program for illiterate adults?" The woman sounded dubious. "The only thing we might have are storybooks geared to young children. I mean, are these adults going to want to read stories about runaway steam engines and anthropomorphic frogs?"

"If that's all I can get, I'll take them."

Marilyn Campbell meditated for a minute. "We ordered new basal readers last year, so I don't know what we've got in storage right now. I'll tell you what—let me make some inquiries and get back to you. Where can I reach you?"

She hadn't said no. The worst hadn't happened. Lila experienced a heady sense of her own success. She'd done what she had to do. She had made a request and hadn't been flatly turned down.

"Actually, I'm not in Wayland at the moment. I'm in Hull," she said, before listing the digits on her room extension phone.

"Hull! What a nice place to work," Marilyn Campbell exclaimed. Lila didn't correct her. "Well, let me get back to you on this, Mrs. Chapin. Give me a few days and I'll see what I can find out for you."

"Thank you," said Lila, meaning it on several levels. She was grateful to the woman for her assistance in obtaining some books, grateful to her for being courteous and not making her feel like an idiot, and most of all, grateful to her for proving that asking for what one needed didn't always have to be so hard.

TWO DAYS LATER, on Thursday evening, Lila learned that the worst sometimes did happen and someone said no. Ken did. And contrary to Claudette's assurances, Lila felt the rejection as strongly as if she *had* been shot.

She'd spent much of the day in Roxbury, and then an hour at the Harvard Co-op in Cambridge, interviewing a clerk there about wholesale distributors of office supplies. The clerk didn't feel his store could donate paper and pens to her project. He thought a wholesale distributor might be able to help her out with some free supplies, however, and he provided her with the names and phone numbers of the distributors with whom he did business.

She was feeling good about herself, proud of her accomplishments and her minor victories. She was feeling so good, even Reverend Munsey's insistence that the church basement was unavailable for her reading classes couldn't get her down. Life was wonderful when you had a goal to work toward. Doing things for others was tremendously rewarding when you didn't feel invisible.

Having no one with whom to share her modest success was depressing, though. As much as she enjoyed working at the soup kitchen each day, she was starting to loathe returning to her solitary second-floor room to spend the night alone. The view from her windows was lovely, but in an empty, impersonal way. The bright yellow walls no longer cheered her the way they used to. Lying in a bubble bath for a half hour without a single interruption was becoming boring.

Last night, after a disappointingly short, efficient telephone conversation with Ken, she'd taken a stroll along the sidewalk bordering the beach. She'd hugged her jacket around herself, listening to the rhythmic whisper of the surf and imagining taking this same walk with Ken. She'd imagined appreciating the sunset with him, and the moonrise, and then bringing him back to her room and welcoming him into her bed. Stripped of their resentments, their inhibitions and their history, stripped of everything but who they were at that very instant, she had imagined them making love. She had imagined Ken's hands on her body, and his lips, and the glorious hardness of him filling her.

The fantasy had been so vivid a heated flush had suffused her body, and she'd opened her jacket to the cool, salty gusts of wind coming off the water. Then she had done an about-face and headed back to Bayside Manor, wondering why some needs were so much more difficult to express than others. Why should she be able to beg a school system for books and not be able to tell her husband she missed him?

She could go home. She could check out of the hotel a couple of weeks early—Mrs. Tarlock already had been paid for the entire month, so she would have nothing to complain about if Lila left sooner. She could pack up and drive back to Wayland, and her family would probably be thrilled to see her.

They would welcome her back into their home . . . and back into her rut. They would see her return as a capitulation. "Mom gave up!" Danny would shriek triumphantly. "Mom decided she'd rather take care of us than anything else!" And Michael would probably chime in, "All right! We don't have to make our lunches anymore!"

She wanted to go back, but not to that. She wanted to be with her children, but not become their handmaiden again. She wanted them to look up to her and see a woman who achieved things, who made the world a better place, who was strong and independent and devoid of bitterness.

It was too soon to go home. But she could ask them to come and visit her. Tomorrow when she called, she would ask Ken to bring the boys to Hull this weekend. Both Saturday and Sunday, if they wanted.

So when she called home on Thursday evening, she asked Ken to come to Hull that weekend—and he said no.

"What do you mean, no?"

"I mean no, I can't," he said. "I'm really backed up in my work, Lila. I'm going to have to be working this weekend."

"How can you be backed up?" she argued, feeling all the confidence she'd accumulated over the past four days disintegrate into dust inside her soul. Her voice quivered; she felt rejected and mortified.

"I'll tell you how. It's a new job, Lila. I've got tons of demands on me—and I can't stay late at the office and finish everything. I've got to get home every night for the kids."

Meaning that if she were home, he *would* be staying late at the office. She would be the primary parent, juggling everyone's schedule, smoothing everyone's paths, coordinating everyone's needs, serving dinner to the boys, cleaning up, serving to Ken and cleaning up a second time. She would be the one who made it all work by doing all the work.

She wasn't going to go home to that.

"I've been bringing work home," he went on. "I'm trying to catch up but it's hard. I may have to farm the boys out to their friends' houses on Saturday so I can go back to the office and get some more work done."

"I don't understand how you could be so far behind," she said quietly. "As you just said yourself, it's a new job. Surely your colleagues can cut you a little slack while you get a feel for it."

"A little slack, yes. Not a lot. They gave me this job because they thought I could handle it, Lila. I have no intention of letting them down."

She sighed, wondering whether Ken's co-workers were dumping too much work on him, or he was accepting too much work voluntarily—or whether Ken's refusal to visit her had nothing to do with work at all. Maybe he was merely testing her, tightening the screws, manipulating her into returning home. Maybe he just wanted to find out how badly she missed the boys—and him.

Not badly enough to let him blackmail her with complaints about how demanding his job was. She'd spent too many days—weekends included—working twice as hard as any vice president of any leading-edge technology firm to feel any sympathy for him.

"All right," she said coldly. "I guess we won't see each other then." She mumbled a farewell and slammed down the telephone, then surrendered to a small moan. *The worst that can happen*... she thought despairingly. He'd said no.

Grabbing her sweater and her key, she stormed out of the room, determined to take another long walk to burn off some of her anger and grief. She managed a feeble smile for the Cavanagh sisters at their usual post around the card table and then hurried out onto the veranda and down the porch stairs.

She was nearly hit by a car as she stepped off the curb; leaping back onto the sidewalk, she watched furiously as the driver sped down to the corner and disappeared.

Grumbling another curse, she crossed the street and stalked along the beach for a while. The exercise proved less cathartic than she'd hoped, however, and the wind was frigid. Attempting to ignore how cold she felt, she focused her mind on the choices before her—and suffered a sense of doom that chilled her even more deeply than the unseasonably nippy night air. She could stay here in Hull and be painfully lonely, or she could go home and take care of everything while Ken knocked himself out for Allied-Tech.

Why couldn't Ken knock himself out for her? Why did she always have to be the one stuck taking care of everything?

Why did she have to be so agonizingly lonely tonight?

When she realized she was shivering, she turned around and retraced her route to the hotel. The bright lights illuminating the veranda gave the impression of warmth, and she quickened her pace. As she started across the street, the front door of Bayside Manor opened and a familiar figure stepped out.

"Hey, Lila!" Jimmy called to her as he closed the snaps on his down vest. "What the heck are you doing outside tonight? It's like winter!"

"I was taking a walk."

"You look like you're freezing."

"I am," she admitted, rubbing her icy fingers together.

He watched her as she neared the steps, then descended and joined her on the sidewalk. Spontaneously, he sandwiched her hands between his and rubbed some warmth into them. "Whoa," he exclaimed. "I think you got a little frostbite here!"

She laughed at his exaggeration, but his kindness touched her. When was the last time Ken had rubbed the numbness from her fingers? When was the last time he'd noticed she was cold?

"How about a drink to warm you up?" Jimmy suggested, continuing to hold her hands within the warmth of his when she didn't withdraw them. "I could sure use some company. Mrs. Tarlock almost drove me to commit murder tonight."

"No! What did she do?" Lila asked. Another exaggeration, but she didn't mind. It was part of Jimmy's youthful spirit to get a little carried away in his description of things.

"She tried to weasel out of reimbursing me for the equipment I had to buy to fix some electrical sockets up on the third floor. Really trivial—wire and clippers and that kind of stuff—but it's the principle of the thing. I spent my own money to get the tools so I could do her repairs for her hotel. She ought to pay me back."

"She certainly ought to," Lila agreed. Recalling her small victories of the past week, she said, "Would you like me to talk to her for you?"

"Nah." He released her hands and looped an arm affectionately around her shoulder. "If you really want to do something for me," he said, "you could buy me a beer."

"All right," Lila said, beginning to feel a little less lonely. "It would be my pleasure."

## *Chapter Twelve*

"Ken? Have you got a minute?"

Ken covered the mouthpiece of the phone and glanced up from his desk. Larry Talbot was standing in the doorway, looking bewildered. "Sure, let me just finish up here," Ken whispered, then turned his attention back to his caller. "Dr. Stein, I really appreciate the information," he said. "It's going to come in very handy when I put together my projections."

"No problem," said the woman on the other end. "Anything else you need, just give me a call."

"I will. Thanks again." Ken hung up and smiled at Larry. "Come on in."

Fingering one of his bright red suspenders, Larry hovered in the doorway for a second longer, surveying the outer room behind him. With a frown, he turned and entered Ken's inner office. "Where's Theresa?" he asked.

Ken pulled a face and shrugged. "She got a call from the day-care center about a half hour ago. Her daughter spiked a high fever."

"And . . . ?"

"And I told her to go pick up her daughter and take her to the pediatrician. Hell of a time to lose Theresa, too," Ken grumbled. "I've got a pile of documents I need faxed out to Sematech. Maybe one of the secretaries downstairs can help me out."

"The downstairs secretaries are downstairs," Larry explained, as if to a child. "This is the third floor, Ken. Theresa's the one who's supposed to be helping you out."

Ken tried unsuccessfully to fathom the point Larry was trying to make. "Theresa left early," he said slowly. "Her daughter is sick. Didn't I just say that?"

"This isn't the first time her daughter's been sick," Larry observed. "The kid spends nine hours a day swapping drool with fifteen other toddlers in a day-care center. Every third week she comes down with a cold, and at least two ear infections a year. Why on earth did you let Theresa leave the office?"

Now it was Ken's turn to frown. Why *shouldn't* he have let her leave? Her daughter was running a fever of a hundred and three. Her husband was in Washington, D.C., on business, so he couldn't pick up the child. Ken supposed Theresa could have arranged for a neighbor to fetch her daughter and dose her with Tylenol until Theresa got home, but that wouldn't have been fair, either to Theresa or the little girl. "Theresa was upset," he said, justifying his decision to send her home early. "She wouldn't have been able to concentrate on her work, anyway. I know if one of my boys got sick at school—"

"Lila would take care of everything," Larry completed the sentence.

Ken disguised a grimace by shuffling some loose papers on his desk. As recently as two weeks ago, Larry's assumption would have been correct. As recently as two weeks ago, Ken would have lacked the sensitivity to urge Theresa to go home and nurse her young daughter back to health. But he knew better now. Monday morning, when Danny had complained of nausea, Ken had suddenly developed a belated insight into the difficulties of juggling parenthood and a career.

"I'm sorry Theresa's kid has a fever," said Larry, "but this is the third floor, Ken. We do things a little differently up here. Our secretaries aren't expendable."

"Right," Ken argued. "And if we don't want to lose them, we're going to have to learn to be flexible and keep them happy on the job. I gave Theresa this afternoon off because she needed it. As a result, she'll be more willing to go the extra mile for me when I need it." He thought it best to temper his impassioned words with a self-deprecating smile. "You heard Aaron Karsch at the powwow on Monday: I'm supposed to bring a new perspective to the third floor. One of my new perspectives is that secretaries deserve to be treated with dignity."

Larry snorted and lowered himself into one of the upholstered chairs across the wide teak desk from Ken. "Why should we treat them with dignity? They never let us into their cute little kitchenette."

"Hmm." Ken concurred with a nod. "We're going to have to demand a little more flexibility from them, too. I know I myself would never dream of leaving a mess in the kitchenette." Not since he'd learned what a dreary chore it was to clean a kitchen.

"So." Larry eyed the telephone. "Who's Dr. Stein?"

"Eleanor Stein. She's a professor over at Boston University, who had some information I needed."

"Eleanor Stein? From B.U.?" Larry contemplated the name and then shook his head. "I don't recall our being involved in any projects with B.U. Is she on the computer science faculty there?"

"The education department," Ken informed him. "She's done a lot of research on adult illiteracy, and she had some figures for me on the extent of the problem in the

Boston area. It's not as bad as it is in some other parts of the country—evidently southern California, with its huge immigrant population—"

"Ken." Larry gave him a reproachful look, even though his tone carried a hint of laughter. "Haven't you wasted enough time on that literacy garbage?"

Ken clung to that trace of amusement as proof that his associate believed he was, at worst, moderately eccentric when it came to the subject of teaching adults to read. "Garbage?" he echoed. "I'll tell you what's garbage: an educational system that lets so many people slip through the cracks."

"Get off the soapbox, Ken—this is *me* you're talking to." He leaned forward, propping his elbows on his knees and his chin in his palms, his round belly seeming to rest in his lap. The gaze he gave Ken over the rims of his eyeglasses was impenetrable. "Have you got a few minutes? We've really got to talk, one friend to another."

What little humor Ken had detected in Larry earlier was totally gone now. He tapped his fingertips together and nodded attentively. "Of course. What's up?"

"What's up is..." Larry paused dramatically, then said, "Some people are a little worried about you."

Ken frowned. "What people?"

"People. You've been at your desk less than two weeks, Ken, so nobody's expecting any miracles from you. But..." He exhaled. "I think one thing people *were* expecting was that you wouldn't be bolting out the door at the stroke of five every afternoon. Back in the old days, when you were a marketing manager downstairs, you were never a clock-watcher. You worked until you were done working. You stayed until whatever you were doing got done. People saw you as diligent and dedicated, a real champion for the company."

"I *am* diligent and dedicated," Ken protested, trying not to sound defensive. He knew Larry was on his side, doing him a favor by sharing the office scuttlebutt with him, warning him of potential trouble. It would be imprudent to erupt in indignation in front of an ally. "You know I am," he said more calmly.

"I know you are," Larry confirmed. "What I don't know is, how come you've been taking off on the dot of five every day?"

"I...uh..." He exhaled. How could he explain that he was racing home each day because he was concerned about the welfare of his sons? Larry was the father of three teenagers, but Ken doubted he'd understand the imperatives of a full-time parent. Larry had Joyce at home to look after his three children.

Damn it all. It was becoming such a strain, not just attempting to balance his enormous responsibilities, but keeping his fractured marriage a secret. Why was he bothering to maintain a pretense of normalcy? What terrible thing would happen if people at work found out Lila had left him? What if he finally broke down and told his coworkers about the pressure he was operating under, the heartache and loneliness and downright panic? He was positive they would rally around him. They would be loyal. They would take his side in any dispute and assume that Lila was utterly in the wrong.

But she wasn't in the wrong. For her sake and the sake of the truth, he couldn't turn to his colleagues for compassion. "Look, Larry," he mumbled, groping for a believable rationalization for his prompt departures from work each afternoon. "There's been—kind of a disruption at home. Lila's cousin—" Why not? The baby-sitter had swallowed that whopper last Saturday. "Lila's cousin just had surgery, and she's been spending a lot of time helping out at her cousin's house. So I've been trying to get home early because the boys have been home alone a great deal lately, and..." Seeing the stony indifference in Larry's eyes, he faltered.

"Too bad about your cousin-in-law," Larry said, sounding not the least bit sympathetic. "You've got a job here, Ken. Do you know what I'm saying?"

"I've been bringing work home with me," Ken noted. "I've been putting in another two or three hours at home every night. Don't tell me I'm not getting things accomplished, Larry, because you know I am. We're moving full steam ahead on this project with Sematech, and I've authorized further discussions with Perkin-Elmer."

"You're letting Cecile fly solo on that one, aren't you?"

"Are you afraid she can't handle it? She used to sit in this chair, remember? I don't think she needs me looking over her shoulder."

"No, of course not." Larry leaned back, appraising Ken through the thick lenses of his glasses. "You wouldn't have to work two or three hours at home every night if you spent more time on your work at the office, instead of pursuing this screwball idea about having the company sponsor a class Lila wants to teach. Give that thing a rest, Ken. Stop wasting time on the phone with education professors from B.U."

"It's a worthwhile project."

"I'm sure it is, but you and I both know it's not going to happen. Aaron likes the glamour charities, the pretty stuff. He likes to be able to seat major clients at a front table at the Pops concerts. How do you think he's going to impress any clients with a group of uneducated losers from Roxbury?"

Ken's mind whirled. He began to comprehend how very much was riding on how he fielded Larry's questions. He couldn't answer emotionally, moaning to Larry that his marriage was in trouble and he was counting on the literacy project to salvage it. He had to respond logically, proving that he was fully aware of his obligations to Allied-Tech.

"My expertise is in marketing," he said, selecting each word with great care. "A large part of marketing has to do with whether a company projects the right image. Education is the perfect image for us to project, Larry. Look at how much mileage Apple got by giving computer systems to public schools a few years back. We're trying to function in a computer-illiterate society. Well, the first step to computer literacy is reading literacy. I don't see what supporting the symphony does for our company. Teaching reading skills gives a much bigger payoff in terms of what Allied-Tech wants to stand for—and as a marketing person, it's my duty to point that out to the company."

"Bravo," Larry drawled, clapping his hands languidly. "Hey, Ken, look—personally, I have no problem with any of this. If you can pull it off, fine. You've got my vote. All I'm saying is, watch your butt, pal. If you keep dwelling on this one thing while your work falls by the wayside, people are going to start wondering whether they made a mistake when they bet on you."

"Okay," Ken muttered, lowering his eyes. "I appreciate the warning, Larry."

Larry nodded and rose from the chair. "Listen, Ken—is there anything we can do for this sick relative of yours? Blood drive, anything like that?"

"No, but thanks for offering," he said, smiling wanly. He was disgusted with himself for having lied. He was also disgusted by the realization that there was, in fact, something the company could do for his home life, something it would never do: be as flexible with its executives as Ken was with his secretary. Acknowledge that they had families, and that it wasn't fair for those executives to expect their spouses to be the sole emotional ballast in those families.

And free up some money so Lila could establish her literacy project.

He watched as Larry left the office, closing the door behind him. Then he let out a long, weary breath.

He should have come clean with Lila last night, when he'd turned down her invitation. He should have told her he was over his head in work because he was trying so hard to get Allied-Tech to finance her dream. He had talked to educational experts, social agencies, even a state representative. He had attempted to put together some estimates for a reasonable budget to run the program. That morning, he had even placed a call to Reverend Munsey. Hoping the Reverend wouldn't remember him as the blasphemous fool ranting and raving in the cellar hallway of his church a week and a half ago, Ken had questioned the minister on how much money it would take to have the use of the church basement for two hours a day. Munsey had given him a song and dance about utility costs and bingo, but Ken had waited him out and at last had received a moderate rental figure. The whole project, Ken was convinced, could be put together for an annual outlay of well under two thousand dollars a year.

So little money, and so much good could come of it.

He had wanted to tell Lila, but something had held him back, some curious, ill-defined fear. What if he went through all this effort and failed? Would she view him as a dud, able to succeed only on his own behalf but not on hers?

What if he went through all this effort and succeeded, and then learned that she didn't want to come back to him anyway? What if she was enjoying her freedom too much, her freedom and her harbor view and that postpubescent blond hunk?

He should have told her he'd come and see her this weekend, regardless of how much work he had to do. He could have worked late Friday night after the boys were in bed, put in a full day Saturday and then driven out to Hull with the boys Sunday.

But damn, he was scared. He was scared by the unfathomable depth of her feelings, scared by the extent of her resentments. Scared by the way she'd smiled at her good friend Jimmy Peele.

Ken was scared enough to understand that he had to approach her from a position of strength. He had to come to her armed with every weapon he could get his hands on. If it was going to take a fight to win her back, he intended to be fully prepared before he entered the arena.

# Chapter Thirteen

Driving into the parking lot adjacent to Bayside Manor Friday afternoon, Lila felt mournful. Ahead of her loomed two barren, desolate days during which she would not have to feed anyone, teach anyone, or help anyone. She would not have to inquire about Mitzie's welfare or assist Michael with a science project. She would not have to take care of anyone's needs but her own.

Two long days during which she would be free, and drearily alone.

She ought to do something, make a plan, take advantage of her liberty. In a couple of weeks that liberty would end and she would be back where she started, wondering how the time had flown by so quickly and regretting the opportunity she'd wasted. She ought to do something this weekend that she might not have the chance to do any other time.

But what? Visit the Plimoth Plantation, where people reenacted the lives of the original settlers of Massachusetts Bay Colony? No, that was an outing the boys would enjoy; Lila should save that for a day when she could bring them with her. Window-shop at Copley Square? No, that would only tempt her to spend money she couldn't afford to spend. Stroll through the Museum of Fine Arts? No, viewing the artwork wouldn't be the same without Ken along to tease her about how her own petite figure compared to the voluptuous bodies of the Renaissance nudes.

She could spend a quiet weekend sitting on the beach, reading and meditating—except that an army of fat, foreboding clouds was advancing across the sky, auguring rain.

Sighing, she entered the hotel and trudged up the stairs. On the second floor she found Jimmy kneeling near the door to her room and tightening a screw on a wall socket. As usual he was wearing a sweatshirt, jeans and sneakers; as usual, his toolbox was close at hand, standing open at the threadbare runner. Hearing footsteps, he looked up and grinned at her. "Hi!"

"Hi, Jimmy." For him she could spare a smile, despite her dismal mood.

He studied her for a minute. "You look like you're in a major funk."

"A minor one," she corrected him, still smiling.

"Bad day at the soup kitchen?"

She shook her head. "No, it was a good day. One of the clients there, this woman Mitzie..." She hesitated. Would Jimmy really want to hear about this? His encouraging grin prompted her to continue. "Well, she told me she hasn't had any booze for two days—not because she couldn't find any to drink, but because she's trying to clear her head a little. I was so proud of her."

"You should be," he said, tossing his screwdriver into the tray of his toolbox and rising to his feet. "So why the funk?"

She shrugged. "It dawned on me that I'm free until Monday. Nobody needs me to take care of them. It's just . . . a strange feeling for me."

"Well, I need you," Jimmy assured her, flashing a dazzling grin. "I've got to get into your room to check the wiring on your sockets. Will you let me in?"

"Of course." She unlocked her door and preceded him inside.

He carried the toolbox into her room and set it down on one of the braided rugs. He scanned the room for sockets, but when his gaze settled upon Lila as she placed her purse on top of the wicker dresser, he paused. He opened his mouth, then closed it and ran his hand through his thick blond hair, shoving it back from his forehead.

Lila watched him, perplexed. She had never seen Jimmy looking uncomfortable before; she had assumed he was one of those fortunate individuals who never suffered a moment's awkwardness or self-consciousness. One of the reasons she found him such delightful company was that he was always so open, so relaxed and natural.

"What?" she prodded him gently, sensing that he wanted to say something.

He smiled again, tentatively. "Last night was real nice," he murmured, bending over and lifting his screwdriver from the toolbox. "I mean, having a drink with you and letting off some steam about my job and all. I don't mean to sound corny or anything, Lila, but I really like talking to you."

"I like talking to you, too," she assured him, removing her jacket and hanging it in the miniscule closet. Going out for a beer with Jimmy last night had worked wonders on her gloomy state of mind. He was so cheerful, so bubbly, even when he was complaining about Mrs. Tarlock. His smile was contagious, and when he gazed at her his expression brimmed with affection and interest. And he didn't think Lila looked forty. "As a matter of fact," she added, eager to vanquish his apparent edginess, "I'd like to thank you for rescuing me last night. I was in another of those minor funks when you came along, and you pulled me out of it."

"I'm glad." He fidgeted with his screwdriver for a minute, then hunkered down in front of the socket plate by the door. While he studied the socket, Lila studied him. The strong contours of his back were visible where the sweatshirt stretched across his shoulders, and his corn-colored hair was long enough to cover the neckline of his shirt. She was pleased that longer hair was once again considered stylish on men. When she'd fallen in love with Ken, his hair had hung nearly to his shoulders, and she had always loved weaving her fingers through it.

"I know it must be hard on you, what you're going through," he murmured.

She was momentarily surprised by the personal direction he'd taken. But she recovered quickly. Jimmy *did* know, because she'd confided in him and because he'd witnessed his parents' marital problems. "Talking to you has helped," she said gratefully. "I don't know if I've thanked you, but—"

"Hey, I don't need thanks," he said, methodically loosening a screw. "I mean, you've really cooled me out a few times, too. Tarlock can get under my skin something awful."

Lila nodded, though she was standing behind Jimmy where he couldn't possibly see her.

"I try to talk to my father about the way she treats me, you know? Or other friends, ladies, whatever..." His eyes remained focused on the socket, as if he couldn't bring himself to face her. "But nobody's gotten me back on track the way you have. I mean, the thanks go both ways, Lila."

Maybe he hadn't been kidding out in the hall when he'd said he needed her. She felt oddly maternal toward Jimmy. In a different context, she would be offering him milk and chocolate chip cookies and assuring him that everything would work out.

As she stared at the arch of his back for another moment, that motherly mental image dissolved. Jimmy wasn't a boy, he was a man.

She suddenly felt old. Tearing her gaze from him, she peered out the window. It was beginning to drizzle. The overcast sky made her feel even older, for some reason.

"Any chance you might be free tonight?" he asked.

Lila turned back to discover that he'd stood up and was gazing at her. She felt a fleeting trill of awareness down her spine, but it faded in the friendly warmth of his smile. This was Jimmy, her pal, her partner in loneliness. And as it happened, she was extremely free tonight, thanks to her neglectful workaholic husband.

She smiled back at him. "What did you have in mind?"

"How about dinner?"

Dinner. That wasn't just going out to a neighborhood tavern for a beer. Her smile waned as another current of awareness swept through her. She realized with a start that Jimmy had also lost his smile.

"It sounds like a date," she said.

His gaze remained unwavering. "It does, doesn't it?"

"Jimmy." She laughed uneasily. "You're a good-looking young man. Surely you can find a nice young woman to take to dinner."

"I've already found one," he maintained, taking a step toward her.

She wasn't afraid. Only disconcerted. "I'm not young," she reminded him with another halfhearted laugh.

"You're nice," he said. "You're great-looking, you're a good listener, you've got a fantastic laugh and an even better smile, and the prettiest blue eyes—"

"And a husband," she reminded him, as he took another step toward her.

"And a husband who you're separated from."

"Well..." She sighed, groping for a way to explain to Jimmy that her separation from Ken wasn't like an actual, legal separation. "We're just taking a little break from each other, that's all," she said, wondering if her claim sounded as feeble to him as it did to her.

"Okay. No sweat." His next step carried him within a couple of feet of her. He tucked the screwdriver into his hip pocket and examined her face. "I'm not asking you to run off with me or anything. I'm just asking you for dinner."

True enough. But it still sounded like a date, and she was still a good fifteen years his senior. It made her uneasy to realize how much more pleasant it would be to have dinner with him than to eat alone. It made her even more uneasy to realize how big he was, how muscular, how strikingly good-looking. She used to view men like him with detached appreciation, wondering whether they would look as good fifteen or twenty years down the road, or whether their bellies would become soft and their jawlines would blur, whether their muscle tone would weaken as they languished in boring desk jobs and stopped for a few cocktails on their way home from work each evening.

For her to go on a dinner date with one of those prime specimens of young manhood struck her as—crazy. Absurd. Perilous. "I don't think so, Jimmy."

"Come on, Lila." He took one more step, this one putting him within arm's reach of her. She could smell his clean, lemony scent. She could feel his height in the long shadow he cast over her. "I thought we were friends."

"We are."

"Then what are you afraid of?"

"I'm not afraid. I just don't think it would be a good idea."

"Why not?"

"I'm practically old enough to be your mother."

"You're not too old for me," he insisted. "Lila, I've really enjoyed getting to know you. I've never met a woman as easy to talk to as you are. If you're a little older than me, so what? I still think you're a knockout. And look at me, okay? I'm not so bad you want to run screaming from me, right?"

She met his piercing gaze. No, he wasn't bad at all. He was kind, funny, congenial, handsome. The times she had spent with him had been among the highlights of her stay in Hull. And to think that a strapping young fellow like Jimmy considered her a knockout... How could she not be flattered by his attention? How could she not be excited?

But going out to dinner would not be a simple comradely jaunt to some local eatery. They both knew that. With his invitation, Jimmy had burdened their friendship with troubling overtones.

"I'm married," she repeated, breaking from his gaze. Throwing her marital status at him seemed a cowardly way to turn him down, but it was the truth. As hurt as she was by Ken's refusal to visit her over the weekend, he was still her husband, and as long as he was, she wasn't about to go out with another man. "You've met my husband. You know I'm married. And in my book, marriage entails certain obligations and certain promises."

He slid his hand under her chin and lifted her face so their eyes met again. His fingers were thicker than Ken's, their tips calloused. "I'm not trying to wreck your marriage, Lila—it's up to you and him whether you want to wreck it. All I know is, ever since I saw you that first day, when you were all wrapped up in your blanket and kind of teary-eyed... I've felt real attracted to you, real close. I think—I think there could be sparks between us." Obviously he was able to read the doubt in her eyes, because he continued before she could refute him. "Don't you see? *I'm* not the one who put your marriage in jeopardy. It was already in jeopardy when we met. Maybe you and your husband can fix things and maybe you can't. All I'm saying is, you'll never know whether or not your marriage is worth fixing if you don't put it to the test."

Logically she couldn't argue. But marriage vows were designed to withstand even the forces of logic. "I know you're not a home wrecker, Jimmy. You're a good person, and I like you. But..." How to explain it? How to tell him that, while the friction of his thumb against the line of her jaw felt good, even arousing, it didn't evoke the deep trust-filled yearning that Ken's caresses awakened within her?

"Just be open-minded, okay?" Jimmy murmured, bowing his head to hers. "Just give us a chance to find out if there's something here."

He brushed his lips over hers. They were warm, firm but not coercive. He wasn't imposing himself on her or pressuring her. This was an experiment between friends. Lila was willing to give him the chance he wanted.

It wasn't bad. His hand was strong, sliding smoothly around to the back of her neck, and his lips coaxed hers, probing the limits of her resistance. She felt his tongue questing—not pushing, but cajoling, satisfied to skim the surface of her lips when she didn't open to him. He looped his other arm around her waist and drew her against his broad, well-muscled frame.

For eighteen years, the only man who had held her this way had been Ken. He knew her size and posture; he knew how to guide her to him, how to entice her with his nearness, how to part the barrier of her lips and slide inside, how to invade and conquer and yet leave her triumphant in defeat. He knew her pleasure points. He knew every inch of her body and a substantial portion of her soul.

But it wasn't just his knowledge of her that excited her when they kissed. It wasn't familiarity, longevity, habit or technique.

She loved Ken. No matter how angry he made her sometimes, no matter how neglected she occasionally felt, no matter how irritatingly self-centered he could be... She loved him. And she responded to him out of love.

Kissing Jimmy wasn't disagreeable. But the most thrilling thing about it, Lila recognized, was that a potent young man like Jimmy could be interested in pursuing a middle-aged woman like her. That was certainly not a good enough reason to let his kiss continue.

Gently she placed her hands against his chest and pushed. He released her at once. His eyes narrowed as he read her expression, and he let out a sigh. "No good, huh," he said with a sad, begrudging smile.

"It's not a reflection on you, Jimmy."

He shrugged and sighed again. "You're my first older woman, you know," he admitted. "It's not my style to go after hotel guests—"

"You don't have to defend yourself." She gave him a quiet hug, feeling maternal toward him once again, anxious to protect his tender feelings. "I do like you."

"Yeah, well..." He returned to the socket he'd been checking, knelt down and screwed the plate back onto the wall. "I like you, too—better than girls my own age. You're a much better listener."

That was probably because she'd had so many years of practice listening to members of the male gender go on and on about themselves, starting with Adrian Pomfret and continuing on through her own sons. Girls Jimmy's age had grown up in an era when women were allowed to think they were the equals of men—which meant they deserved equal time when it came to talking about themselves.

"I'll bet once you move up to Boston you'll find lots of nice women to date," she reassured him. "The only reason I look good is because there's no one else around."

"No," he declared, placing the screwdriver in his toolbox and fastening the latch. "Don't put yourself down, Lila. You'd look good anywhere, and I'm not just talking about your appearance. And if your husband doesn't figure that out soon..." He drifted off for a moment, then straightened up and lifted the toolbox. "I'll take care of the rest of the sockets some other time," he concluded, striding out the door and leaving her to realize that checking the wiring had been only an excuse to get into her room.

Meditating on their encounter, she felt bewildered but also touched. If she'd wanted to put herself down, she would have interpreted the pass Jimmy had made at her as simply an attempt to make an easy score. She would have taken his dinner invitation as an insult, not a compliment.

She was complimented, though. She knew that for a woman her age, despite her crow's-feet, silver hair and abdominal stretch marks, she was tolerably pleasant-looking. She also prided herself on being reasonably good company. That Jimmy could find her attractive wasn't beyond belief, and she wasn't beyond appreciating his interest.

If only Ken was as interested. If only he cared less about his work and more about saving his marriage...

If he didn't, Lila would have to make him care. She loved him, and if he didn't return her love, if he was still confused or enraged by her temporary defection, if he intended to continue taking her for granted—she would just have to convince him he was wrong. If he had too much work to come to Hull this weekend, she would have to go to him. When love was at stake, you couldn't stand on ceremony or nurse your pride. You did what had to be done.

TWO HOURS LATER, Lila was on the highway, staring at the road through a blur of rain. Her suitcases lay on the back seat and her wallet held a wad of twenty-dollar bills that she'd received from Mrs. Tarlock. At first, Mrs. Tarlock had been adamant about not refunding any of the money Lila had paid in advance. But Lila had wheedled, negotiated, asserted herself. To her amazement, after about ten minutes of haggling, Mrs. Tarlock had muttered, "All right—I'll split the difference with you," and counted one hundred and forty dollars into Lila's palm.

Lila was learning, slowly but surely, how to make demands—how to make them loudly and clearly enough to bring results.

The rain and the last of the rush hour traffic slowed her progress on Route 128. She didn't arrive home until well past seven o'clock. The garage door was closed and she got wet unlocking and opening it. Shaking the raindrops from her hands, she climbed back into her car and drove inside.

Evidently the boys had heard the rattle of the garage door sliding along its track. By the time Lila climbed out of the car, the door to the mudroom was open, and Michael and Danny were screaming, "Hey! It's Mommy! Yo, Dad! Mom's here!" Danny leaped down the steps to the garage and barreled into her, nearly knocking her over as he enveloped her in a joyous hug.

She eagerly returned his embrace, but a small part of her brain couldn't help worrying. Would Ken be glad to see her? Would he have a hug for her?

As soon as Danny released her, Michael wrapped his arms around her. "Look, Mike—her suitcases!" Danny shrieked, his strident voice echoing against the concrete floor. "You gonna stay, Mom? Are you coming home to stay?"

"Yes," she answered, giving Michael a crushing hug and wondering whether Ken would agree to her return.

"Yay! I'm gonna get this suitcase," Dan yelled, hoisting the heavier one from the seat and grunting under its weight.

Michael considerately pulled it out of Danny's hands and pointed him toward the smaller bag. "You take that one, Danny. I've got this one."

"It sure is heavy, Mom," Danny babbled happily. "Have you got presents in there for us?"

"I'm afraid not," she said. She should have picked up some trinkets for them. A couple of Bayside Manor postcards, or something...

Jimmy's voice echoed inside her head: *Don't put yourself down*. Just because she'd neglected to bring any goodies for her children didn't mean she was a bad mother.

Indeed, after a moment's disappointment, Danny seemed to forget all about presents. "Come on in," he ordered her, lugging her suitcase up the steps to the mudroom. "Hey, Dad! Mom's home!"

Given the high-decibel fuss the boys were kicking up, Ken must have heard the news by now. Where was he? Why wasn't he in the mudroom, or at least in the kitchen, bracing himself for her arrival? Whether he greeted her with a smile or an ultimatum—why wasn't he greeting her at all?

Michael dropped her suitcase near the kitchen table. "Yo! Dad! Stop working, would you?"

"I've stopped," Ken said as he materialized in the family room doorway.

Lila devoured him with her gaze. He looked fatigued, his hair mussed, his brow lined and his shoulders slumped. He had on a pair of jeans and a flannel shirt with the sleeves rolled up; one hand clutched a pen and the other was propped against the doorjamb. His lips hinted at a vague smile, but Lila couldn't tell whether its lack of warmth was a result of revulsion at seeing her, or simply exhaustion.

His eyes met hers, and for once in her life she couldn't read his thoughts in their luminous depths. She couldn't tell what he felt, what he wanted, what he intended to do.

Her anxiety building, she shifted her attention to the kitchen. While cluttered, it wasn't as messy as she'd expected. The sink was empty of dishes, the cabinet doors were closed and only a few random crumbs rested on the floor beneath the table. The room was not as clean as she preferred to keep it, but really, it wasn't bad.

Inhaling for fortitude, she turned back to Ken. For some reason, her gaze latched onto his hand holding the pen. His fingers were long and blunt-tipped, and she was suddenly visited by an image of those fingers on her, running down the smooth skin of her back, twining through her hair, curving around her bottom and holding her against him, around him. Poor Jimmy—he'd tried and been unable to ignite even a flicker of passion within her. Ken could turn her on without even trying. Just looking at him—just loving him—was enough to excite her.

She wished she could think of something to say, some way to demand that he put down his damned pen and shove his damned job and *talk* to her, *love* her, figure out how to put their lives back together again. She wished making demands of Ken was as easy as demanding her money back from Mrs. Tarlock. When it came to her marriage and her future, the worst thing that could happen—Ken's saying no—would demolish her.

Drawing her out of her ruminations, Michael said, "Hey, Mom, wanna check out my mold?" He grabbed her hand and dragged her back toward the mudroom, explaining, "One of the slices of bread just went stale, but the others are awesome. I got black mold, white mold, green and turquoise. I've been looking up the different kinds of molds in this book I got out of the library, and I'm gonna make a label for each mold and write up some stuff about it, like its Latin name and stuff like that. It's going to be real neat, Mom. Better than Mark Nugent's project, even."

Lila tossed an uncertain look at Ken as Michael ushered her away. Ken remained in the doorway to the family room, fingering his pen and staring at her, his gaze enigmatic.

She made the appropriate oohs and ahhs over Michael's bread mold, and then accompanied Danny upstairs to his bedroom so he could show her the pie graph he'd drawn depicting Massachusetts's state income: one slice manufacturing, one slice agriculture, one slice tourism and one slice service. "Service industries are, like,

Pizza Hut," he explained. "I guess that's because the waitress *serves* the pizza."

She exclaimed over his graph as she had over Michael's mold, genuinely impressed by her sons' masterpieces and relieved that, despite her temporary abandonment of them, they still wanted to share their school projects with her. But a part of her mind couldn't let go of her image of Ken, the rugged grace of his forearms, the rangy length of his body as he lounged in the doorway, the weariness and wariness darkening his eyes.

For some reason, all her justifications for having left home no longer seemed as important to her as her justification for coming back. But what if he refused to let her stay? What if he couldn't forgive her for having left? What if he'd take her back only on the condition that life would return to what it had been before she'd left?

"These projects are terrific," she finally said, laboring to keep the anxiety out of her voice. "But it's getting late, boys. Shouldn't you be getting ready for bed?"

"Tomorrow's a weekend," Michael objected. "Dad's been letting us stay up late on Friday nights."

"Well, now I'm home and I say it's time for you to get into your pj's," Lila declared, silently worrying that the boys might despise her for not being as lenient as Ken.

*Don't put yourself down.* As long as she was home, she had a right to set limits on her children's behavior. If they hated her for it, they could align themselves with Ken when he decided to give her the boot.

Hardly a consoling thought. With a sigh, she tuned out the boys' grumbling and steered them toward their bedrooms. Then she returned downstairs. Ken was no longer in the family room, and her suitcases had vanished as well. If she wanted to imagine the worst, she could believe he was out in the garage, shoving her bags back into her car.

She couldn't let herself think that way. She had come home to fight for Ken and her family, not to present him with her terms of surrender.

Squaring her shoulders and doing her best to shake off every last trace of pessimism, she went back upstairs in search of him. Before she could reach the master bedroom, however, the door to Danny's bedroom swung open and he dashed out, clad in his underwear, with one sock on his foot and one in his hand. "Will you tuck us in tonight, Mom?"

His words bolstered her more effectively than any of her internal sermons about fighting for the future of her family. "I'd be honored," she said.

"All right! Hear that, Mike? Mom's gonna tuck us in!"

The adjacent bedroom door opened and Michael appeared, already dressed in his pajamas. He glanced briefly at his brother and then at Lila. Impulsively, he went to her and gave her a hug. Then, apparently embarrassed, he darted into the bathroom.

She could have headed to her own bedroom until the boys were through washing up, but she opted to remain in the vicinity of their bedrooms. At least with the boys she knew she was welcome. No matter what Ken thought of her, they still loved her. If their love was all she had left, it was a great deal. She wanted to stay with them for as long as possible, to savor their love before she marched off to face the unknown with her husband.

In a couple of minutes, Danny exited his bedroom in his pajamas and joined Michael in the bathroom. Lila listened to the familiar ruckus as they squabbled over the toothpaste, and her heart swelled. She knew she would eventually find their trivial bickering annoying, but right now she considered it the sweetest sound in the world.

After a while the boys emerged from the bathroom. "Into bed if you want to get tucked in," she commanded with a bright smile.

The boys raced each other down the hall to their rooms. Lila entered Danny's room first. He had buried himself under the cover, just as he used to do. And just as she used to do, she pretended she couldn't figure out where his head was beneath the blanket. She groped his back and belly while he giggled, then bent down, kissed his foot and exclaimed, "My goodness, Danny—your nose is enormous!" while she wiggled his big toe.

Squirming and laughing, he peeked out from under the blanket and gave her a long-suffering look. "This is my nose, Mom!" he said, jabbing at it with his index finger.

It was their standard game. Lila realized how much she'd missed playing it with him during the time she'd been away.

Once she'd kissed him, she shut off the light and left the room, leaving his door slightly ajar to let the dim hall light filter in. Then she went into Michael's room. He lay neatly on his back, his blanket arranged with precision over his body and his head centered squarely on the pillow. "I love your mold," she told him. If she expressed her love for him instead of his science project, she would undoubtedly gross him out.

"Yeah, it's pretty awesome, isn't it," he agreed. His smile informed her that he knew she wasn't really talking about his mold, and that he appreciated her for sparing him a maudlin display of sentiment. "Are you going back to the beach again, Mom?" he asked.

She wished she could give him a definitive answer. She wished she could tell him no, she was never going back unless the whole family came with her. But she couldn't bring herself to lie to Michael. She wanted to be home with her family, with her husband. But what if a year or two elapsed and she found herself fading from sight again? What if her love began to wither as her needs remained unfulfilled?

She just didn't know.

"I'd like to stay here with you," she said truthfully. "I'd like that more than anything, Michael."

He digested her statement, then said, "I want you to stay, too. It's not as much fun when you aren't around."

Lila wished she could devour him with kisses and hugs, but wisely she continued to exercise restraint. "I love you boys so much," she murmured. She gave him a single light kiss on his forehead, then whispered, "Sweet dreams, Mike," before she left his room.

Now what? The open affection she'd shared with Danny and Michael had strengthened her, but she still wasn't sure she had enough courage to face Ken. What should she say to him? That she loved him enough to tolerate the inequities of their marriage? That she actually enjoyed taking care of others? That if only he would put her needs first on her birthday, she would put his needs first the other three hundred and sixty-four days of the year?

If she said such things she wouldn't mean them. She couldn't buy her way back into this family with lies. Acknowledging the truth with Ken was terrifying, but it couldn't be avoided.

Taking deep breaths, she walked down the hall to her bedroom. She spotted her suitcases standing by the closet door. Ken hovered near the window, gazing out at the overcast night sky. At her entrance he turned to face her.

It dawned on her that her entire future—the remaining half of her life—depended on what happened in the next minute, and she had no idea what to do.

"Did you check out of the hotel?" he asked.

She opened her mouth, but the muscles in her throat didn't seem to want to function, so she answered with a nod.

She sensed a subtle change in Ken, a softening in his stance, as if some of his tension had drained away. "Thank God," he whispered.

The tension began to drain from her, too. She felt her muscles unwinding, her breathing returning to its normal rhythm, her legs coming to life, carrying her across the carpeted floor to his open arms. He folded them around her, but the hug he gave her wasn't like the exuberant bear hugs with which her sons had welcomed her home. Ken's hug was cautious and restrained, as if he considered her fragile.

Resting her forehead against his shoulder, she closed her eyes and took another deep breath. She reveled in the familiar scent of him: a trace of Old Spice, a hint of balsam shampoo, and the warm, musky aroma of healthy masculinity. When he slid one hand up her back to the nape of her neck, she nestled closer to him, longing for him to know how much she loved him, aching to hear him swear that he loved her just as much.

"I've tried very hard for you, Lila."

His words drifted down to her, slow and faltering. It took several long seconds for their dire implications to register on her. As soon as they did, she sprang back from him, her muscles tightening all over again and her breathing becoming faint. She risked peering up at him, and the sorrow she read in his eyes devastated her. This was it, then. He'd tried, but he couldn't change, or forgive her, or love her anymore.

Whatever it was, whatever he was about to say, it was going to hurt. It was going to destroy her.

Unless she could preempt him. Unless she could stop him, before he said something he couldn't retract. Unless she could convince him that their marriage was worth trying harder for. "Ken—"

He brushed his fingers across her lips, silencing her. A shy smile crept across his mouth and he shook his head. "Let me finish, okay?"

*Okay. Sure. Finish annihilating me. Finish off our marriage. I'll sit here politely and keep my mouth shut.* She eyed him furiously and waited with as much dignity as she could muster to hear him announce the end of their marriage.

"I've tried as hard as I could to get some funding for your reading class in Roxbury," he said.

She frowned. "My reading class?"

He seemed to share her confusion for the moment. "Remember? The class you want to teach to those illiterate people at your soup kitchen."

Of course she remembered. She just hadn't expected to be discussing that topic with him right now. Didn't they have more important issues to work out? "Ken—"

"I've been trying to get money out of Allied-Tech's charity fund," he cut her off, seemingly anxious to unburden himself. "They give money to all sorts of cultural organizations, and now that I'm a vice president I thought I should have some input into how that money gets disbursed. Lila, I've tried. I've pointed out the public relations aspects, the relatively low cost of your project, the need for it. I've talked to Reverend Munsey. I've done whatever I could. . . ." He drifted off.

Tears filled her eyes. To know that Ken had exerted himself that way for her reading class was worth infinitely more than any actual funds he might have raised. "Oh, Ken, thank you," she whispered, hoping he knew how grateful she was—and how relieved. "But that's not important. What's important is us."

"This *is* us," he insisted, his eyes darkening with frustration. "It's a part of us. It's why you left."

"The reading project is not why I left. I left because—"

"You left because you were afraid I didn't take you seriously, because I was getting all the strokes and you weren't. And you deserved them. You deserved to get funding for that project, and you deserved to get the funding from Allied-Tech. If we're supposed to be a team, you ought to benefit from my promotion. It's supposed to belong to both of us. And, damn it, if I can't get it to work for you..." He closed his eyes and wrestled with his emotions "I failed, Lila. Don't thank me. I've blown it. I've failed."

"You tried."

"It's not enough. If it were, you'd be content to find yourself back where you started. You don't want that, and neither do I, Lila. We can't go back to that."

A few tears trickled through her lashes and down her cheeks. *He understands,* she thought, realizing that, whatever became of her literacy project, her most important dream had come true. Ken understood. He accepted. He saw her, heard her, recognized her needs. He understood her.

"I've knocked myself out on this—I've spent time on it that I should have spent on my job," he confessed, his anger dissolving into regret. "I failed, Lila. You put up with my business trips, my late hours, the loss of your career, and now that I've finally reached some sort of pinnacle, you come out of it with zilch. And it's not fair. I wanted to be able to give you this, and I can't."

She stared at him in wonder. How could he possibly feel that he'd failed? He had given her the most valuable things one human being could give another: his effort, his attention, his concern.

"Why didn't you let me know what you were doing?" she asked. She had only just told him last weekend about her idea to teach reading to the soup kitchen's clients. He must have spent the entire week attempting to get funding for her project. She had talked to him every evening, and he'd never breathed a word about what he was up to.

"I wanted—I wanted to give it to you," he insisted. "I wanted to be able to come to you and say, 'Here, Lila, here's your birthday present from me. Here's your dream.' And now..." A frown line creased his forehead. "I can't do that. I haven't been able to pull it off. I haven't come through for you."

"You tried," she repeated, wishing she could console him. "That's all that matters."

"Not to the folks at the soup kitchen. They still can't read, and Allied-Tech thinks I'm a flake—"

"A flake?" Her eyes widened with dismay. "Ken, you haven't risked your job for this, have you?"

His silence was all the answer she needed.

"Oh, no." She lowered herself onto the bed, shaken by the magnitude of what he'd done. He had sacrificed his own dream in an attempt to fulfill hers. "What are they going to do to you?" she asked anxiously.

"They haven't fired me," he replied. "I've made them nervous, though. I'm going to have to work twice as hard to win their approval. That's why I wasn't going to go to Hull this weekend, Lila. I'm up to my eyebrows with work. Thank God the boys have been helping out around the house, cleaning up after themselves and keeping out of trouble while I've been working. They've grown up so much in the past couple of weeks, Lila."

"We all have," she said, extending her hand to his. When he wove his fingers through hers, she pulled him toward her, drawing him down onto the bed beside her. "I came home tonight to tell you I love you," she murmured, clasping his hand between hers. "But I didn't realize how much I loved you until now." She brought his hand to her lips and kissed the inside of his wrist, then lifted her head as he lowered his.

Their lips merged, and she understood in the most profound way what love truly meant. It wasn't about the sort of flattery you felt when a younger man like Jimmy made a pass at you. It wasn't about demanding attention and respect. It wasn't about seeing that your own needs were met.

It was about meeting the needs of the person you loved and having faith that your lover would reciprocate. For a while Lila had lost faith, but she had it now, full and strong and solid. The details might not be smoothed out; the day-in-day-out of their relationship might contain flaws, but if the faith was there, if Lila knew that Ken was listening to her and trying for her, their love would survive and grow.

Right now she and Ken needed each other in the most fundamental way. Their kiss grew in intensity, Ken's tongue penetrating her mouth and engaging in an erotic duel with hers. She circled her arms around him and they tumbled backward into the bed, still kissing, pulling at each other's clothes and sighing, gasping when a button gave way, when Ken's hand cupped Lila's breast, when her fingers slid the flap of his belt through the buckle. At some point he rose to lock the door, and then he was with her again, sliding off her skirt, shucking his trousers, flicking her bra out of his way and burying his lips in the sensitive hollow between her breasts.

Holding his head to her, Lila felt her love for him expanding inside her, filling her with the comprehension, both sweet and painful, of how precious this emotion was, how easy it was to lose faith if you were careless or confused. She had faith now, faith that Ken saw her and knew her and loved her.

She knew him, too, yet he seemed different to her. She knew his body but it seemed changed, his skin more sensitive to her caresses, his motions more urgent, his response more desperate. He was still her husband, Ken Chapin, the computer scientist and businessman, the sports enthusiast, and father of two, someone who worked hard and eschewed sentimentality and sailed through life on an even keel. But the past two weeks had changed him. He, too, had lost and then regained his faith in their love, and his unbridled passion proved it.

They moved quietly, muffling their responsive moans and kissing each other into silence as Lila's hands roamed through the wiry hair adorning Ken's chest, as his hands explored the pliant curves of her bottom, as she skimmed down his abdomen, as he massaged her thighs, as her fingers curled around his hardness and his entered her softness, touching and teasing and awakening every nerve, every desire, every want and hope and hunger.

The boys were within earshot—probably asleep, but awfully close, and Lila and Ken loved each other in a soundless ballet, speaking only with their eyes and their bodies. They'd been parents for so long, the silence seemed natural to them. It excited Lila to think of Ken holding back his groans as he held back in other ways, straining to contain the fire in one place while it flared out of control in another. She too had to contain herself, smothering her ecstatic cry as he thrust into her.

His body stroked hers in strong, rhythmic surges and hers tensed around him, increasing the pressure, increasing the pleasure until she lost herself to it. She muffled her moan against his shoulder as her body convulsed around him, wringing her with blissful spasms. Above her she heard his ecstatic gasp as he released himself into her.

Spent, he rested heavily on top of her, his ragged breath ruffing her hair and his fingers brushing gently over her shoulders and throat. She felt the muscles along his spine slacken beneath his perspiration-damp skin. He gasped again, a hushed exhalation of contentment. "It's not supposed to be this good, is it?" he whispered hoarsely, his lips moving against the tip of her earlobe as he shaped the words.

"It's supposed to be as good as we make it," she answered, ringing her arms around his waist to prevent him from moving off her.

He obeyed her unvoiced command and remained where he was. Lifting his head, he peered down at her. "Maybe we try harder when we're not so sure of each other."

The candor in his words moved her. She wanted to be sure of Ken, and she wanted him to be sure of her. But that often led to complacency. They could no longer take each other—or their love—for granted.

Apparently Ken discerned the somber path her thoughts had taken. He broke into a crooked smile. "Or maybe it's just that you're forty years old. Women are supposed to enter their prime at forty, aren't they?" he joked, stroking his thumb along the graceful edge of her jaw.

She mirrored his smile. "If you think forty is great, wait till you see me at fifty."

"I'm looking forward to it," he murmured, covering her mouth with his. He kissed her deeply, slowly, then raised his head again. All traces of his smile were gone. "I'm really sorry about the reading project," he confessed, caressing her jaw again, and her cheek, touching her with a quiet obsession, as if he couldn't get enough of her. "In my dreams, I imagined you coming back to me—like this—and I would greet you with this gift, this wonderful surprise. I wanted to do that for you, Lila."

She tightened her arms around his waist. "I had dreams, too," she confessed. "In one of them, I came home and you accepted me back with love. You've made that dream come true for me."

"Yes, but—"

"Another dream is the reading project, and that dream can come true for me, too. *I'll* make it come true. I'll get the funding somehow. Sometimes a person has to make her own dream come true, Ken. You don't have to do it for me. I'll do it for myself."

"But we're a team."

"We were a team when you were climbing the corporate ladder," she conceded. "But you were the one scoring points at Allied-Tech. All I did was stand behind you."

"You did more—"

She silenced him with a shake of her head. "Stand behind me, Ken—that's all you have to do. Stand behind me and love me."

He smiled tentatively. "You make it sound so easy."

She contemplated his words. "Some days it's easy and some days it's not. Standing behind someone sometimes makes you feel like you're in second place."

"Then we'll have to stand side by side," Ken resolved. Abruptly he rolled onto his back, carrying Lila with him and holding her on top of him. "Although there's a lot to be said for changing positions every now and then."

Feeling him revive beneath her, she smiled. The hell with younger men; Ken seemed to be very much in his prime, too.

"I missed you," he whispered before pulling her down to him for a kiss. "Don't ever leave me again."

"Don't ever give me a reason to."

"I'll try, Lila. I'll try anything. But you've got to help me, you know that. You've got to tell me what the red light means on the vacuum cleaner, and you've got to tell me when you think I'm heading the wrong way. I'll be listening. Always. I swear."

"Then we'll be fine," she promised, inclining her head for another kiss. His body tensed beneath hers and hers melted in readiness for him, and they locked together, wedded by love and law, the past and the future. And Lila knew that if love was supposed to be as good as they could make it, it would be very, very good indeed.

# *Epilogue*

Ken found the bottle lying on its side on his workbench shelf in the cellar, where he'd left it a month ago. He occasionally purchased wine by the case because the liquor store gave him a discount for buying in quantity, and he kept the extra bottles racked on a shelf along one cool concrete wall.

He hadn't stashed the champagne with his other wines, though. It had been special from the moment he'd bought it. More than once since the night he'd stashed it in the cellar, he had found himself wondering whether he would ultimately be stuck drinking it all alone, extravagantly drowning his sorrows in the overpriced bubbles. He had wondered whether he would ever have anything worth celebrating again.

But tonight he did, something more exciting than his having been named a vice president at Allied-Tech. The promotion had been for him alone. Tonight's celebration would be for both of them, Lila and Ken, the team, the equal partnership.

He wiped off the thin layer of dust that had accumulated on the bottle and carried it upstairs to the kitchen. Fortunately the cellar tended to be cold, especially in November, so the wine wouldn't require much chilling. He placed it inside the freezer, then pulled a couple of fluted champagne glasses from the cabinet where Lila stored the crystal.

A month ago, Ken wouldn't have known in which cabinet to look. He'd learned a lot about the kitchen in the past few weeks. Along with the crystal, he'd learned where the potato chips were kept, the microwave manual, the spices and the sponges and, of course, the coffee filters. It struck him as strange to think that he could have lived in this house for so many years without knowing such basic things.

Lila was upstairs. He'd hollered a hello up the stairway when he'd gotten home, and she'd shut off the vacuum cleaner long enough to holler a return greeting. Danny had shouted something, too, something about how Mom was making him and Michael clean the bathroom, and they'd already cleaned it a week ago so they really shouldn't have to clean it again so soon, and what was worse, Michael wasn't letting him use the toilet brush. Now that Lila was working five days a week at the soup kitchen, she was usually gone from home until just before the boys got off the school bus, which meant she had to put off her housework until late afternoon.

That worked out well, because the boys were now expected to help her with the cleaning. They were currently assigned to maintaining their bathroom as well as their bedrooms. Lila also had them on a rotating schedule in the kitchen; they took turns wiping the table and sweeping the floor under it, while Lila and Ken took turns cooking and putting the dishes away. Ken had a tendency to rely heavily on frozen dinners and pizza when it was his turn to fix supper, but tonight's meal was Lila's responsibility and the kitchen was redolent of the aroma of roast chicken and baked potatoes.

A good thing, too. Pizza didn't go well with champagne.

Loosening the knot in his necktie, Ken headed up the stairs. As he reached the second-floor hall, he was assailed by the all-too-familiar sound of his sons bickering. "You're suppose' ta put the soap in before you do the brushing part," Michael scolded.

"But Mom said we're not suppose' ta use this stuff, because it scratches the sink."

"You use it in the toilet, not in the sink. Don't you know anything? The sink is fiberglass so you have to use this liquid scrub-free stuff. You use the powder soap in the toilet."

"But what if it scratches the toilet?"

"Who cares? Are you gonna stick your head in the toilet to look for scratches?"

"Your head belongs in the toilet!"

"Yeah? Well, your head belongs flushed down!"

Rolling his eyes, Ken bypassed the bathroom and headed for the master bedroom. He found Lila there coiling the electrical cord from the vacuum cleaner. Her hair was pulled back in a barrette, but several tendrils had escaped from the clasp and fell delicately around her face. She wore a pair of old, snug-fitting blue jeans, and Ken decided that she looked as good in jeans today as she'd looked back in graduate school.

Maybe better, he amended, because these days she wore jeans so rarely. When she wore slacks nowadays, they were usually tailored trousers, loosely cut, with high waists and pleats. She looked nice enough in them, but it wasn't the same as wearing soft, well-worn denim that clung revealingly to her thighs and bottom and gapped slightly at her narrow waist.

Damn, but she was sexy. Even tired and disheveled from her chores, she was an unbelievably sexy woman.

Ken would never tell her so, but he'd considered her just as sexy when she had appeared before the upper echelon of Allied-Tech's management during its Monday morning powwow this past week. She'd worn a chaste woolen dress to the meeting, nylons, pumps and modest gold earrings, yet Ken had caught a whiff of her perfume and his nervous system had shifted gears, right there in the third-floor conference room as he'd handed her a cup of coffee.

She must have sensed her impact on him. Her eyes had met his and the anxiety she'd been suffering all weekend long seemed to wane. "Do I look okay?' she'd whispered, knowing the answer.

"You look great."

"I'm nervous," she'd admitted.

"Don't be. You're going to bowl them over."

She had. She'd given his hand a subtle squeeze, then taken the coffee he'd prepared for her and allowed Aaron Karsch to escort her to a seat at his left, halfway around the conference table from Ken. As soon as she'd been introduced she had stood, exuding poise and confidence, and distributed copies of the budget she'd compiled detailing the financial needs of her literacy project.

Then she'd spoken. Her voice had resonated in the elegant room, steady and full of conviction. She'd talked about the cost-effectiveness of her program, the need for it, the failure of other, more bureaucratically oriented literacy programs and the trust she'd built up among the soup kitchen's clientele over the years. She had asked the assembled executives to spare her project whatever money they could—as a public relations gesture if nothing else. Then she'd answered a few questions, thanked the group for their time and glided out of the room.

Once she was gone, the others had all commented to Ken on the excellence of her presentation. He'd agreed and then expressed the hope that they would put the Mt. Zion Reading Program right alongside the Boston Symphony Orchestra on the company's charities list. But one small corner of his mind had lingered on how incredibly sexy a woman could be when she was competent and determined and ambitious, and when she carried a hint of that amazing perfume. And how sexy he could find her when he no longer took her for granted.

Right now she smelled not of perfume but of a pine-scented cleanser. He wrapped his arms around her and gave her a loving kiss. "I bet you'd like a bubble bath tonight," he murmured.

She shot him a cagey look. Whenever she took a bubble bath—and Ken had made it a point to spare her a stretch of uninterrupted time for one on a regular basis—they wound up making love afterward. She always emerged from the bath with her skin so soft, her body so warm and relaxed, her flesh ultrasensitive to his touch.

"Keep it clean," she whispered teasingly. "It's hours till the boys get to bed. We haven't even eaten dinner yet."

"Would you like some wine with dinner?" he asked, sounding less nonchalant than he'd planned. He wanted to surprise her with the news, but he was having a difficult time keeping it from her.

Naturally, she became suspicious. "Why would I want wine with dinner?"

He slipped into the walk-in closet to avoid answering, but she chased him, joining him in the crowded space between her dresses and his suits. "I don't know," he mumbled evasively as he hung up his jacket. "It's the end of the week. Why not?"

She watched him slide his tie free of his button-down collar and drape it over the tie rack. "They didn't take away your third-floor office, did they?"

"No." He stepped out of his loafers and unbuttoned his shirt. "If they did, I'd be wanting to drink something a lot harder than wine."

She sized him up for another minute, then broke into a smile. "They're funding my literacy class," she guessed.

He feigned annoyance. "I wanted to surprise you."

"You blew the surprise when you mentioned the wine." She gathered him into her arms and let out a whoop. "Thank you, Ken! Thank you!"

"Don't thank me," he countered, although he happily returned her hug. "It was your presentation at the powwow that did the trick."

"It was your position that got me into the powwow so I could make my presentation."

"But *you* were the one who convinced them." He brushed her forehead with a kiss, then tossed his shirt into the hamper and donned one of his comfortable around-the-house flannel shirts. "Anyway, they aren't giving you much," he cautioned as he buttoned it. "Eight hundred and forty dollars, enough to cover the rent on the basement room in the church. You're lucky Reverend Munsey isn't charging more."

Lila refused to be disappointed by the skimpy donation. She did a little victory dance within the cramped interior of the closet, then hooked her hands around the back of Ken's head and kissed him again. "I'm lucky, all right. I've got you."

She let her lips linger on his, seductively sweet, but before he could get too caught up in the kiss, he heard Danny's shrill voice piercing the air. "Hey, Mom—you wanna inspect the bathroom?"

Laughing, Lila released Ken and left the closet. Through the half-open door he heard Danny interrogating her on what she and Dad had been doing in the closet. "Talking," she told him. "Just talking."

By the time Ken had finished dressing and emerged from the closet, Lila and the vacuum cleaner were gone. He hurried down the stairs and found his family in the kitchen, the boys setting the table and Lila sliding a roasting dish of chicken from the oven, her hands encased in insulated hot-mitts. She angled her head toward the crystal stemware. "Champagne flutes?" she asked.

He pulled the bottle from the freezer and grinned. "At least that much is a surprise."

"Ken—you got champagne?" After setting the chicken down on a trivet on the table, she pulled off the mitts and crossed the room to examine the bottle. Then she gazed up at him. "You bought champagne just for this?"

He couldn't lie to her. "I bought it a while ago," he confessed. "I was saving it for the right moment. This seems pretty right to me."

"How come?" Michael demanded to know. "What's going on, Dad?"

"Your mother is embarking on a new career."

"Does that mean we're gonna have to keep cleaning our own bathroom?" Danny asked sullenly.

"Either that, or your bathroom is going to get so filthy you'll have mildew growing in the corners and spiders dropping from the ceiling."

The boys exchanged a look, as if the possibility appealed to them. Then Michael shrugged. "I'll do my share if Danny does his. I guess Mom deserves it, huh."

"I guess so," Ken confirmed.

Uninhibited by the presence of the children, Lila gave him another hug and another kiss, a long, leisurely, nerve-shattering one. Danny made a gagging noise at the back of his throat, and Michael muttered, "Don't look."

"It's gross, all that mushy stuff," Danny declared.

"I know. Really sickening."

"It makes me want to puke."

"They can't help it," Michael explained grimly. "They're in love."

*You'd better believe it,* Ken concurred silently, closing his arms around Lila in a firm, possessive embrace. *We're in love, and we can't help it.*

And he went right on kissing her.

## PASSPORT TO ROMANCE VACATION SWEEPSTAKES

# OFFICIAL RULES

### SWEEPSTAKES RULES AND REGULATIONS. NO PURCHASE NECESSARY.

### HOW TO ENTER:

**1.** To enter, complete this official entry form and return with your invoice in the envelope provided, or print your name, address, telephone number and age on a plain piece of paper and mail to: Passport to Romance, P.O. Box #1397, Buffalo, N.Y. 14269-1397. No mechanically reproduced entries accepted.
**2.** All entries must be received by the Contest Closing Date, midnight, December 31, 1990 to be eligible.
**3.** Prizes: There will be ten (10) Grand Prizes awarded, each consisting of a choice of a trip for two people to: i) London, England (approximate retail value $5,050 U.S.); ii) England, Wales and Scotland (approximate retail value $6,400 U.S.); iii) Caribbean Cruise (approximate retail value $7,300 U.S.); iv) Hawaii (approximate retail value $ 9,550 U.S.); v) Greek Island Cruise in the Mediterranean (approximate retail value $12,250 U.S.); vi) France (approximate retail value $7,300 U.S.).
**4.** Any winner may choose to receive any trip or a cash alternative prize of $5,000.00 U.S. in lieu of the trip.
**5.** Odds of winning depend on number of entries received.
**6.** A random draw will be made by Nielsen Promotion Services, an independent judging organization on January 29, 1991, in Buffalo, N.Y., at 11:30 a.m. from all eligible entries received on or before the Contest Closing Date. Any Canadian entrants who are selected must correctly answer a time-limited, mathematical skill-testing question in order to win. Quebec residents may submit any litigation respecting the conduct and awarding of a prize in this contest to the Régie des loteries et courses du Quebec.
**7.** Full contest rules may be obtained by sending a stamped, self-addressed envelope to: "Passport to Romance Rules Request", P.O. Box 9998, Saint John, New Brunswick, E2L 4N4.
**8.** Payment of taxes other than air and hotel taxes is the sole responsibility of the winner.
**9.** Void where prohibited by law.

---

## PASSPORT TO ROMANCE VACATION SWEEPSTAKES

# OFFICIAL RULES

### SWEEPSTAKES RULES AND REGULATIONS. NO PURCHASE NECESSARY.

### HOW TO ENTER:

**1.** To enter, complete this official entry form and return with your invoice in the envelope provided, or print your name, address, telephone number and age on a plain piece of paper and mail to: Passport to Romance, P.O. Box #1397, Buffalo, N.Y. 14269-1397. No mechanically reproduced entries accepted.
**2.** All entries must be received by the Contest Closing Date, midnight, December 31, 1990 to be eligible.
**3.** Prizes: There will be ten (10) Grand Prizes awarded, each consisting of a choice of a trip for two people to: i) London, England (approximate retail value $5,050 U.S.); ii) England, Wales and Scotland (approximate retail value $6,400 U.S.); iii) Caribbean Cruise (approximate retail value $7,300 U.S.); iv) Hawaii (approximate retail value $ 9,550 U.S.); v) Greek Island Cruise in the Mediterranean (approximate retail value $12,250 U.S.); vi) France (approximate retail value $7,300 U.S.).
**4.** Any winner may choose to receive any trip or a cash alternative prize of $5,000.00 U.S. in lieu of the trip.
**5.** Odds of winning depend on number of entries received.
**6.** A random draw will be made by Nielsen Promotion Services, an independent judging organization on January 29, 1991, in Buffalo, N.Y., at 11:30 a.m. from all eligible entries received on or before the Contest Closing Date. Any Canadian entrants who are selected must correctly answer a time-limited, mathematical skill-testing question in order to win. Quebec residents may submit any litigation respecting the conduct and awarding of a prize in this contest to the Régie des loteries et courses du Quebec.
**7.** Full contest rules may be obtained by sending a stamped, self-addressed envelope to: "Passport to Romance Rules Request", P.O. Box 9998, Saint John, New Brunswick, E2L 4N4.
**8.** Payment of taxes other than air and hotel taxes is the sole responsibility of the winner.
**9.** Void where prohibited by law.

 RLS-DIR

## VACATION SWEEPSTAKES

MONTH 2 ENTRY

# Official Entry Form

Yes, enter me in the drawing for one of ten Vacations-for-Two! If I'm a winner, I'll get my choice of any of the six different destinations being offered — and I won't have to decide until after I'm notified!

Return entries with invoice in envelope provided along with Daily Travel Allowance Voucher. Each book in your shipment has two entry forms — and the more you enter, the better your chance of winning!

Name ______________________________

Address ______________________________ Apt.

City ______________ State/Prov. ______________ Zip/Postal Code

Daytime phone number ______________________________
Area Code

☐ I am enclosing a Daily Travel Allowance Voucher in the amount of $__________ Write in amount revealed beneath scratch-off



PASSPORT
WIN
1 of 10 Vacations
SEE INSIDE
TO ROMANCE

## VACATION SWEEPSTAKES

MONTH 2 ENTRY

# Official Entry Form

Yes, enter me in the drawing for one of ten Vacations-for-Two! If I'm a winner, I'll get my choice of any of the six different destinations being offered — and I won't have to decide until after I'm notified!

Return entries with invoice in envelope provided along with Daily Travel Allowance Voucher. Each book in your shipment has two entry forms — and the more you enter, the better your chance of winning!

Name ______________________________

Address ______________________________ Apt.

City ______________ State/Prov. ______________ Zip/Postal Code

Daytime phone number ______________________________
Area Code

☐ I am enclosing a Daily Travel Allowance Voucher in the amount of $__________ Write in amount revealed beneath scratch-off

CPS-TWO